M

By the Same Author

Menachem's Seed

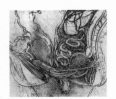

MENACHEM'S seed

a novel by
Carl Djerassi

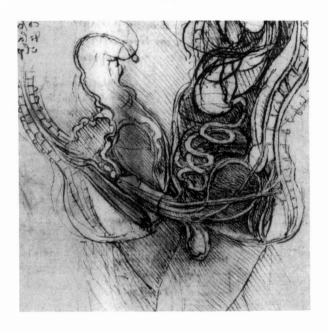

The University of Georgia Press   Athens & London

Published by the
University of Georgia Press
Athens, Georgia 30602
© 1997 by Carl Djerassi
Set in Bodoni Book
Printed and bound by
Maple-Vail Book Manufacturing Group
The paper in this book meets the guidelines
for permanence and durability of the Committee on
Production Guidelines for Book Longevity of the
Council on Library Resources.
Printed in the United States of America
97 98 99 00 01 C 5 4 3 2 1
Library of Congress Cataloging in Publication Data
Djerassi, Carl.
Menachem's seed : a novel / by Carl Djerassi.
p. cm.
ISBN 0-8203-1925-2 (alk. paper)
PS3554.J47M46   1997
813'.54—dc21   97-12749
British Library Cataloging in Publication Data available

Title page illustration: Leonardo da Vinci,
Coition of Hemisected Man and Woman (detail), c. 1492–94.
The Royal Collection ©1997 Her Majesty Queen Elizabeth II.

In memory of

SHALHEVETH FREIER

Preface

Menachem's Seed is the third volume in a projected tetralogy in the genre of "science-in-fiction," which by my definition requires that everything I specify does or could exist. Most of my characters, fictional as well as real, are scientists. By exposing their lives, I try to make comprehensible the culture and behavior of scientists — uncommon in contemporary fiction.

In the first volume, *Cantor's Dilemma*, I dealt with the kind of trust without which the research enterprise would sink; with ambition and even Nobel lust, which fuel the hottest research but at times also taint it; and with scientists — young and not so young, and not exclusively male — for whom trust and ambition are the hidden engines of their work. In the second volume, *The Bourbaki Gambit*, I focused on a rapidly increasing subset of the scientific community: retired though intellectually alert scientists and linked them with another, much rarer phenomenon, the anonymous cooperative, an apparent contradiction in a culture that is so steeped in the cult of celebrity.

Although my emphasis lies on scientists as persons, I also want to explain to the general public, in the guise of fiction, some of the cutting-edge science performed by the scientific elite — the top 5 percent or so of the hundreds of thousands of scientists and technicians working throughout the world. Thus in *Cantor's Dilemma*, insects flutter through various chapters, because recent advances in invertebrate endocrinology and pheromone-based means of communication form an integral part of the story. *The Bourbaki Gambit* attempts to make comprehensible the discovery of PCR, the acronym for "polymerase chain reaction," which was honored with the 1993 Nobel Prize in Chemistry. Among the myriad of applications of this method for replicating fragments of genetic information, its role in the fantasy science of *Jurassic Park* is most widely known (although perhaps least relevant to everyday life).

In this third volume, *Menachem's Seed*, sex — more precisely, human male reproduction — occupies a key position. A goodly portion of my own professional life over four decades has dealt with research and teaching in certain areas of reproductive biology, with virtually exclusive attention to female contraception. In *Menachem's Seed*, however, I focus on one aspect of male reproduction currently receiving attention from the scientific community: treatment of male infertility (rather than male contraception — a field that is ignored to a disgraceful extent). The science I describe in this novel is the real thing, with one important chronological exception: to fit my plot, I predated by over a decade the development of single-sperm injection (ICSI or intracytoplasmic sperm injection) — a technique pioneered in Belgium by André C. Van Steirteghem, who allowed me to use his name for one of my cameo characters.

In the first two volumes, my exposition of the tribal culture and behavior of scientists was sited primarily on familiar turf: laboratory and home. In *Menachem's Seed*, I explore venues of international policy — an arena associated much less frequently in the public mind with scientists. For this purpose, I invent the Kirchberg Conferences on Science and World Affairs, supposedly initiated by Bertrand Russell and financially realized through the family fortune of the famous Austrian philosopher Ludwig Wittgenstein, whom Russell first brought to England. Kirchberg am Wechsel is a small village in Austria in whose environs Wittgenstein spent several unhappy years in the 1920s.

The inspiration for my Kirchberg Conferences was provided by the annual Pugwash Conferences on Science and World Affairs, named after the small village of Pugwash in Nova Scotia, where the first meeting (1957) was held and funded by the wealthy industrialist Cyrus Eaton. Though barely known until recently, the Pugwash Conferences were honored in 1995 with the Nobel Peace Prize. The impetus for these conferences did indeed originate with Bertrand Russell, and what transpired at my fictional 1977 Kirchberg Conference in Kirchberg am Wechsel could well have happened at the real Pugwash Conference that I attended in Munich in 1977. I also frequented many earlier Pugwash Conferences ranging from Ronneby (Sweden) in 1967 to Warsaw in 1982. The 1981 Pugwash Conference was held in Banff, Canada, from August 28 to September 2, not far from the Lake Louise setting of my fictitious 1981 Kirchberg Conference. It is not inappropriate that I have borrowed excerpts of the text of the official Pugwash resolution condemning Israel's bombing of the Iraqi Osirak nuclear reactor on June 7, 1981, for my own Canadian Kirchberg Conference. The characters in *Menachem's Seed* — foremost the Israeli nuclear engineer Menachem Dvir, the French physicist called *le gourou*, and all other Kirchberg Conference participants — are fictional, but the events of the 1970s in the Middle East, notably those associated with the acquisition of a nuclear arms capability by Israel and the eventual bombing of Osirak, are factual. I am indebted to a number of Israeli scientists — foremost the late Shalheveth Freier — who were also active Pugwashites, for helpful advice and information on that topic. In addition, several past and present staff members of the Hadassah Medical Center in Jerusalem and of Ben-Gurion University in Beersheba responded gracefully to my requests for somewhat intrusive interviews and visits.

And one last caveat, this one musical in nature: As described in my novel, George Frederick Handel's last opera (and the first based on an English-language libretto), entitled *Thalestris and Alexander*, had its world premiere in Vienna in September 1977. Handel's librettist, Charles Jennens, based it on the virtually unknown tragicomedy, *The Amazon Queen; or, The Amours of Thalestris to Alexander the Great*, by the Restoration playwright John Weston; the score was discovered only recently in a Dublin library where it had rested misfiled since 1742. My hope is that all of this musical invention will seem quite plausible. But that world premiere, and in fact that opera and specific libretto (but not Weston's play), are figments of my imagination. Nothing would please me more than to learn that somewhere there is still hiding a Handel score dealing with such a feminist reading of the story of Thalestris, Queen of the Amazons. But until it does, readers will have to hum my text to some imaginary music of their own.

Menachem's Seed

1

"What he doesn't know about the queen of Sheba isn't worth knowing."

"That's Menachem Dvir?" she asked in a low voice. "White beard and glasses? He does look like a biblical scholar."

"No," *le gourou* whispered back. Unlike the subject of their conversation, the Frenchman was one of the few participants without a name tag. He didn't need one. Everybody at the Kirchberg Conference knew who *le gourou* was. "That's one of the Russians. Dvir is the other one." He chuckled. "The Israeli looks like a Russian, and the Russian like a rabbi. Even his appearance mistakes you."

"We say, 'fools you.'" Melanie Laidlaw couldn't resist correcting *le gourou* — after all, how often did one get the chance? "But what would Wittgenstein have thought of all this?" she added, working perhaps a little too hard at keeping the conversation going.

"Wittgenstein?"

"Ludwig — the philosopher."

"I do not see the relation."

"He taught around here in the twenties."

"Here?" The Frenchman looked as astonished as only a Frenchman can. "In Kirchberg? In this . . . ," he waved his hand, "How do you say, *trou perdu?*"

Laidlaw shrugged helplessly. During the past quarter century, her high school French had abandoned her to the extent that she barely could ask for the lady's washroom.

"*Le boondog?*" he asked tentatively.

"I see," she said, relieved. "You mean boondocks. Still, great things can happen even in the boonies, as we call them sometimes. This conference, for instance."

"So you're the mysterious Dr. Dvir." She'd sidled up to him at the end of the coffee break as the group had started to shuffle back into the conference hall. "I understand you're one of the world's authorities on the queen of Sheba."

Dvir slowly turned his head toward his questioner. "*Mister* Dvir," he said deliberately, the voice seeming to issue from a formidable depth. "Not Doctor."

She gestured toward the label fastened to his sweater. "Ben-Gurion University," she read. "I thought you were an academic. A Shebaist," she added quickly. "If there is such a specialty."

Dvir broke into laughter, and for a moment sounded a good deal less formidable. "I've been called all kinds of names in my life, but never that. May I borrow it?" He glanced at her name tag. "The REPCON Foundation?"

Melanie Laidlaw laughed self-consciously. "I'm afraid so."

He shrugged his shoulders. "And is it *Doctor* Laidlaw?"

"I'm afraid so. I'm an ex-academic."

"You're too afraid: first the foundation, now your title."

Laidlaw started to flush. "It's just a figure of speech."

"Relax," he said, simultaneously steering her by the elbow to one of the empty seats in the back of the hall. "I'm not an academic, just an administrator."

"Of what?" she asked as she sat down.

Dvir waved his hand. "I'm a vice president in charge of all kinds of things. Ben-Gurion is a young university and a small administration is one way of saving money."

"You're in Beersheba, aren't you?"

Dvir nodded.

"That's in the Negev, isn't it?"

Dvir's attention had wandered; he nodded absently.

"Isn't Dimona also in the Negev?" Laidlaw persisted.

Dvir's attention snapped back to his interrogator. "So?"

"Isn't that where you keep your atomic arsenal?"

The man in front of Melanie Laidlaw had turned around. "Shh," he put a finger across his lips. "Don't you see the program has started?" he hissed.

Dvir ignored the interruption. His attention was now focused entirely on Laidlaw. "So?" he asked again.

"I understand you were one of the first directors there," she whispered in his ear.

Dvir turned his head so rapidly that her lips brushed his ear. "First the queen of Sheba; then Dimona. Who told you this?" She couldn't tell whether he was annoyed or curious.

"Later," she whispered.

2

"Do you have any family?" Melanie Laidlaw asked after they'd been served the soup.

"Sure. Or is immaculate conception more common in America?"

Very funny, she thought, but it serves me right starting out that way. "I mean, do you have any children?"

"Is that really what you mean?" he said, playfully.

"All right. A wife, then. Lots of people brought their spouses to Kirchberg. You seem to be alone."

"Where is *your* man?" He had turned inquisitional.

"Man? You mean my husband — "

"Don't be Talmudic," he interrupted. "I meant 'man.' "

"My husband is dead."

"Sorry." The twinkle had left his eyes.

"What about you?"

"I'm not a widower. But why these circuitous questions?"

"Circuitous?" Melanie was not an easy blusher, but the first tinge of rose started to appear. "What do you mean?"

"Why didn't you ask directly whether I was married?"

"And are you?"

"Are you asking because you want to sleep with me?"

Melanie's cheeks had turned litmus red. Quickly, she glanced at the neighboring tables, partly to hide her embarrassment, but mostly to see whether they were being overheard. She had no reason to be concerned. As in most dining rooms occupied by academics or by political types — and the Kirchberg Conferences were notorious for mixing both — the decibel level ensured total privacy.

"I think it's time to change the subject," she said, trying to sound prim. Yet something about his bluntness, his obvious disdain for conversational manners, left Melanie feeling . . . unrestrained. "I gather you're a regular at these things. What do you get out of it?"

Menachem shrugged. "I'm here because I do get something out of it: I run into people I don't usually meet. I can talk about subjects that interest me."

Melanie knew why she had come to this, her first Kirchberg. A newly admitted member of the notoriously closed circle of Western and Eastern European scientists, she was curious what had brought other people here, especially the ones who all seemed to know each other, the ones who belonged.

She knew the facts: they had first congregated in the late fifties, at the height of the Cold War. Originally, the only common denominator had been their fear of a nuclear arms race spinning out of control — a fear shared openly by a surprising number of scientists from both sides of the Iron Curtain. On July 9, 1955, at a public meeting in London, Bertrand Russell had read the manifesto he and Einstein had composed: "In the tragic situation which confronts humanity," it had begun, "we feel that scientists should assemble in conference to appraise the perils that have arisen as a result of the development of weapons of mass destruction, and to discuss a resolution. . . ." In the audience was a visiting physicist from Austria, who, in a moment of inspired synthesis, grasped that it would take politically unstained money to realize Russell's vision in a manner acceptable to East and West. Himself Teflon-clean of Nazi contamination, the Austrian physicist decided to make the Russell-Einstein Manifesto bear fruit.

At that time, Austria had only recently been declared a neutral country, a potential new Switzerland, as the result of a peace treaty that had negotiated the mutual withdrawal of both Soviet and Western occupational forces. The physicist had returned to this newly neutral nation convinced that there was one name in Austria capable of making Russell's vision a reality. Not himself, but Austria's greatest philosopher, Ludwig Wittgenstein. Around the turn of the century, the Wittgenstein family had become so rich that many referred to them as Austria's Rockefellers or Krupps. Ludwig, the philosopher, never cared for money. Indeed, his disdain for inherited wealth was so great that in his early thirties — years after he had published his *Tractatus-Logico-Philosophicus* — he quit to become a grade-school teacher in the remote countryside around Kirchberg am Wechsel, in the hamlets of Trattenbach, Hassbach, and Otterthal. He refused all support from his family, even presents of food when he was ill. The man was practically a recluse.

The Viennese physicist recalled the name of an acquaintance — a Wittgenstein cousin — and called her. Why not use some of the Wittgenstein money for a noble purpose of which even Ludwig might have approved, had he not died four years earlier? he asked. And why not pay discreet homage to Bertrand Russell, by now in his eighties, who had launched Ludwig on his philosophical path, however much it eventually diverged from Russell's? And why not pick Austria, whose newly born neutrality status was one of the few examples of Cold War political cooperation between West and East? And with a final stroke of insight, the Viennese physicist suggested that instead of Vienna, with its enormous historical baggage, they pick for the site of the first Conference on Science and World Affairs the unknown village of Kirchberg am Wechsel in whose surroundings the famous philosopher had once tried to educate the peasant children. With consummate diplomacy, the physicist stopped there; the rest of the story involved Wittgenstein's abrupt departure from the Kirchberg area, after having beaten a student too severely even by local standards.

The first conference was held in Kirchberg am Wechsel in 1957, followed in successive years by meetings in other Austrian locations: Kitzbühel, Badgastein, Vienna, and then Zell am See. By that time, the conferences had acquired the generic title *Kirchberg Conferences*, with the participants self-anointed as *Kirchbergers*. Menachem Dvir did not belong to the first group of Israeli Kirchbergers, nor to any other Kirchberg contingent from Israel during the 1960s. The Israelis, generally no more than three at any one conference, were not invited until 1962. By then, nuclear proliferation had risen to the top of the Kirchberg agenda, and the

French-Israeli cooperation in the nuclear field had moved from rumor to fact: involving Israeli scientists in Kirchberg affairs made sense. Menachem Dvir's position back home was much too sensitive to permit any but the most clandestine foreign travel. Not until 1969 — by which time he had turned formally into an academic administrator at the University of the Negev, later renamed after Prime Minister Ben-Gurion — did he accept an invitation to the next Kirchberg Conference.

———

"What sort of people can *you* meet here and not elsewhere?" Melanie asked.

Menachem had just pushed his soup plate away. He was one of those diners who punctuate the completion of a course by giving the empty plate a push. In his case, it wasn't even a discreet push. One couldn't help but notice. It meant *finished, fini, fertig*.

"All kinds of people," he said, "but especially Arabs. As you can imagine, the ones that interest me I'm not likely to bump into in Beersheba. Or anywhere else in Israel," he added with a shrug.

Menachem had started to cut his schnitzel. At conferences where room and board is included, the choice of menu is usually made in the kitchen. Except for catering to vegetarians — a custom introduced one year when the Kirchberg met in Udaipur, and all but the Indians had ended up with diarrhea — it was strictly table d'hôte and people ate what was put in front of them. This year was no exception; and not surprisingly, the fare was standard megacaloric Austrian cuisine.

"I noticed you're in the Working Group on Local and Regional Conflicts," Melanie continued. "Is that what brings you here?"

"Let's eat before this gets cold," Menachem said. "I've learned how to talk with a full mouth," he added, "even though it's not supposed to be good manners. At least that's what they taught me in Africa."

"Africa?"

"Later," he said. "You wanted to know about local and regional conflicts. Israelis were born in both, and we still wallow in them. In the early sixties, we were the underdogs, but now?" He chewed his schnitzel as if it were a local conflict to be decimated. "We're always on the defensive. It's all in the title of my paper." He waved his fork as if the conference proceedings were suspended in front of them. "'Some Comments on a Paper by M. M. El-Gammal Entitled *Israel Military and Nuclear Alternatives to Peace*.' I wrote it because I can already imagine how the British and Dutch will be nodding when El-Gammal spouts his views tomorrow morning. Have you read his paper?"

Melanie shook her head. "I'm in the Working Group on Population Issues."

"Don't bother," he said dismissively, before scooping up a forkful of mashed potatoes. When he spoke again, he seemed to Melanie to be addressing a somewhat larger audience than herself. "I won't be surprised about the Brits agreeing with El-Gammal," he said. "Scratch most of them here and you'll find Lawrence of Arabia under their rumpled tweed jackets. But the Dutch? This worries me. So I took it seriously and put my rebuttal on paper. But this is not the only local conflict on our agenda. It used to be Vietnam, and Biafra, and Czechoslovakia; now it's Cambodia, Northern Ireland, and, of course, as always the Middle East. But tell me, why were you invited?"

"I'm with the REPCON Foundation. The American group decided to include me."

"Never heard of it. What does it do?"

"Give away money."

"Well," Menachem grinned, pretending to move his chair closer. "How much money?"

He's like all the others, thought Melanie.

"I'm joking," he said, as if he'd read her mind. "But like any university vice president, I make it my business to know about foundations. Why have I never heard of yours?"

"Perhaps we're too small for you. Or too specialized."

"How small and how specialized?"

"By Ford or MacArthur standards, small. Annually, we give away less than twenty million dollars."

"You call that small? You must have an endowment of at least four hundred million dollars. By Negev standards, that's huge."

Melanie shrugged. "We're highly specialized. Our exclusive focus is human reproduction: REPCON stands for reproduction and contraception. And we're much smaller than you think, because we don't live on our endowment. Our founder stipulated that all of the money had to be spent in twenty years. Once we've done that, REPCON will be liquidated. If solutions can't be found in twenty years, she said, the world will go belly up anyway."

"She?"

"Athena Campobello. A remarkable woman. I'll tell you her story some time." She eyed him speculatively. "So can we expect an application as soon as you return to Ben-Gurion University?"

"Reproductive biology?" he mused. "I'll have to check what we have going on in that field."

Melanie raised her index finger. "*Human* reproductive biology. Or at least work applicable to humans. To be frank, our founder thought primarily about birth control, but since I've been on board, I found that most of our grant applications have come from the opposite side: infertility, in vitro fertilization, ex-utero manipulations — "

"Don't you pay any attention to men?" he demanded, his voice suddenly loud enough to turn heads at other tables.

Melanie Laidlaw was taken aback. "Of course," she said quietly. "We support work in the field of male reproduction. In fact, our Mrs. Campobello was especially interested in male problems: male contraception for the world; male infertility in her home."

"Really?" he said, and moved his chair closer. "Tell me more." The outburst, or whatever it was, had gone as quickly as it had come.

"About Athena Campobello?"

"No. What you're doing about male infertility."

"We're *doing* nothing. We just support the work of others."

3

"Reproductive biology? You must mean *female* reproductive biology. Why don't you men ever pay attention to *your* role in reproduction?"

Even though the question was addressed to her neighbor, the woman's voice was meant to be heard by the rest of the people at their table. It was the annual fund-raiser for Brandeis University, where the guests felt entitled to register complaints. Invariably, they were handled politely, especially when raised by potential donors.

The woman's neighbor, and the subject of her complaint, was Professor Felix Frankenthaler, one of Brandeis's stars, invited this evening to demonstrate to the guests the kind of value they could expect from their donations. "A fair enough question," Frankenthaler responded diplomatically. "I have to admit that I made my reputation in the fallopian tube. Even though," he raised his hand to stop any interruption, "that work dealt, in fact, with sperm motility."

"So?" the woman asked, her tone now less aggressive than amused. "What have you done for me lately?"

"Well," he announced, loudly enough that the rest of the table turned his way. "We are now hot on the trail of the biological function of nitric oxide."

Her disappointment was audible. "Laughing gas? What's that got to do with — "

"Madam!" Frankenthaler was fast losing his diplomacy. "Laughing gas is ni*trous* oxide. N_2O to the chemist, or *di*nitrogen oxide. We work with ni*tric* oxide, NO, also known as nitrogen monoxide. Or, more precisely, mononitrogen monoxide. In fact — " Frankenthaler, without realizing, had moved onto the slippery slope of chemical pedantry — "to be really precise, we — and many other competitors — are working on the biological role of different redox forms of nitric oxide. . . . 'Redox forms,' " he explained hastily, "simply involve the shuffling of electrons, which is not important for what I want to describe."

It probably would have taken Frankenthaler only a few more seconds to realize that he was in the process of losing most of his audience, but the man across from him saved the situation.

"I thought nitric oxide was an industrial gas, and a poisonous one at that. Isn't it involved in auto emission, ozone destruction, acid rain?"

"Precisely!" exclaimed Frankenthaler. "But do you know that it is also produced by fruit flies, chickens, trout, horseshoe crabs? Even man? It's amazing that a molecule with such a simple chemical structure and such a variety of biological functions should have escaped detection until very recently. In spite of its very short half-life — the chief reason why the production of NO in the body was overlooked for so long — it is now recognized that in minute amounts NO is one of the most important biological messengers." He paused, wanting to be sure that the statement had sunk in. It had. His audience, whether or not they understood what a biological messenger might be, had abandoned their meals. This was, after all, precisely the kind of thing they had come to hear.

"Nitric oxide is involved in blood clotting, in the immune system's destruction of tumor cells, in neurotransmission, and most importantly for our purposes," Frankenthaler looked directly at the woman who had questioned his interest in male reproduction, "in blood pressure control.

"One of our problems," he smiled conspiratorially, as if his circle of listeners actually did understand, "is that we don't know yet which of the various forms of nitric oxide — the neutral, negatively charged, or positive one — plays what biological role."

"I'm sure this is all absolutely fascinating," said his woman neighbor, "but what has it got to do with male reproductive biology?"

Frankenthaler was taken aback. Was she pulling his leg? "Do you know what the corpus cavernosum is?" he inquired, a faintly lupine smile around his lips.

"No," she replied. "Spell it."

"Never mind the spelling. It is the major erectile tissue of the penis."

"Well, well," she said, and grinned for the first time. "Tell us more."

"Nitric oxide is involved in the relaxation of the smooth muscle of the corpus cavernosum — "

"Relaxation?" she interrupted. "But don't you want it to — "

"Madam!" Thank God she isn't one of my students, he thought. "Let me finish. As I was about to say, nitric oxide-mediated relaxation of the smooth muscle of the corpus cavernosum permits increased blood flow *into* the penis, which," he bowed in the woman's direction as if he were inviting her to dance, "accomplishes precisely what you were so anxious to achieve: tumescence of the penis. In other words, you get a stiff — " She'd irritated him sufficiently that he was tempted to say *prick*, but he caught himself in time. "Penis," he finished, somewhat lamely.

"Go on," she said. "As you can see," she waved her hand around the table, "we're all listening. So what are you — at Brandeis — doing about stiff pricks?"

Frankenthaler flushed. "One of my brightest postdocs," he said, speaking as calmly as he could under the circumstances, "is trying to design nitric oxide-releasing substances that might be applied to the penis. As a way of treating impotence," he explained.

"I knew it!" the woman exclaimed triumphantly. "All female reproductive biology means to you is contraception. But when you men work on your own sexual apparatus, all you worry about — "

"Now wait a moment." By now, Frankenthaler didn't give a damn that he was supposed to be buttering up prospective donors. "If you can't get it *up*," he hissed, "you can't get it *in*. Only then do we start worrying about birth control. And for your information, the person in my lab doing the work is a woman!"

The conversation never did recover.

———

"Renu," Frankenthaler asked, a few weeks after the fund-raising debacle, "would you consider going to Israel for a few months?"

"Why Israel?"

Whenever Renu Krishnan needed time for deliberation, she asked a question.

———

13

Frankenthaler levered himself onto a lab stool. "You're working in one of the hottest labs in nitric oxide biology, but let's face the facts. Brandeis has the great Rosenstiel Basic Medical Sciences Research Center in which you're privileged to work," he gave her a benevolently conspiratorial wink, "but no medical school. And, as both of us know, most of the clinicians in Boston are interested in women, not men." Good God, he thought, I sound like that damn woman at the dinner. "But in Israel, you'd have one of the best andrologists in the world to draw on: Yehuda Davidson, at the Hadassah Medical Center. He's a clinician, a real master in male infertility and male impotence."

"And how long would you want me to work there?"

Frankenthaler produced a disarming flutter with his hands. "You be the judge. However long it takes you to determine how nitric oxide releasers are best administered to humans. A few months, perhaps half a year?"

"When?"

"I suppose early spring. Jerusalem is nice at that time of the year. And it's likely to take me until then to raise the funds."

"How will you do that?" Renu Krishnan was only in her second postdoc year, but she had already figured out that grantsmanship was as important a skill as anything she could learn in the lab. "You've just missed the last NIH deadline. Isn't the next one in January? By the time they reach any decision, it will be summer or autumn."

He nodded approvingly. It's nice to see a postdoc, he thought, who appreciates the subtleties of raising money. "I'm not bothering with government agencies. We are not talking about much money, maybe 25K. I'll try REPCON. I bet they'll go along, especially when they hear that they'll support a woman working in male reproduction. Even if it deals with impotence rather than contraception," he added as an afterthought, as if he were still addressing the female critic from the banquet.

"And why would REPCON respond so much faster, even if they should approve your application?"

Frankenthaler looked at the young woman with an appraising eye. Time to do some mentoring, he thought. "First of all, as a private foundation, REPCON has much less red tape. Second, they only fund research in reproductive biology, preferably with applications to humans. In fact, in our application, we'll point out that this will be precisely your area of concentration." He raised an admonishing index finger. "And most important, 25K still falls within the director's discretionary budget. So it doesn't have to go through committees and deadlines."

"Do you know the director?"

Professor Felix Frankenthaler permitted himself another conspiratorial wink, something he would not have done in the presence of the other postdocs. But he thought that on this afternoon Renu Krishnan deserved one.

"As a matter of fact I do. I've known her ever since she was married to Justin Laidlaw."

4

"How about joining us in the sauna after the evening session?" Menachem said as he pushed his chair back from the table. People were getting up all over the dining room to head for the school where the evening event was being held.

"*Us?*" Melanie asked. "Who is *us?*" His question had sounded offhand, as if he'd asked whether she wanted to join him for a coffee. But Melanie's mental radar started to sweep, though not as actively, she noticed, as it usually did. This time, its sweep seemed almost perfunctory.

Menachem's answer sounded disarming enough. "Who knows?" he said. "But it's bound to be amusing company."

"You make it sound as if it were a tradition."

"So it is," he nodded. "I was there when it started — at the 1973 Conference in Aulanko, north of Helsinki. That year, the Finnish hosts had, as a matter of course, made available on the shores of an adjacent lake a wood-burning sauna with all the accoutrements, including the obligatory birch branches." He snickered. "I skipped the sauna-flagellation part. In the beginning, the only women to use the sauna were the Scandinavians — spouses, or student staff, and all of them unself-consciously naked." Menachem grinned boyishly as he recounted this, his thumb and index finger making a circle of approval. "But soon the word spread; and by the end of the Conference, the large sauna had become the 'in' place for mixed company after the evening session — at least for the hardy types who enjoyed diving into the nippy lake." Menachem slouched back in his chair as if he had forgotten that they had to leave.

"Someone, I think it was Karl Popper, said that most natural scientists are modest. Or maybe he said only the great ones were. Either way, it's a laudable fiction — but a fiction all the same. Just look around this conference. Of all the human qualities, and you find plenty of them here, modesty is mostly absent. It's just not part of their intellectual baggage." He gave a disarming laugh. "I don't know why I say, 'their'; it includes me. But whatever the opposite of modesty is, it gets lost when people appear naked in the sauna. In the dim steamy light, a potbellied naked man with thick glasses is reduced to the real fundamentals." Again he laughed. "I never used a sauna in Israel, but now I'm hooked. And the local organizers somehow managed to fix one up. I can hardly wait to see who'll be there."

"And women will also come?" she asked.

"I'm sure some of the Scandinavians and Germans will." He shrugged his shoulders. "What about you? Have you ever been in a sauna?"

Of course she had. Ever since she had moved to midtown Manhattan two years ago, jogging — her favorite form of exercise — had become too complicated. She was too busy during the day and too single to be jogging evenings. So Melanie had joined a women's athletic club for aerobics and swimming, followed by a sauna. She understood what Menachem meant, when he said he'd gotten hooked. Melanie had gotten hooked not just by saunas, but also by the nudity as well — a nakedness only slightly tempered by the scrim of steam, where makeup and physical pretense could not be maintained.

Melanie enjoyed inspecting the diversity of bodies in her club's sauna and was not ashamed of her own. Indeed, it rather pleased her. Firm to the touch and well proportioned, her muscles had, as they say, "definition." There were no excesses where they mattered most: belly, thighs, buttocks, even her smallish, alpine breasts. But men? She had not seen a naked man since Justin's death. And seeing naked the man who, just a short while ago, had asked whether she'd thought of sleeping with him: the thought appealed to her. It appealed to her because, as soon as she'd passed through a phase of acute embarrassment, it had dawned on her that his basically crude remark had turned her on as she hadn't been turned on for months, or was it years? In her capacity as director of REPCON, she met men constantly, but all of them, in one way or another, wanted money. On more than one occasion, she had felt empathy for the Doris Dukes and Barbara Huttons of this world, who could never be sure that a man saw anything but their wealth.

Menachem had been different. When they met, he hadn't a clue what REPCON stood for. For Melanie, that had made Menachem so rare an academic bird that she was willing to overlook all kinds of imperfections in his plumage. But what was the dress code in a mixed sauna at the Kirchberg? Or in any mixed sauna, for that matter. Melanie had never been in one.

"So will you come?" Menachem asked as they headed for the plenary session in the gym of the *Volksschule*, the local grammar school, which the conference had taken over for the week during the long summer vacation. The smaller working groups, consisting of no more than twenty participants each, were held in the classrooms.

"I may," she said.

———

Melanie did not see Menachem during the evening plenary session. She nearly discarded the idea of the sauna when she asked a lawyer from a Washington think tank whether she'd join her for a late-night sauna. The woman had seemed willing to consider the idea, until Melanie had added that it would include men.

"I don't think so," the woman said after a pause. "Besides, I didn't bring a bathing suit."

The word "bathing suit" raised Melanie's energy barrier even higher. Would people be wearing bathing suits? In her exercise club, bathing suits in the sauna were *déclassé*; women too self-conscious about cellulite simply hid the offending areas with a towel. Forget the sauna, she thought, it's not worth the bother.

But back in her room at the *Gasthof zur Steinwand*, after having stripped off her slacks, she stopped. Her hesitancy may have been associated with a sense of irritable unfulfillment or with the view she caught in the full-length mirror on the open bathroom door. Melanie was always scrutinizing herself in a mirror, whenever she happened to chance on one, with a normal mixture of self-satisfaction and insecurity. Tonight, as she gazed at the reflection looking back at her, she found herself trying to imagine how she might look to a man. With her slacks she had worn silvery Lurex knee-high socks with black, medium-high T-strap shoes. Pantless, there was nothing but bare flesh between the top of her glittery socks and her bikini briefs. In her present state of partial exposure in her black turtleneck, she looked positively stripteasish. The transformation from professional quasi-academic to elegant tart, produced by just stepping out of well-cut slacks, startled her. Slipping out of her sweater, she resumed the examination, turning slowly while discarding her bra to display her breasts.

It took her only minutes to put back on the same slacks and sweater, brush her teeth (Why do that for a sauna? she might have wondered under less impulsive circumstances), grab a bath towel, and slam the door behind her. Although ordinarily compulsively neat, Melanie didn't even bother to put the discarded brassiere into the drawer. She left it on the bed. While this omission was unconscious, the fact that she kept the room key rather than leaving it at the front desk was not.

———

The common dressing room was a mess. The pools of water on the floor and the clothes scattered on the bench or hanging from the hooks on the wall gave the distinct impression of a male locker room. Melanie resisted the urge to glance through the small window of the heavy wooden door of the sauna, with its dim light barely illuminating the scene inside. Instead, she inspected the clothing.

With one exception — a green woolen skirt, carefully folded over some more private items — the remaining garb was a unisex assortment of jeans and sweaters. A quick count of the shoes pointed to the existence of eight occupants, at least one of them female.

What the hell, she thought, I might as well strip. The bath towel, not the most luxuriant, just barely provided combined cover for her dense pubic hair and her breasts, but in a sitting position, she judged it would be adequate.

In the steamy, low-lit sauna, Melanie could scarcely see. Hesitating at the threshold, peering blindly before her, she held the door open too long. The curt command, "Quick. Shut it!" propelled her inside. She had to proceed by feel.

The lower bench seemed overcrowded, with one body reclining in back and another four sitting bent over. The upper shelf, presumably too hot for the rest of the company, was occupied by a single supine denizen whom Melanie joined by crouching near his legs. The sex of her upper berth companion was unambiguously displayed, but the lower row, arranged in waiting room fashion, was less obvious. The bare breasts and toweled turban of the person below her consoled Melanie that at least one other female was present. But who were the rest? From her upper vantage point, the occasional low murmur of one pair and the vaguely discernible outlines of the rest offered little help.

"It sure is hot," she announced to no one in particular, hoping that her voice would raise someone's awareness of her identity. And where was Menachem? she wondered. Almost by command, the door opened, two dripping, naked men pushing in.

"It's cold," Menachem exclaimed. "Excuse us," he said, reaching past the turbaned woman for the water bucket and throwing its contents on the hot stones. The whoosh of steam nearly obscured her view of the two men climbing up into her balcony, which suddenly promised to turn populous. "I hope you don't mind," Menachem murmured, trying to reach the recesses of the upper shelf behind Melanie.

"Oh, it's you," he exclaimed. "I didn't think you'd come."

"I wasn't sleepy when I got back to my room," she replied.

"I can think of much better reasons for coming here, but anyway, welcome. Do you know each other?" he asked, pointing to the naked man, who quickly offered his hand.

"How do you do," said Melanie and found her towel slipping off her wet breasts as the man, reaching past Menachem, kept shaking her hand without letting go. His manner of eyeing her breasts made her wish she could tuck her towel tighter.

"Enough," Menachem laughed, separating their hands as if he were a referee. "Let's sit here for a few minutes until I'm hot again. You can then join me for another dip. You do swim, don't you?"

Melanie just nodded. Two of the men below them departed and so, finally, did the recumbent silent type behind, allowing them to spread out. Melanie swung around, knees clamped together, the towel around her waist. Covering her breasts at this stage seemed almost pointless. Whoever wanted to ogle her breasts, Melanie concluded, had had ample opportunity to do so. Besides, they made her look younger. Or so Justin had told her.

As if on cue, the other woman rose, causing the upper gallery to turn their attention toward her. Melanie judged her to be around sixty and Scandinavian, given the nonchalant manner in which she now stood naked, towel over one arm, as if she were about to leave a salon. Her departure left just three of them in the sauna.

"Do you know any of those people?" Melanie asked, searching for some neutral conversational subject, now that they were almost alone.

"Just a few," Menachem replied, matching her earlier movement by pivoting around, his arms now clamped around one raised knee. His penis, clearly visible to Melanie, was sufficiently erect to emphasize his circumcised glans. For a long moment, his eyes glided over her in a drawn-out, visual caress. Though neither lecherous nor even intrusive, his gaze kept her from scrutinizing him. "You look great," he finally said approvingly. "Just great. But by now you must be boiling. Let's jump in the water," he said and then turned around, speaking some rapid sentences to the man behind.

———

"What language were you two speaking?" she asked. They were swimming in the pond, both of them doing the breaststroke, rising rhythmically in cetacean fashion to gather air.

"Arabic," he said, turning over to float on his back.

"Who was he?"

Menachem rolled over and eyed her humorously. "You mean his name? You have to press him for it. He's a chemist from Tunis. Even if he hadn't told me, I would have guessed the chemist part. He washed his hands *before* he stepped up to the urinal. Only chemists do that."

"Where did you pick up this useful piece of information?"

Menachem, who had started treading water, grinned back. "I have learned to be observant."

"Hmm," she said. "But I didn't know we had a Tunisian representative at this conference."

"He's not a Tunisian. He's just from Tunis."

"Oh?"

"He's a Palestinian; a last-minute addition to the Arab delegates. That's why he's not on the original registration list. Let's go back to the sauna once more. Maybe we'll have it to ourselves."

―――

"In the Middle East, the hand you cannot cut off you kiss," said Menachem while pulling on his socks. "There are plenty of people in my government who want to cut off one of their hands, but I don't believe that's realistic. Nor the PLO's obsession with cutting off both our hands. I think Ahmed Saleh is a kisser, and I intend to find out.

"But enough of that. I want to tell you something. When I saw you in the sauna, I was surprised and happy."

"You showed that," Melanie said dryly.

"After dinner, when I asked you to come to the sauna, my motive was somewhat Solomonian."

"Oh?" Melanie drew out the sound to give it a coy twist.

"Not unlike when he invited the queen of Sheba to approach him."

"Well, well. So I am finally hearing the famous Menachem Dvir lecture. The one *le gourou* said I shouldn't miss."

Menachem had just finished tying the laces of his shoes. As he straightened, Melanie caught an unexpected expression, almost of shyness.

"Here?" he asked. "In this dressing room?"

Melanie broke out laughing. "You're right. It isn't very romantic or even clean. Tell it to me while you walk me to my hotel."

———

It was a clear night. Menachem proposed that they take the path through the woods. "You seem to know your way around," remarked Melanie.

"I've been here at an earlier conference. And the one thing we don't have in the Negev are forests like these. So whenever I come to Europe, I explore them."

They walked on in silence for a few minutes more before Menachem continued. "I usually walk alone — even at home. But this time. . . ." he hesitated and then groped for her hand. "May I?"

"Of course," she said, squeezing back. "And now," she pressed his hand once more, "tell me about Solomon and the queen of Sheba."

"All right," he chuckled in the darkness, "but only the short version. I can't give a lecture walking hand in hand with a woman."

Melanie withdrew her hand. "If that's your only problem, let me unleash you."

"No," he said quickly, reaching again, "now that I have touched you, without physical contact I would be struck dumb."

Strange, she thought, we both behave like romantic adolescents after having sat naked next to each other. But she understood, indeed was certain that Menachem also understood the difference between then and now. When they had run out to the pond, she only dropped the towel just before diving into the water. When they returned, she'd asked him to stay in the water, "Menachem, wait here a couple of minutes. Let me run in and first get dressed."

"Sure," he had said and floated back into the darkness.

———

"Of the many versions, this is the shortest, yet it tells you most about the king as a man. Solomon had heard that the queen of Sheba was very beautiful, but her legs and feet were hairy like the legs of an ass."

"Oh, come now, Menachem," Melanie exclaimed. "How do you know the feet of an ass are hairy?"

"You obviously underestimate my credentials as a Shebaist," he said playfully. "But as every Shebaist knows, one of the juicier versions of this story comes from the Koran and that's precisely what it says: 'Her legs and feet were hairy like the legs of an ass.' The Koran also describes the approach to his throne and again I quote." He squeezed her hand and stopped to draw breath.

She could only see the outlines of his strong face with his deeply set eyes, the high cheekbones and below them deep grooves. They were like the mistakes of a sculptor, who, in trying to insert dimples, had slipped with his thumb to produce heavier indentations, thus elevating dramatically the cheekbones.

" 'It had a floor of white, transparent glass, beneath which was running water, wherein were fish. And when she saw it, she imagined it to be a great water, and she uncovered her legs, that she might wade through it; and Solomon was on his throne at the upper end of the palace, and he saw that her legs and her feet were handsome.' "

"A lovely story, but what happened then?"

Menachem reached over to move some hair away from her eyes. The fleeting touch of his fingers on her forehead made her shiver — pleasantly so.

"You tell me," he said. "Here in the woods."

"Before I do, tell *me* whether that's why you invited me to the sauna. So you could see whether I had hairy legs?"

"Not quite."

"Well?" she coaxed.

"Well," he echoed, "when we met earlier in the day, your body was covered like that of the queen of Sheba — "

"So you couldn't tell in slacks and sweater what I looked like?"

"Not the details."

They had reached the point where the path through the woods entered the main road. As they passed a streetlight, Melanie disengaged her hand from his.

"You didn't mind, did you?" he asked.

"You mean your interest in physical details?"

"That, and my asking about the sauna."

"If I had minded, I wouldn't have come."

She wondered what he would say next, but Menachem had turned silent. His hands were in his pockets, his steps audible on the cobblestones.

"Where are you staying?" she finally asked. "My *Gasthof* is just up the road."

"Back there, by the school." He motioned with his head. One of his hands moved out of the pocket to touch her ever so lightly on the sleeve. "You were going to tell me how *you* imagined the queen of Sheba story ended. I'd like to hear your version."

"All right," she said and resumed walking. "You'll get an even shorter variant because we're almost at my place: Solomon instantly fell in love and proposed marriage."

"You're either a romantic or you're cheating," Menachem exclaimed.

"A romantic I am — that is when circumstances allow it — but why accuse me of cheating?"

"Because the passage I was quoting says exactly that." He sounded disappointed. "Had you heard it before?"

"No," she said quickly. "I just put myself on the throne instead of Solomon."

"Rather than in the place of the queen of Sheba?"

"How could I? She hasn't said anything so far."

"True," he said, partly mollified. "Actually, the Koran isn't quite as romantic as you. But here we are." He halted a few yards away from the lit sign *Gasthof zur Steinwand*.

"You can't stop now," Melanie exclaimed. "I want to know how close I came. I want to hear the rest of the story. And why you — a Jew — are quoting the Koran instead of the Old Testament."

She had said it banteringly, but Menachem's expression did not mirror hers. "It's late," he replied, "and it would take too long."

"Are you sleepy?" she asked.

"No, but I thought — "

"Come in then," she pointed to the entrance. "I'm wide awake."

———

"You take the chair," she gestured to the only one in the sparsely furnished room. "I'll sit on the bed." They both saw the discarded brassiere at the same time. Nonchalantly, she sat on it, legs crossed.

"And now the rest of the story. I want to hear how Solomon proposed marriage."

"Ah yes." Menachem leaned back in the chair and laced his fingers together behind his head, clearly enjoying stretching out the tale. "As a romantic, you may be disappointed. 'He desired to marry her; but he disliked the hair upon her legs' — "

"Wait a moment," Melanie cried out. "You said her legs were handsome."

"I'm talking about the *hair* on her handsome legs. The Koran says, 'so the devils made for him a depilatory of quick-lime, wherewith she removed the hair.' You look disappointed, Melanie."

"I guess I am." She gave a mock pout.

"Well, *you* have nothing to worry about with *your* legs."

Melanie raised a warning finger. "Let's stick to the queen of Sheba. What happened next?"

"According to the Koran, 'He used to visit her every month once, and to remain with her for three days' — "

"Is that all? How typical of a man."

"Consider the quality, not the number of visits."

"Are you still quoting the Koran?" she asked skeptically.

"No," he said, and started to rise from the chair. "This part of the story is mine."

"And the marriage proposal?" she asked, looking up at him as he stood in front of her.

"Melanie, I'm not Solomon."

5

"Wait," Melanie commanded. "What about a condom?"

"If you keep talking, this will be all academic."

She clutched his rapidly softening penis as if she wanted to arrest any further shrinkage. "We really should," she murmured.

"I don't use rubbers," he gasped. "I'm infertile."

Many weeks later, Melanie would remember his choice of word:

infertile, rather than *sterile*. But at this moment in Kirchberg, it registered only in her deep subconscious. "But what about — "

"We Jews in the Negev don't have your American problems," he interrupted. "In any event, not yet. And before they come — " She could feel his member hardening. "Lead me into you," he urged.

"Please, Menachem!" Her hand did not let go.

"All right." He slipped off her hand. "My tongue then."

———

Late that night, as they lay naked on the narrow single bed, the breeze from the open window cooling their moist, warm bodies, Melanie whispered, "Earlier this afternoon, you really shocked me with that question about wanting to sleep with you."

Melanie's head was lying on his left arm. Gently, he ran his right index finger along her cheek, as if he were following a marked path, until his finger reached her lip. "You did, didn't you?" he murmured, brushing her lip once more.

"Yes," she laughed. "But I could never have answered 'Yes.' Was I red in the face when you asked?"

"I don't remember. You took me by surprise: you're too prim to be sexy, and much too sexy to be prim."

Melanie turned onto her side, propping up her head to face him. "Will you believe me if I tell you I've never done this before?"

"Define *this*."

"Sleeping with a man I barely know."

"Sure. I believe you."

"Really? Honestly?"

"Honestly."

"How come?"

"Because it also applies to me."

"*You*? You've never slept with a woman you barely knew?"

"Well," he hedged. "Not one I met only a few hours ago."

"Hmm." She rolled over on her back, hands folded on her stomach. "Tell me something about your life. For instance Africa."

"Africa?"

"At dinner, you said you learned good table manners in Africa."

Africa! I spent the first eighteen years of my life there, yet I've hardly talked about them. Spending so much of your adult life on secret pursuits means that your personal history turns into a barely opened book. It would have to be someone like this to ask about Africa: the first woman since leaving Dimona with whom I've had . . . what should I call it? . . . An affair? . . . A one-night stand? And why can't I give her a simple answer? Is it the usual problem of us Jews? You ask Gentiles where they're from and you get straightforward information. You ask a Jew and he starts with an explanation.

I used to be crazy about the Congo. But I haven't thought about it for a long time. Or about Leonid. How would I tell her that story?

It's a strange one. How many Polish Jews ended up in the Congo? I don't mean Léopoldville or Stanleyville or even Costermansville out east on Lake Kivu, where the colonials used to spend their holidays. I mean out in nowhere, in the real Congo of the twenties and thirties, not the Kinshasa, Kisangani, or Bukavu of today's Zaire. I'm talking about Kutu, that outpost of King Albert's empire just large enough to be entitled to one Belgian administrator, one sergeant, twelve soldiers, and one Greek shopkeeper. It was much too small to get a Belgian name. I was born there. In my time, Kutu was untouched by road or railroad, but it was near water and surrounded by oceans of hard wood. That's where Leonid established his giant sawmill operation, employing hundreds of natives, at Kutu on the southern edge of Mai Ndombe, Lake Leopold II on the maps of the Belgian Congo. Mai ndombe, black water, was inky because the Lukenie and Lokoro rivers draining into the lake were black from all the copal trees in the flooded forests surrounding Lokolama. Once a month a steamer came from Léopoldville — a trip that took eight days during the rainy season and five during the dry, and that was all our communication with the outside world. Kutu had no radio or electricity. Except for the kerosene for our lanterns and the precious gasoline for Leonid's outboard motor, everything, including the monthly steamer, was powered by wood. Of which there seemed an unlimited supply.

What distinguished Leonid from ordinary human beings was his ability to make things out of nothing — or at least out of nothing that resembled in any way the final product. He had learned engineering at Ghent, but his mechanical wizardry and ability to learn new skills on the fly must have been genetic. Even his flying was picked up that way.

The rivers were fine for transporting the logs and timber — he'd even constructed his own steam-powered barge — but Leonid was much too impatient to depend on water for his personal travel to and from the capital. He learned how to fly on early biplanes, made out of a lattice of fine wood — I'm almost sure it was ash — canvas, and lots of steel wire. By the time I was thirteen, Leonid had taught me how to pilot a Coudron-Latécoère — the same model Antoine de Saint-Exupéry had made famous. I'd been solo flying and troubleshooting biplanes years before I learned how to drive a car. But that wasn't all Leonid taught me.

He must have assembled one of the most extensive private libraries in Central Africa — how, I'll never know — and maintained it in the face of a climate that turned more substantial things than paper into mold and rot. We had a big, spacious residence of handmade brick, raised about one meter off the ground, tin-roofed, with a wide veranda circling the entire building. The floors were of polished cement, waxed in red, and while termites were an ever present hazard, the inside construction was such that termite tunnels could be spotted easily. In those days before DDT, insects were controlled with Flytox, which one of the houseboys applied daily at dusk with a hand-pumped sprayer. Our food was kept in a garde-manger, a caged cupboard made out of mosquito screening; it stood in the central room, the kati-kati, its legs set in empty tin cans filled with water and topped with a bit of kerosene. Leonid declared the medium-sized cans of Olida ham ideal — one of many items of esoteric information I never forgot, but one I could never share with any rabbi. To this day, I can see the changing blue and yellow interference patterns on the water surface that so fascinated me as a child.

Compared to keeping a library, the logistics of food storage and preservation were simple, because the ultimate purpose of food is physical consumption, whereas books are meant to be preserved indefinitely. According to Leonid, the best way of maintaining his library mold-free was to keep it dry, a formidable task at any season,

requiring air circulation. In the absence of electricity, this was pro-
vided by a houseboy, whose function it was to open and move the
books, which were kept on simple wooden shelves, as often as possible.
Thoth, as we called him after the Egyptian god of learning, flipped
the pages with a sound like a professional cardsharp shuffling his
deck — a sound that any cockroach ootheca breeding there must have
taken for Armageddon.

Thoth's dominion was multilingual — the books were in French,
Flemish, English, and German — because Leonid was a linguist,
who, to my good fortune, insisted that my mother and he speak both
French and English in front of me. We used to do Shakespeare, not
just read him, with roles assigned irrespective of gender. One of the
greatest memories of my Kutu youth is the bloody-hand scene as
Leonid, not even in drag, entered the lantern-lit room from the ve-
randa as Lady Macbeth, his hands stained with grenadine.

But even then, in the middle 1930s, my English was not good
enough for Leonid. He believed in accentless, multilingual compe-
tence, and my Kutu-acquired English, though burnished by
Shakespeare, Dickens, and the Brontës, was not accentless. Leonid
also insisted on my taking table manners seriously: serious *table*
manners that Leonid, the Polish Jew, pursued in the depth of the
Congo with preposterous Anglomimetic stubbornness: we would dress
for dinner in the tropical humidity wearing clean white shirts, ties,
long pants, and freshly polished shoes. Middle-aged conviction,
rather than childhood fantasy, makes me believe Leonid must have
put on a tie even when faced by just sardines and toast. When I turned
fourteen, he shipped me to Cape Town, to one of the best South Afri-
can English-language boarding schools, which he picked less for its
Etonian scholarship than for its emphasis on table manners, its dress
code, and its rugby. In Leonid's opinion, a high-contact team sport
would make up in express time for my prior lack of exposure to white
children.

I spent four years in South Africa without once returning to the
Congo. In early 1940, Leonid called me back because he knew the
war would eventually spread south. We flew together from
Léopoldville to Kutu using a combination of map and visual navi-
gation until we reached our aerial marker: the black and yellow line

near Mushie where the yellow Kasai river meets the black Fimi. For kilometers, these waters do not mix, until the ebony Fimi wins out as it flows from black Lake Leopold II carrying the latter's copal ooze. It was the last time I landed on the dirt strip near the sawmill in Kutu. A year later, not yet 19, but claiming to be 21, I convinced the RAF in Nairobi to accept me. Even though I knew more about planes and flying than most of their recruits, it was my South African table manners and accent that got me into officers' training.

Leonid would have loved that interview. "You see," he would have gloated, "I knew that school was right for you," never realizing that his mania for the English colonial dress code would not stick.

It was the war that did that. I never told him — too afraid, even at that distance, of his disapproval. Still, I like to think that Leonid would have approved of the Palestinian Jews I met during the North African campaign — all of them Zionists — who persuaded me to get some engineering training at Manchester as a RAF veteran before joining the Hagana — tieless though they all were. But I couldn't put this into the letters I sent to Kutu, and we never met again face to face.

God bless you, Leonid, my father, whom I never once called "father."

"You ask about Africa?" murmured Menachem. "Some other time." He leaned over and kissed her. On her forehead, like an uncle. "I must get back to my room. I expect a phone call very early in the morning."

6

The real work at Kirchberg Conferences occurs in the working groups.

Now, on this second day, with the opening ceremony and initial plenary talks out of the way, the working groups were assembling in the classrooms of the *Volksschule*. The classrooms were more than big enough: each held a couple of dozen pupil's seats now arranged around the teacher's table — the only piece of adult furniture. In this Working Group on Population Problems and Economic Growth, some of the bigger men refused to even try using them; chairs were fetched from the outside. People were still drifting in, while Melanie, who was lithe enough to manage one of the students' seats, sat with her cheek resting in her hand and gazed through the window at the sunlit copper steeple of St. Wolfgang's church. As was her custom, she had chosen a place at the periphery of the group. It offered a certain physical distance from the smokers, who seemed to constitute the majority among the Europeans, as well as a better perspective. Ordinarily, she would use that perspective to advantage, taking time to observe her prospective colleagues, titrate their intellectual depths, figure out who was who, before entering into the discussion. This morning, however, her gaze wandered out the window. She wondered whether Menachem could see the church from his classroom. She also wondered whether he was thinking of tomorrow.

"Let's skip the Wednesday tour to the Semmering," she had proposed back in her *Gasthof*. "Let's go to Vienna instead."

"And do what?" he asked

"Leave it to me," she said and ran her finger along his lips until he caught it between his teeth. It almost hurt.

———

"You permit me?" Luc Morand's voice brought her back into the classroom. "Or you wish to be *seule?*"

"No, please," Melanie pointed to the adjacent seat. Morand, a thin, ascetic Frenchman with closely cropped, salt-and-pepper hair, folded himself into the small space without apparent effort.

"It does not disturb you?" He waved his cigarette.

"Go ahead," she said, not really meaning it, but appreciative of the courtesy. She might have changed her mind, had she known that *le gourou* was essentially a one-match-per-day man, lighting each cigarette from the flickering corpse of its predecessor.

"I have seen you last night in the *salle à manger* with Dvir."

"Yes," she said. "How well do you know him?"

"Me-na-shem?" She liked the way he pronounced Menachem's name. He made it sound so much gentler. "At one time, very well."

———

"And now?"

Morand wagged his head, finally terminating the movement with a dismissive Gallic puff. *"Moins.* Less so." He blew smoke through his nostrils. "Did he recount the queen of Sheba story?"

"Yes," Melanie laughed.

"In which *version?*" he asked, ending the word with a nasal *o.* But before Melanie could answer, Morand raised a warning finger. "It commences," he pointed to the group's chairman, who was tapping a water glass with his pen.

"Let's have lunch together," Melanie whispered. "I would like to hear your version of Menachem Dvir." After all, she thought, in the final analysis, it was *le gourou* who had led her into bed with Menachem. The least he could do now was answer a few questions about her lover.

———

It did not take Melanie long to discover that Luc Morand stuck to one thing at a time. And food came first, Melanie noticed, with a mixture of awe and censure, as she watched *le gourou* attack his salad.

His fork had turned into a weapon, stabbing two, three, or even four shreds of lettuce at a time. As soon as the first forkful had entered his mouth, the hunt was resumed: cherry tomato, slice of cucumber, garnish of carrot, more lettuce. He did not select; he stormed from the right edge of the dish to the left, piercing whatever was nearest, and then swallowing the prey, with just a chomp or two. Only when he'd cleared his plate did he look up, catching Melanie's surprised stare.

"Yes?"

"I was just wondering," she recovered quickly. "You're a nuclear physicist from Saclay, aren't you? I'd have thought you'd be with the disarmament bunch."

Le gourou picked up the smoldering cigarette balanced on the side of the ashtray and revived it with a deep puff. "Yes," he nodded, "that made me come first to Kirchberg when there were few avenues of intervention between East and West."

Avenues of intervention. What a wonderful expression, thought Melanie. It sounds like one of the *grands boulevards* of Paris.

"And Kirchberg has produced results. The Test Ban Treaty would perhaps never have been signed in 1963 if the Russians had not had *confiance* during those conferences in us and in the *Anglais* and above all in the *Américains.*"

Melanie had heard that story before. Every new Kirchberger was informed of this early and most dramatic success of the Kirchberg conferences. "So you're a nuclear dove, Luc? May I call you Luc?"

Le gourou grinned. "Yes. But do not say it *Look.*" He mimicked Melanie's enunciation, adding a few more *os*. "It is *Luc.* And yes, I am now a dove."

Melanie leaned forward. "But not always?"

"*Non.* At one time I was like Dvir."

"You mean you and he were nuclear hawks?"

Melanie had caught *le gourou* in a matchless cigarette transfer. He took a deep puff, the new Gauloise still in his mouth, its glowing end pointing at her like a lit missile as he extinguished the burning stub of the old one in the ashtray. She interpreted the whiff of smoke drifting toward her as affirmation. "And is he still?"

He shrugged. "You must ask him. What I always liked about Mena-shem, and still do, is he never hesitates to say anything he believes." He stopped for several draws on his cigarette. "What I like less now is that he also seems to believe every word he says — at least when it comes to Israel and *les armes nucléaires.*"

"But how could he be a hawk? He isn't even in the Nuclear Arms Group." She waved in the direction of some imaginary classroom. "He's in Regional Conflicts."

"*Précisément!* That is why he is always a hawk. But then, he is an Israeli and a Jew, and I am a French *catholique. Ex-catholique,*" he added, stubbing out his cigarette for emphasis. He stared at it for a moment, as if surprised at what he'd done, before beginning a general search of his pockets for a match.

Melanie waited patiently while *le gourou* set fire to another cigarette. "Where did you two first meet?"

"In Beersheba," he said matter-of-factly.

Melanie was taken aback. All along, she had assumed that they'd met as fellow Kirchbergers. But in Israel? "When was that?" she asked.

A new puff of smoke sailed in her direction. "In the sixties."

"By the way," Melanie asked, purposely not looking at Morand, "is Menachem married?" Her timing was off by only a few seconds, but it took minutes before she received her answer. The waitress had just set the next course in front of them. *Le gourou*'s attention was focused wholly on his plate.

I could kill that waitress, Melanie thought, but then found her own attention drawn to the food. She had barely finished her first *Spinat Knödel mit Champignon Sauce* — a tasty spinach dumpling — when another cloud of smoke blew across her plate, followed by Morand's voice.

"Yes," he said. "Why do you ask?"

Melanie busied herself with the second dumpling, cutting it into pieces, then depositing the knife near the upper edge of her plate before switching the fork from left hand to right. For once, she was thankful for the inefficiency inherent in American table manners. A European non-switcher of cutlery would have had less time to stall.

"Just curious," she said, piercing a morsel of dumpling with more care than the act required.

Morand took a long draw on his cigarette and held it a long time. Melanie was beginning to wonder if he had swallowed it all, when he leaned back and slowly released the smoke toward the ceiling.

"You have not asked him? Why?" The way he looked at her, his sharp, intelligent eyes examining her through the smoke, unnerved her.

"I thought it would be intrusive," she said. What the hell, she thought, if he can see through that, let him. "What's she like?"

"She?"

"Menachem's wife? Have you ever met her?"

"The second *Madame* Dvir, yes."

With an effort, Melanie held herself still. She couldn't possibly pursue a cross-examination, much as she'd like. Instead, she lifted her water glass and took a few sips.

Morand kept inhaling deeply, his eyes on the circles of smoke rising slowly and then dissipating as they headed toward the ceiling. To Melanie, the silence had started to feel awkward.

"So there were two wives," she said at last.

Morand turned one eye down toward her, and nodded. "Me-nashem had a *liaison* with his *assistante*. In Paris," he shrugged his shoulders, "who knows? It could have become a *ménage à trois*. But in Dimona? It became, as we say, *un scandale compliqué*. What about you?" He looked at Melanie. "Would you have a liaison with your *chef* or *professeur*?" He shook his head. "*Non*. Looking at your face, I would say you would not do it. You are not even capable to imagine such a thing."

Not imagine it? Perhaps not at age 23. Not as a second-year graduate student at Columbia. I'm a Scorpio, born in 1939, who missed the entire sexual revolution of the sixties. I've often thought about that, especially since Justin's death. If I had been a swinger in my middle twenties, would my sex life as a widow have been different? And if so, would I still have ended up in bed with Menachem, just a few hours after having met him? I doubt it. It's so unlike me: I am too measured, even too cagey, to indulge in a simple sexual escapade, and also much too self-sufficient. Not sexually — although I acquired a capacity for self-gratification at a remarkably early age. Rather, I'm thinking of professional independence — the problem that stared me in the face the day after Justin's cremation.

My high school and college days were all during the pre-Pill era. When I graduated from Mt. Holyoke in 1960, I was still a virgin. But so were many of my classmates. Going to a woman's college, of course, made that somewhat simpler (simpler, that is, if maintaining your virginity is one of your objectives. And to many of us, it was). Holyoke was always strong in chemistry — I'd say best among the Seven Sister colleges — and when I graduated, I knew that I'd first want to get a Ph.D. before even thinking of getting married. I had my pick of graduate schools, but I preferred to stay in the East and chose Columbia. I haven't thought about that first year in grad school for ages. That's when I decided on biochemistry, which at Columbia meant that I'd be working in the medical school at West 168th and

Broadway. If I'd picked straight chemistry, which was on the main campus some fifty blocks south, I wouldn't even have bumped into Justin, but already before meeting him, I'd lost my virginity. I don't know what makes me use that quaint expression, because I didn't really lose *it. I gave it away fairly willingly to a very bright, but, more relevantly, also brashly sexy TA in the departmental darkroom. It seemed very illicit and even dangerous: what would have happened if a professor or even worse, my new thesis advisor, Justin Laidlaw, had walked in and turned on the light, finding Melanie Sutherland bent over the developing tray, the skirt raised over her hips, its hem gripped between her teeth, while the TA thrust into her from behind? It was by no means romantic, but it was fun, at least from the second or third time onward. Over the next few months, that sexy TA and I had picked other, potentially even riskier spots in the lab. Now that I reflect upon it, the danger of getting caught was almost more exciting than the act itself.*

In my second year, I joined Justin's lab group, which fluctuated in size between eight to ten grad students and postdocs, with a couple of technicians. Justin was marvelous: a biochemist's biochemist — a deep and original thinker — who, not yet forty, had already acquired a major reputation in enzyme research. He saw every one of us at least once, and sometimes twice daily in the lab, but he always seemed to be spending a bit more time with me. I ascribed it to my status as the newest and least experienced grad student. Initially, I'm sure that this was the only reason. One day, halfway through my second year at Columbia, I was finishing an experiment. It was close to 7:00 P.M., a time when the lab was at its emptiest, when Justin appeared. He asked whether I'd join him for a bite at a nearby Italian place. I was hungry and I was flattered by the invitation, so I accepted. There was nothing special about the restaurant, but I still remember the dinner, even what we ate. When the waiter came around and asked what I wanted as a starter, I ordered minestrone. "I'll have the same," said Justin. For the main course, I selected mushroom lasagna. "The same," said Justin. And when it came time to order desserts, I beat him to the draw. "Two zabagliones," I said. "Right?" He just laughed.

Justin, of course, was obsessed with his work. But then it's impos-

sible to be a full professor at a place like Columbia and a member of the National Academy of Sciences by age thirty-seven without being something of a work fanatic. While workaholism may be great for one's professional life, in my opinion, it's usually the pits for the rest of the time, whatever little may be left. Not surprisingly, Justin was still a bachelor and, on the surface, not even a dissatisfied one.

It took a couple of months before we took our first outing together. It was on a Sunday, the only guiltless day off for lab scientists. We drove north along the Hudson during one of those enchanting October days, when the trees along the road seemed to be draped with oriental carpets. We wound up at the Storm King Art Center. It had just opened, and we had it almost to ourselves as we gamboled among the David Smith sculptures. We kissed there for the first time, while picnicking on the crest of a hill with the multicolored tesserae of the fall foliage all around. That's when I kidded him about his eyes rather than brains having first attracted me to him. But it was true: his personal magnetism first shone through his eyes. They caught yours in a fashion that allowed for no disconnection. When he talked research, they sparkled with verve; when he talked about love, they caressed. How many men have caressing eyes?

It was weeks, maybe months, before we went to bed together. Justin didn't want anyone to know that he had a "relationship" with a graduate student, even a consenting adult, and we met very discreetly in his apartment. Our consummation was touchingly conventional: lit candles, an open bottle of a very good red wine (that had been breathing for just the right time, I learned later from my oenophile husband-to-be), Vivaldi in the background, and a package of condoms, with its plastic cover cut open, by the bedside stand — strikingly different from the dark room and the other daring lab locations of my short-term liaison with the TA — yet, in some sense, more valued, because of Justin's consideration for my feelings: even in bed, he didn't take me for granted.

I don't believe my coworkers in the lab suspected anything for at least a year. I spent more and more time with Justin, sometimes four or five days in a row. But I retained my own room in Bard Hall on Haven Avenue and I stopped there every day to at least pick up my mail. Only during the summer, at the end of my fourth year, did we become careless. *One morning, when we entered the building at the same time, the only other female in our group, a Californian named Kim, confronted me: "Have you and Justin got something going between the two of you?" Most of the others called him Prof or Doc, but to Kim, who came from Santa Barbara and still looked like a beach bunny, he was Justin. Her question so startled me that my face turned a give-away pink.*

Strange. I remember the details of our first meal or where we kissed for the first time. I even remember the first wine-tasting he took me to and the winespeak he could emit without the slightest embarrassment: "The smashingly intense, exotic nose, the passionately entwined pepper and black currant flavors, the faint whiff of horse shit. . . ." When he first said "horse shit," I nearly choked on my mouthful of wine. Justin rarely used four-letter words, and I certainly didn't know that for some French wines, a faint equine spoor is actually a plus. And I never heard him say or write "passionately entwined" or even "smashingly intense" without a wine glass in his hand. Certainly never in bed.

Melanie looked *le gourou* straight in the eye. "I have a good imagination," she said quietly. "Sometimes, such an affair — "

"We say *liaison*, not *affaire*," he interjected.

Melanie shrugged. "I didn't realize I was speaking French. *Liaison* sounds more . . . consequential."

"Consequential?" He laughed. "A *bon mot* and quite *juste*: Menachem married Shulamit."

I can't recall precisely when or even whether Justin proposed marriage. One morning, it was more or less settled that we'd get married. But instead of doing it and thus promoting me instantaneously into the rank of professor's wife, he placed me — quite innocently — into a much more ambiguous situation by presenting me with an engagement ring. Even in the middle sixties, engagements among mature academics had started to go out of fashion, but I, of course, was touched.

Justin suggested that we get married the day after I got my Ph.D. and while this was an incentive for both mentor and disciple to ex-

pedite matters, our engagement still spanned nearly two semesters, which, in retrospect, were collegial purgatory. A lab group, and especially one as small as Justin's, is very intimate. You only realize the extent of that intimacy when it suddenly evaporates, and evaporate it did as the first glimmer of light reflected from my engagement ring.

And le gourou *wonders whether I can imagine what it's like to have a* liaison *with my* chef! *Justin was a popular and respected chief. And yet, the underlings do talk, most often in good humor. His affectation for describing wines was well known in the lab: Justin's winespeak — by then elegant music to my ears, but prissy affectation to beer-guzzling postdocs — could make even a Gallo jug wine sound classy by describing it as "well structured with a generous palate." One day, a British postdoc in our group had constructed a letter of recommendation for an academic position in a parody of Justin's winespeak — a potpourri of descriptors like "balanced" and "impressively, well-structured" juxtaposed with "slightly coarse finish" and "needs some maturing." I had just walked in and heard enough to judge it rather funny. But when the man caught sight of me, he stopped, clearly embarrassed. I learned very quickly that the person sharing pillow talk with the professor is excluded from gossip or even banter in the lab.*

The trouble with engagements is that you're neither wife (conventional and committed) nor lover (reckless and legally unbound), but the worst combination: conventional, yet legally unbound. So I concentrated on finishing the last few experiments and on writing my thesis, while bedding my fiancée and mentor. I may yet write an essay on the pros (really only one: ad libitum sex) and cons (numerous, and much more enduring) of being engaged to one's Ph.D. supervisor.

On our honeymoon, my new and very dear husband, in one of his many moments of insight, said something truly important: "In a successful marriage, the partners can be lovers, friends, and companions. Achieving even one of these is pretty good. Combining two is enviable, but three!" He could have used one of his enological flowery superlatives, but I preferred the ocular and facial exclamation point. We were married in 1965, when I was nearly twenty-six and

Justin barely thirty-nine. Ten years later, I became a widow for a reason that left me unprepared and enraged: a doctor's sloppiness during a basically trivial operation.

If I were asked to define our marriage on Justin's scale, I'd say that to me it appeared, at the very least, enviable. The lover phase was relatively brief, perhaps already over by the time we tied the legal knot, but the companionship was deep, considering that it had started in the lab and persisted there as well as in the home. For the rest of my marriage, I worked with my husband as a research associate without feeling that the shadow of his reputation in any way diminished me. It was this feeling of mutual respect that was the basis of our profound friendship.

As my peer cohort from graduate school days left, my position vis-à-vis the new group members turned into that of professor's surrogate; I even gave some of Justin's lectures when he was absent. I didn't mind because in some sense I became Professor Laidlaw. And Justin found it extraordinarily useful: gradually, he stopped feeling guilty if he didn't pay daily visits to the lab as a result of more consulting, more committee service, more this and more that. "Administrative oomph. That's what keeps the world going," Justin used to say. "Especially in science. And you, Melanie, have such oomph." When it came to international travel, to the big congresses, to the NATO workshops or award lectures — I always tagged along.

Tagged along sounds bitchy — probably because it is a widow remembering, rather than a wife. In fairness to Justin, he always asked that I accompany him, not only as wife and as companion, but also as the scientific collaborator he respected, with whom even pillow talk or pillow laughter could be about biochemistry. It was my husband's respect that had blinded me to the realization that my position as a research associate, depending as it must on "soft" money from my husband's research grants, might lower or demean me in other people's eyes. But it did, as I learned within weeks of my Justin's death.

We had no children. Justin never said he didn't want children. He just never expressed a desire for fatherhood. And I, who foremost wished to establish a scientific name for myself, found it easy to tem-

porarily sublimate ideas of motherhood. There was plenty of time for that in another few years, I thought, but as time passed — with our private life becoming more and more intertwined with our lab existence — the idea of motherhood receded. But the urge to procreate was always there.

The absence of children had an enormous impact on our social life. Schools, children's sport activities, scouts — you name it — are all potential social meeting places that our path never crossed. Most of our social friends were also academic colleagues, and because Justin was exceptionally young for a professor of such high stature, his peers were generally in their late forties or fifties — in other words a different generation from mine.

Again, as wife I didn't mind. In fact, I was flattered to find myself the youngest and frequently, professionally, also the most advanced woman in such settings. In my pride, I ignored that this was so only because the majority of the other spouses belonged to the earlier generation, when wives offered domestic rather than laboratory support. When I became a widow, they dropped me overnight.

One exception was the Frankenthalers, but they lived near Boston and even during our married life, Justin and I saw them only sporadically, primarily around scientific meetings; or when they came down to New York for Metropolitan Opera performances. I had seen the odd opera prior to my move to Manhattan, but it was Felix and Shelly Frankenthaler who always urged us to come along and who eventually converted me into the opera buff I now am. When Justin died, Felix and Shelly didn't just send condolences. They stayed in touch and have done so to this day — a gesture I will not forget.

The first few months of widowhood weren't as traumatic as I might have thought. I was extremely busy taking on the full responsibility for Justin's scientific research and his collaborators. Deep down in my psyche, I probably hoped that Columbia would elevate me from my "soft" research associateship to a "hard" tenure-track position. I know I had the credentials, but most of the faculty only saw the shadow Justin's enormous reputation cast on my own independent contributions. Perhaps I should have published as "M. Sutherland," rather than "Melanie Laidlaw," because the surname "Laidlaw" —

at least in our department — carried no given name other than "Justin." But without a formal academic slot, I could not serve as principal investigator — and without that title I had no access to independent funding. Operationally, I was indistinguishable from any other principal investigator in our department, but legally, I was nothing. And when Justin's grant money ran out, I found myself for all practical purposes on the street.

I had two choices: seek an academic position elsewhere, which was by no means impossible, but which nevertheless meant that I'd have to start near the bottom rung, or look for something more substantial outside academia. But I had been spoiled: I had tasted authority, even though it may have been sham influence as the surrogate of a powerful man. I decided that I wanted both: some degree of independent power and the ability to exert it within the academic milieu. In the final analysis, money is the ultimate currency of power. I was lucky to put my hands on quite a pile.

The REPCON Foundation's legal counsel had encouraged the founder, Athena Campobello, to spend her prospective legacy — corpus he called it with a certain lack of delicacy — over a period of twenty years rather than establishing the conventional type of endowment. He carried the day by arguing that in this fashion, Campobello's foundation would be able to distribute much more money annually, thus carrying more clout — especially in so chronically underfunded a field as contraceptive research. Felix Frankenthaler, who was like a boar sniffing for buried truffles when it came to new grant money in his field of reproductive biology, had heard about REPCON practically on the day of its conception. Sniffing closer to parturition time, he learned that they were looking for a director and promptly called me. The rest is history: my personal history. Athena and I hit it off famously. I had three important advantages: I was a woman; I was young enough to still be pre-geriatric when REPCON was scheduled for liquidation twenty years hence; and I was a scientist. I had done all of my advanced training and research under the umbrella of Columbia's College of Physicians and Surgeons, and for Athena Campobello, whose primary concern was medicine, the initials P & S tipped the scale.

It seemed that the REPCON job had solved all my problems: it gave me professional satisfaction, financial independence, and no tenure hassles. Yet at the same time I was being courted assiduously by all the cocks of the academic walk. It seemed an answer to all of my problems but one: the increasingly louder ticking of my reproductive clock.

"Any children?" The question popped out before Melanie had time to reflect. Melanie had a fleeting moment of worry, remembering how Menachem had persuaded her to forget about *rubbers*, as he had called them with such disdain.

"*Non.*" Morand shook his head. "They had other problems."

Melanie pondered this one, wondering how she might inquire about the nature of those problems without appearing overly inquisitive.

Le gourou closed that opportunity.

"You ask so many questions about Me-na-shem. Why?"

She waved the question away with an airy gesture. "You are right." She leaned toward him, smiling what she hoped was her disarming smile. "Let's talk about you. What *did* bring you into the Population Group?"

Le gourou raised both hands, palms open. It wasn't a guru's benediction, not with a cigarette suspended between two fingers, but a disclaimer. "It is not my *spécialité*. But if the world does not blow itself up with *la bombe H*, then *la bombe de la population* may do it. I wanted to hear what your group had to say about that. For the rest of the conference, I have to return to my *bombe*.

"I want to concentrate on *les risques du terrorisme nucléaire*, because this should be of common interest, even to hawks like *notre ami* Me-na-shem. Just ask him about the Israeli definition of *prolifération nucléaire* to see how divisive some other problems are." He snorted. "But I am an optimist. It is necessary in this business. Also in yours." He pointed his cigarette at Melanie. "Maybe even more in yours."

"And what are your grounds for optimism?"

"Number one: the Partial Test Ban Treaty of 1963. Kirchberg

helped here, as I told you, probably more than people realize. Number two: The 1968 Treaty on Non-Proliferation of the *Armes nucléaires.*"

"But you just pointed to Israel. And what about India, South Africa — "

"*Bien sûr.*" He gave his cigarette a reflective puff. "Still, we are making some progress. Take Number three: The Anti-Ballistic Missile Treaty four years later. I know, the progress is very slow, but still. . . . That is why I want us to focus on something new — *un problème terrible*, but also *un problème d'optimiste*: One day, we will agree about gradual dismantling of nuclear weapons. That is *la bonne nouvelle* of the *optimiste*. But how do you say '*mauvaise nouvelle*,' the opposite?"

"Bad News?" Melanie ventured.

"*Exactement*! The bad news is the storage and ultimate disposal of the dismantled warheads *nucléaires*: five kilograms of plutonium for each! Some technologists say, use it for *l'énergie nucléaire*, for breeder reactors, for *je ne sais quoi*. It is like with cobalt *radioactif*, they declare: it causes cancer, but it can also be employed to fight cancer." Suddenly he stopped.

"Enough from me." He mashed the cigarette against the ashtray's bottom. "Ask others. Ask Me-na-shem. Or perhaps you have more interesting questions for him?"

7

"I see you had lunch with *le gourou*," remarked Menachem. He had bumped into Melanie on the way to the afternoon sessions. "What do you think of him?"

"He's an interesting man," she replied noncommittally. "Do you know him well?"

They'd been walking side by side down the corridor. He stopped to face her. "Did you ask Luc that?"

His unexpected directness flustered her. "Yes," she reddened, "but you can get different answers — "

"So what did he say?"

"That at one time he knew you quite well."

Menachem gave a curt nod. "So far so good. That applies to both of us."

"And when did you meet him?" she persisted.

"You didn't ask him that?" They were still standing face to face. Melanie was surprised by the direction the conversation had taken. To hear them, one wouldn't think they were on exactly friendly terms. Had she trespassed on chancy ground? Judging from his wary look, she'd have to say yes.

She decided to be straightforward. "I asked him where, and he said 'Beersheba.' But to the 'when?' he gave a vaguer answer."

"I'm surprised he said that much." He smiled briefly. "And even the little he told you is not completely correct."

"He called you a hawk," Melanie said. "A nuclear hawk," she added quickly, feeling she was getting in deeper with each word. "An *Israeli* nuclear hawk. I don't think he meant it accusingly."

Menachem glared. "Maybe not. Still, I don't like to be placed into pigeonholes. Only pigeons belong there, not a *mensch*."

The word seemed to cheer him up. He took her elbow and started to steer her down the hall. "I think you should forget about population issues this afternoon," he explained. "Come to Regional Conflicts instead. This morning, I had to listen to too much Arab verbiage. Our chairman is one of those Austrian Bruno Kreisky types: leans over backward so far that he practically lies on his back. I asked him to lean forward a bit this afternoon." Menachem bared his teeth in what might have been a smile. "Your Israeli hawk intends to display his hawkish nature." He winked. "Or maybe I'll just flap my wings." To Melanie, Menachem Dvir suddenly looked very engaging, almost a teenager posturing before his girl.

"This, I've got to see," she said and followed him.

———

" 'The great wish of some is to avenge themselves on some particular enemy, the great wish of others is to save their own pocket,' " the man read ponderously from the single page in his hands. " 'Slow in assembling, they devote a very small fraction of the time to the consideration of any public object, most of it to the prosecution of their own objects.' I am using a chairman's prerogative to start this afternoon's proceedings by quoting from Thucydides. He ended by saying: 'and so, by the same notion being entertained by all separately, the common cause imperceptibly decays.' I might add that this was in 400 B.C. Let us hope that in A.D. 1977 we act differently in Kirchberg." He put down his glasses and turned to Menachem.

"Only a neutral idealist without problems for survival can afford to say that," grumbled Menachem. "Not even the modern Greeks follow Thucydides."

"*Also, Herr Kollege* Dvir," the Austrian chairman said in a resigned tone, "the floor is yours." He took off his wristwatch and put it, somewhat ostentatiously, on the table. "We have only three hours this afternoon — "

"Don't worry," Dvir interrupted, tilting his chair to such an extent that Melanie, who had taken her usual place on the peripheries of the group, worried that he'd crash backward. "I won't take too much time . . . if I don't get interrupted too much. I didn't notice any concern on your part this morning about time. However — " he raised his hand in a conciliatory gesture to stop the chairman from responding.

"This morning, our Egyptian colleague," Dvir leaned forward, still balanced precariously on the two rear legs of his chair, to nod in the direction of El-Gammal who studiously ignored the acknowledgment, "expanded at some length, Mr. Chairman . . ."

Come on, Menachem, Melanie thought silently. Stop paying back the chairman and get to the point.

". . . about Israel's military and nuclear alternatives. So let me start there." His chair came down on all four legs as Dvir suddenly leaned forward to catch the attention of the half-circle of men around him. He spoke slowly, his raised index finger ticking off points. "Nuclear capabilities are linked to chemical weapons; chemical weapons to conventional arms; and conventional arms to political fabric." He stopped and tilted back to return to his balancing act on two chair legs.

"All these threads are woven into a seamless fabric of fear and insecurity and to unthread it all in one swoop through NWFZ is preposterous."

"Mr. Chairman," El-Gammal interrupted, "do we have to go through all this again?"

Before the Austrian could answer, Menachem exploded. "*Again?*" Melanie had never heard him use such a threatening tone. "Just because we have listened most of the morning to the Egyptian position — "

"Not just Egyptian," countered El-Gammal. "Our British friend here, our colleague from — "

"Mr. Chairman!" This time Dvir waited until he had the undivided attention of the group. "If I'm going to be interrupted all the time we are not going to make much progress, even if we use the entire afternoon. Good," he said, seeing the chairman's resigned nod, "so let's get back to NWFZ."

Melanie leaned across to the man next to her, who was idly doodling. "What is NWFZ?" she whispered.

He looked up startled. "What?"

"What does NWFZ stand for?" she repeated.

"Nuclear-Weapon-Free-Zone" he replied, astonished as if she'd asked for the definition of U.S.A.

"If the Middle East is to become *and remain* nuclear-free, then this fabric must be cut into manageable pieces and dealt with piece by piece. And as an Israeli, even if every other person in this room disagrees, I must insist that arms control focus first on conventional arms. Israel will never sign a NWFZ accord until peace is assured."

"And how does our Israeli colleague propose to achieve that?"

Menachem nodded curtly to the Englishman. "I'm getting to that. The problem is too complex to be solved in a single comprehensive settlement. Too little time, which supposedly heals all wounds, has passed since the state of Israel was born. While history, which always keeps wounds open to bleed again, is all around us. We have to deal with the separate elements and we have to do that concurrently, because you won't be able to settle the smallest piece — let alone on the scale of NWFZ — unless *both* parties," to Melanie's surprise, Menachem, after pointing to himself, directed his index finger at the Tunisian from last night's sauna, "are persuaded that progress is also occurring on all other fronts."

"Which are?"

Melanie started to wonder why the Englishman had replaced El-Gammal as Menachem's foil.

"Good point." Menachem almost looked pleased by the question. "First: Israel must be accepted by all Arab states as a normal state. And you cannot . . . *must not* . . . expect any concession from Israel for that recognition of normalcy. All our wars — in 1948, 1956, 1967, and 1973 — were about the very existence of Israel. Just name me one war in this century that had as its objective the total annihilation of a nation other than ours? Our enemies even think they will choke if they pronounce the name of our state. To them, we're just the 'Zionist entity.' "

"Would you care to define 'normalcy?' "

Menachem shook his head in mock wonderment. "You really do sound as if this were an Oxford debate. Surely you, a citizen of the country where the Balfour Declaration originated that made the Zionist entity possible," his voice had turned deeply sarcastic, "ought to know the answer. Normalcy certainly means public recognition and acceptance of Israel as an integral state of that region. Until now, no regional group accepts us: not the Middle East, not Asia, not Europe — except for some special purposes, like football," he snapped sardonically.

"Need I emphasize that Israel has always affirmed its recognition of the Arab states? Even of its bitterest enemies?" He raised his hand to stop any interruption. "That, of course, is not all. We need accredited representations by all states in Israel and vice versa. And we need public renunciation of any attempts to enforce boycotts or to delegitimize Israel's international standing."

"Is that all?" Melanie couldn't tell whether the Englishman meant it sarcastically, he carried such a deadpan mien.

"It will do as a first step," replied Menachem. "Point two: In parallel with negotiations on a political settlement, confidence and security building measures must be implemented and *tested over time*." Menachem tapped the table sharply as he pronounced the last three words. "Kirchberg is a good example. Over the years, since the late 1950s, nuclear scientists and other people coming to these conferences from East and West have started to have confidence in each other . . . and you know the rest."

" 'Confidence building.' " This time, the Englishman's sarcasm was clear. "What's that supposed to mean in your part of the world?"

" 'Your part of the world!' " Menachem's echo resounded with derision. "We won't make much progress until people in *your* part of the world begin to realize that *our* part includes yours; or do you still subscribe to the English myth that everything beyond the Home Counties is peripheral? You remind me of a headline in one of your country's newspapers: 'Fog in English Channel; Continent isolated.' " Menachem waited for the chuckles to die down — amusement in which even the Egyptian had joined. "More sad than funny, these days," he added. "But I will give you an example of confidence building. Just one, because otherwise our chairman's watch might break." Menachem did not take his eyes off his British interrogator. "An example that in its early planning stages could even be initiated at a forum like our Kirchberg Conferences. Take regional cooperation," he said, again tapping the table for emphasis. "Cooperation that need not be based on good will — of which there is hardly any — but on mutual needs: on environmental degradation in the region, on critical shortages, notably water. On desalination and irrigation techniques . . . ," his voice trailed off.

"But of course, that's not enough," he continued. "The rejectionist states — right now Libya and Iraq and Syria, but God knows who else will join that clique — must participate in the ultimate peace process. Practical arms control measures are inconceivable unless these confrontation states join in the negotiations. Once *that* happens, almost everything else can follow."

Menachem stopped, his eyes sweeping around the table and beyond, his chair now resting solidly on four legs. For the first time this afternoon, Melanie and he exchanged glances, though only for a moment.

"Would you enlighten us about your view of 'practical arms control measures'?"

Menachem made a dismissive gesture with his hand. "As I said at the outset, it has to start with conventional and then chemical arms. Israel will never sign a NWFZ agreement until peace is assured."

"Ha." El-Gammal's interjection was clear and loud. "I knew it."

"You may *know* it," Menachem said evenly, "but I don't think you *get* it. Maybe you don't either," he pointed to the Englishman. "I continue to be amazed at the naiveté of the Arab insistence to have the nuclear arms issue lifted out of context and moved to the UN and the IAEA. . . ." The way Menachem slurred the letters they almost sounded *oy vay.*

"What's that?" Melanie whispered to her neighbor.

The man had long since stopped doodling. "International Atomic Energy Agency," he whispered back.

". . . where majority resolutions take the place of negotiations, and where, of course, they dispose of overwhelming majorities. I cannot conceive that Israel will ever agree to such a demand, be it from the Arab or even American sides, because — as all of you here must realize — in 1977 Israel is the sole guarantor of its security. What the Arab states must do is to make peace with Israel. Only by way of peace will NWFZ be established in this region, which in turn will enable Israel to eventually sign a Nuclear Nonproliferation Treaty. I'm sorry that no one from the People's Republic of China is in Kirchberg, because their position on NPT might be enlightening. And what about the views on NPT by our friends from India?" Menachem turned to his neighbor once removed and to the man sitting behind Melanie. "You openly exploded a nuclear device three years ago, even though I know of no one wishing to exterminate your country. Or should I be calling India the 'Gandhi entity?' " he asked ironically, when he received no reply. "States are not uniform in their intentions or performance. So what makes you think that complicated political conflicts can be dealt with uniformly?" Menachem had really built up steam. "Don't forget: in 1964, our prime minister, Levi Eshkol, declared that Israel would not be the first state to introduce nuclear weapons to the Middle East." He looked around the table, finally fixing his gaze on El-Gammal. "But the Zionist entity certainly doesn't plan to be second."

"I was fascinated to hear our Israeli colleague's exposition." It was the man from Tunis, who was not a Tunisian; the man who last night had inspected the sweat running down Melanie's naked breasts. Until now, he had not said a word. Melanie could sense the controlled fury behind his accented but otherwise fluent English. Still, he called Menachem *colleague*. Is that how incremental progress is measured at Kirchberg? "There is one word — or dare I say two words? — that I have not heard from our colleague's mouth. Actually, from no one else's either: 'Palestinian' and 'PLO.' Are these words forbidden in Kirchberg? I am a newcomer, unlike my colleagues here from Egypt and Israel, but what brought me here was the assurance that every topic germane to a working group can be raised. And how can you discuss the Middle East conflict," his controlled, low voice suddenly rose to a pitch, "without these two words? Or let us start with just one. *Mister* Dvir . . ."

Ah, thought Melanie. So I was not the only one to hear Menachem's rejection of any formal title.

". . . let us take Palestinians. Not Arabs in general, but Palestinians in particular. At what point do we enter your logical order of conflict resolution? *After* confidence building? *After* conventional, but *before* chemical arms control? Or maybe *after* NWFZ or maybe *never*? And if we are permitted to participate, who will speak for us? Will you let the Dvirs of our PLO enter the room?"

The ping of the chairman's tap on his glass could be heard clearly in the silence. "It is time for the *Jause* — for tea and coffee." He pointed to his watch. "We shall continue in thirty minutes."

The mood seemed somber, almost shocked, as people rose to leave the classroom.

Melanie went out to join the line for coffee. When Menachem did not appear, she returned to the classroom, cup in hand, to find him arguing with her neighbor, who seemed Dutch, one of the Indians, and the Palestinian.

"You," the Palestinian pointed at Menachem, "are not any different from your government: 'What is mine remains mine; what is yours is up for negotiation.' Sure, you have the power. Now. But power is just another expression for illegitimacy."

"If that is so," replied Menachem in an even voice, "then the power of propaganda is the ultimate illegitimacy. And you have certainly learned how to manipulate that."

"While you Israelis have not learned that?" The Arab's tone had turned vicious. "You Jews, who control the media?"

To Melanie's surprise, Menachem replied quietly. "We have botched it. Totally so. Look at our lousy public image. In spite of it, they all believe what you believe: that we control the media."

"Ha!" The word was spat out. "I repeat: you are not different from your government; you're just more subtle, *slightly* more subtle. That's all."

"Just a moment," Menachem said, disengaging himself from the Palestinian, who was jabbing his chest for emphasis. "Don't leave. I'll be back in a moment."

He went over to Melanie. "Are you not staying?"

"I think I'd better get back to my group," she said. "But I'm glad you asked me here. There's lots to talk about. How about at dinner?"

"I can't. Not this evening. I'm meeting the man off campus, so to speak. But later."

"Shall I come to your room tonight?" she asked.

"My bed is wider than yours," he grinned. "But are you sure you can come — "

"I can come anywhere," she said under her breath, not wanting to be overheard, yet wanting to tease him. But he hadn't gotten it. Had she spoken too low or did Menachem just not know the idiom? Or was it something else? There's so little I know, she told herself. Is that what attracts me so much? Or is it the way he carries his intrinsic maleness, with so little peacockery? The counterpoint between his rough manners and his surprising tenderness in lovemaking? She thought of last night: the gentle strokes over her skin and nipples; the slow, patient, almost precious, cat-like licks of his tongue; and then his full penile thrusts.

"Around nine?" she asked, this time louder.

"Too early. Make it ten to be safe. I wouldn't want you to stand in the corridor pounding at my door while other people wander around. There are many more participants staying at my hotel than in your *Gasthof*."

The area for the afternoon *Jause* was common to all five working groups. As people began returning to their respective classrooms, through the thinning crowd Melanie caught sight of Luc Morand.

"Luc," she waved him down, "can we talk before dinner? I've spent the afternoon in Menachem's group. I'd like to ask you some more questions."

"*Bien sûr*. When?"

"Do you swim?"

"Yes," he said, surprised. "Why the question?"

"I've been sitting all day and it's so warm. There's a big swimming pool just up the road from this school. I'd like to swim some laps. Let's meet there after five."

Melanie caught sight of Luc as she stood dripping by the pool, shaking her head to get some water out of her ears. Judging from the way he was slouching, the cigarette dangling out of one side of his mouth in the proverbial French movie manner, it was obvious that he'd been there for some time.

"You are a *bonne nageuse*," he said approvingly. Seeing her bafflement, he mimicked a crawl.

"You mean a swimmer," she laughed. She pulled up a poolside chaise and stretched out, gesturing to him to take the chaise at her side. The setting sun shone into her face, making her squint. "Back home, I swim almost every day. And you?"

"Mostly in *La Méditerranée*. I like your *coiffure*."

Melanie automatically ran her hand through her short hair. She knew it became her.

"And you have *des jolies jambes*." He pointed with his cigarette. "Great legs," he explained, forming a circle with his thumb and index finger around the cigarette.

"*Merci*," she laughed, crossing her legs. "But enough of this inspection. I told you I sat in on Menachem's group, the one on regional conflicts. Yet most of the discussion revolved around NWFZ agreements and IAEA inspections." Melanie felt pleased about the ease with which the acronyms poured forth. "Is that what took you to Israel? Is that how you and Menachem met?"

Le gourou chuckled and took a long draw on his cigarette. *"Ee Ah Eh Ah."* He pronounced each letter slowly and chuckled again. *"Non.* Not *Ee Ah Eh Ah,"* he said. *"Au contraire.* In 1977 it is no more a question of *informations secrètes.* But around 1960, when our *force de frappe* dominated our thoughts and we even cooperated with some Israeli *techniciens* at our *nucléaire* test site in the Sahara, Me-na-shem was there."

"So you met him first in the Sahara?"

Morand shook his head. "Later. He came to the Sahara not only because of this," he tapped his head several times, "but because of his perfect *français.* Almost perfect." He grinned. "Me-na-shem had no hesitation to *tutoyer* every Frenchman, even those who *vouvoient* everybody." He shrugged his shoulders. "Maybe they *tutoient* everybody in the *Congo Central."*

"So you met in Beersheba. How come?"

A short pause intervened while *le gourou* performed his cigarette version of in-flight refueling. After giving the new one a kick-start puff, he continued. "It is no more a *ha'anoseh ha'adin."* A nostalgic grin crossed his face as he noted Melanie's bewilderment. "I still remember some Hebrew. And certainly an expression so *nuancée.* It means 'sensitive topic.' After the Suez War of 1956, De Gaulle was so *furieux,* he canceled officially," Morand rolled his eyes skyward, "all *coopération militaire* with Israel. But unofficially," he laughed as if he'd just pulled the wool over the General's eyes, "we cooperated for several more years with the Israelis on the construction of their chemical reprocessing plant in Dimona. I was then a hawk and we — Me-na-shem and I — became friends." He waved his cigarette at Melanie. *"Les Américains* were very unhappy with us. But *c'est la vie* or perhaps *la guerre.* I still remember how careful we were. I even changed my name on my mailbox. It was *très élégant.* I eliminated one letter. There is a pure Hebrew name, you see: *Morad."*

"Luc Morad? I doubt it would fool the CIA."

"Melanie!" Morand pretended outrage, as if she had insulted his ingenuity. "It was written *Mishpachat Morad* — family Morad. It would fool everybody, even the Mossad, who we all know is *plus astucieux* than your CIA. Except that it is precisely the Mossad in Beersheba who suggested the name."

Melanie felt that some defense of the CIA was indicated. "And what accentless language did you speak to fool anyone?"

"*Touché*," he said and saluted Melanie with his Gauloise. He pointed to his watch. "It is necessary to go."

"Wait," she said quickly. "Let me get dressed so we can walk together. I want to ask you something else."

⸻

"What is the second *Madame* Dvir like?"

"She was *très charmante*."

"But what's she like?" Melanie persisted.

"*Une belle femme*," he said. "But I have not seen her for many years."

"And she does not travel with him?"

They had been walking side by side, with Melanie trying to catch *le gourou*'s eyes. But he had become inscrutable, his eyes fixed to the ground. "She does not travel."

"But why?" Melanie could not refrain from asking.

"Ask Me-na-shem."

8

"Menachem, my private hawk," she murmured, "and how does that feel?"

He was lying supine on the bed, eyes closed. Melanie, with arms spiked straight next to each shoulder, rode him slowly.

"Stop!" he exclaimed suddenly and grabbed her thrusting hips. "Stop," he commanded. "Not yet."

Menachem leaned forward so quickly that his slippery penis slid out. Still holding her hips, he fell back against the pillow.

"Look," he pointed at his erect phallus seemingly rising out of Melanie's pubic hair as she straddled him. "I've turned you into a man. Now stroke him. Pretend he's yours. But do it slowly."

"Like that?"

"No," he removed her cupped hand. "You're pulling too much. Like this: stroke; don't pull."

"Like that?"

"Not quite." Again he took over. "Look, like this. Move all the way to the tip."

Melanie saw his curved hand move past his ring of circumcision, glistening and red. "I'm not very good at — "

"You don't masturbate?"

"I mean a man."

They had both stopped touching his penis, which had started to soften. "What about you?" he asked again. "Do you . . . ?"

"Yes," she said, holding his curious gaze.

"Often?"

"It depends," she said, running the tip of her left middle finger along Menachem's penis; it stiffened between her thighs.

"On what?"

"Lots of things. First, my mood — "

I don't even know how I should start: "I'm right-handed, but I use the middle finger of my left hand?" If I know Menachem, he will interrupt me with "Why the left?" That would get us off on a tangent.

But tangentially is the only way I could talk to him about masturbation. I am the ultimate masturbatory autodidact, who is quite capable of presenting a chronological record of her skill. It started before puberty, before my first period, for which my mother had prepared me so well and kindly that I looked forward to it with anticipation as some sort of menstrual bat mitzvah. Another good point for tangential departure: why do I, Melanie Sutherland Laidlaw, a New England WASP, use a Hebrew word I never recall uttering before? It's a subject worth exploring with Menachem.

Even though I cannot date the discovery of my autoerotic talent, I can confidently attribute to myself a degree of inner sexual precocity. Playing tetherball was the unconscious beginning; climbing other poles and ropes a conscious extension; but the epiphany came through the power of my middle finger. When? Probably in my early teens.

Certainly before age fifteen, when my mother surprised me one afternoon on my bed with a pillow between my legs. By then, I had developed various techniques, like mounting a pillow held tightly between my thighs, preferably a satin pillow that felt even smoother than the inside of my own thighs when I stroked them with my right hand. ("Because I'm right-handed," I would say if I had the courage to say anything).

Usually, I would indulge only at night, under a blanket, in what I then called rather primly "attempted pacification," thrusting against the pillow with my face buried in another one. But this one time, it was in daylight, late afternoon, shades drawn, but still light enough so that my naked buttocks moving slowly and held tight must have been visible as my mother entered the bedroom. She didn't knock, but why should she have? She had some freshly laundered towels in her arms and she had no way of knowing that I was upstairs. "I'm sorry, Melanie," she started. My buttocks relaxed, my thighs separated, and I turned over. "Melanie," she repeated. "What are you doing? Are you . . . ?"

It was the first and last time I'd ever been surprised that way. I don't think anyone has ever observed me masturbating, although I've been at it for over twenty years, right through my marriage and especially the last three years. For me, masturbation is far more pleasurable than sex with the wrong person. Even when the right sexual partner has been found, masturbation in his absence is extolled in my personal Kamasutra; at the very least, it recalls the desire and memory of the earlier carnal experience.

Of course, it's not just hands or finger anymore. I have never used mechanical devices — dildos, vibrators — but I indulge myself with surfaces and protuberances: knobs on drawers, edges on tables, rims of bathtubs . . . the bronze shoulder of a reclining nude. That, of course, was risky, because the Henry Moore sculpture was in a park, which leads me to another tangent: a disclosure of my desire, by now an addiction, of pleasuring myself surreptitiously in public places. All it requires are two skills: a noiseless orgasm and no hands. I've even had a soundless orgasm at a REPCON board meeting during the treasurer's report. I always conceal my eyes, which I can do with very dark glasses, though not at a board meeting. There, I pretended to rub them with my clenched fists.

Not that I do it all that often. The locale has to be novel, the risk of detection real. Otherwise, why not do it at home? There's nothing wrong with home: masturbating there not only eliminates the need for having to subdue my reactions, it also allows me to satisfy a sense that public venues hardly ever permit. I taste my honeyed moisture when I masturbate at home; when my middle finger dips, not strokes, ever so often past my clitoris until it can't go any deeper, after which I turn it into my digital popsicle. During my marriage I doted on cunnilingus — more than intercourse, I suspect — because I adored kissing Justin when his mouth and chin were soaked with my juices. I also fancied the slightly acerb taste of Justin's semen, but I was always afraid to have him come in my mouth. Only after he'd ejaculated did I take his softening penis into my mouth to lick it, like my middle finger.

So what came first? Masturbation in public or my ability to perform it undetected? I suspect it was the latter. My transition from pole climbing to middle finger to pillow (and later to hand showers) led quite logically to the more sophisticated and subtle exercise of pressure. I'm one of those millions of women who find crossing her legs pleasurable. Isn't that why the earlier censors of our mores discouraged women from crossing their legs, knowing where this might lead? Why girls in convent schools, even now, are asked to sit with legs uncrossed while they cross themselves?

My revelation came to me fairly early in college when I read about Kegel exercises, which are recommended for women in pregnancy and prior to menopause, to prevent loss of genital muscle tone and incontinence. I came across those exercises when the problems alleviated by them were of no concern to me. Even though my muscles, genital and elsewhere, were firm and my bladder in great shape, I was intrigued by the technique; and as other autodidacts have found, building up vaginal muscle tone by exercising the pelvic floor muscles à la Kegel increases arousal. The formal description of these exercises seemed dry enough — even the analogy of the pelvic floor to an elevator and of the deliberate contractions to stopping at each floor of a five- or six-storied building — but operating my internal elevator produced to my surprise ample honeyed moisture. After that, it became a question of practicing isometric pressure of the vaginal lips

and clitoral stimulation with my upper thighs until one day, I had
my first Kegel orgasm. For me, it was the ultimate breakthrough in
my masturbatory repertoire because it extended the range of my au-
toerotic grazing into territory about which, until that day, I could
only fantasize.

One other refinement I discovered not long after: well-cut pants
with raised middle seams. The right kind of seam raises the pressure
induced by my love muscles another notch.

This seems to take care of all operational details, except one: I also
have to be in the mood.

"Tell me." Menachem was lying with hands clasped behind his
head.

Melanie slid off his body. "I can't," she said. "It's too private."

"Do you fantasize?"

"Yes."

"What about?"

"The sort of things I haven't done or can't do or can't talk about."

"Will you do one of them with me?" he asked, drawing her toward him.

Melanie could sense his excitement. "Yes," she said.

"Now?"

"No. Tomorrow. In Vienna. What I want to do with you can't be
done here in this room."

9

"Melanie, for the director of a foundation anxious to spend itself
into oblivion, you've certainly made yourself unavailable." Felix
Frankenthaler's chuckle sounded almost spontaneous. "What exactly were you doing in Kirchberg? I had trouble even finding the
place on the map."

"Spreading the contraceptive gospel to physicists, engineers, and
the like — "

"But why Kirchberg?" he interrupted. "Surely you can be more effective doing that from here."

"Well . . . ." She knew Felix Frankenthaler well enough to realize his curiosity wasn't anything particular, but even so, the question had momentarily discombobulated her. She wondered what his expression would be if she told him the truth: *I slept with a married man on the first day I met him.* "For one thing — it's more intimate. You can concentrate on important issues — "

"Come now — "

"What brought you to Manhattan, Felix?" It seemed safest to fall back on professional efficiency. After all, it wasn't as if she had time to waste on social niceties — or embarrassment. She had come back to her office at REPCON to find her desk overflowing with accumulated business. "It sounded urgent. Was there no one on my staff that could have helped last week?"

He shook his head. "I wanted to ask you something directly. . . ."

Melanie waited, while Frankenthaler paused, as though collecting his thoughts — or his courage, she thought. Then suddenly he stopped and changed his mind. "Before I do, let me invite you to something interesting."

The invitation could have been handled easily enough over the phone. But he never resisted the slightest professional excuse for visiting Manhattan during the Metropolitan Opera season, especially when the schedule included an opera's Met premiere. *The Makropoulos Case* had been staged once before in the States, in the late 1960s, but he had missed it. And now the Met was doing it with none other than Geraint Evans and Anja Silja in the lead roles.

"I am going to the Met tonight to the new Janáček. Shelly couldn't make it down from Boston. How about joining me?"

Melanie's physiological clock had not yet recovered from jet lag, but seeing *The Makropoulos Case* — an opera she'd never heard of before — tempted her.

"Sure," she said. "Sleep I can always get later."

"Good," he said. "Now that we have taken care of the important question, let's turn to something trivial: could you support a project of mine through your director's discretionary fund? You know I've never approached you before about such special handling. It isn't much," he made a deprecatory gesture with his hand, "about 25K."

"I didn't know you even dealt in such paltry sums, Felix," she said. Surely he isn't trying to use an opera invitation as bribe? she thought; it's not like him — and he knows that he doesn't need to grease my palm. "But why not go through our regular application process? We're not some government agency; you know we haven't got much red tape — "

"I'm in a hurry."

"I could arrange for an expedited review — "

"I'm sure you could," he said impatiently, "but I have a reason. To be quite frank, I'd rather not have the competition see what we've got up our sleeves."

"Competition?" She leaned back behind her desk, ready to listen. Personal motivation among scientists, especially superstars, always intrigued her.

"You know how small a community we are in male reproductive biology. Your panel must be full of — "

"Okay," she interrupted. "So what's so hot about your project?"

"We may have a new approach to male impotence . . . ," he began, but Melanie Laidlaw didn't let him finish. The half-done work in front of her had made her impatient, which in turn made her prone to interrupt. With Felix, at least, she masked her restiveness with banter.

"Are you trying to cause impotence or cure it?"

"Be serious. We're trying to cure it, of course." It was his turn to display irritability.

"That's all you men ever think of. Why don't you work on prevention rather than performance, for a change? In other words, pay some attention to contraception."

"Christ," Frankenthaler started to mutter, remembering the recent Brandeis fund-raiser debacle, but then decided to swallow the rest. "I've heard that before."

"So why don't you? We get fewer and fewer applications dealing with contraceptive research. And virtually none when it comes to new approaches to male birth control. All the reproductive fraternity is interested in these days seems to be treatment of infertility."

"Hot advice; and not one to be spurned from a fountain of unrestricted money," he countered, realizing he wasn't going to get his 25K without working for it. "But it's not a fraternity any more. We're getting more and more women in the lab. So what would you work on if you were in my shoes?"

"How about releasing hormones of the hypothalamus? RH research is really hot just now. Take the announcement about the Nobel Prize to Guillemin and Schally for their RH work."

Frankenthaler snorted. "A good reason not to touch it."

"What do you mean?"

"The Swedes are unlikely to give another Nobel in the same field."

"Felix, are you serious? Is that how you pick your research?"

"No. Or maybe semi-serious. But go on. What releasing hormones do you want me to study?"

"Take one that affects both male and female reproduction: LHRH — "

"Come on, Melanie." Frankenthaler's impatience grew deeper. "I have nothing against the luteinizing hormone-releasing hormone or even the follicle-stimulating releasing hormone" — in eschewing the acronyms, his disdain had acquired professorial dimensions — "but why bother? The structure of LHRH has already been established — that's what this year's Nobel in medicine is all about — "

"Puh-lease Felix!" Melanie was not going to let him weasel out of this field that easily. "I mean LHRH *analogs* or FSRH *antagonists*. Either one would stop sperm production, wouldn't it?"

Frankenthaler let out an audible sigh. "I suppose so. It would also shut off libido."

"You could offset it with testosterone administration."

"A real pain."

"You poor men: having to take a pill all the time, like women. Still — what about occasional injections of long-acting testosterone esters?"

"A pain in the butt. Sorry," he said quickly, "I just couldn't resist it."

Melanie shook her head. "I guess you just aren't interested in birth control."

"Melanie, that isn't fair!" His voice had started to rise. "I'm just being realistic. Even if you could come up with a lead from a synthetic LHRH analog — and I'll grant you," he raised his index finger for emphasis, "that theoretically you have a perfectly valid point — just think of the development times required; the years and years of clinical tests. We'd have to make sure it was reversible. Because if it isn't, why bother? Why not just have a vasectomy and be done with it?"

"What about your male impotence? Won't that take just as long?"

"The eventual application in wide clinical practice? Perhaps — especially considering the psychological component you have to account for. But the initial research, the testing of our concept?" He thought of his contretemps with the virago at the Brandeis banquet and snapped his fingers. "Either you get an erection or you don't. The time is measured in seconds or minutes — not years."

"Is that why you picked male impotence for your research?"

"I didn't *pick* it; it picked *me*."

"Oh Felix, I'm so sorry."

"What?" Felix Frankenthaler felt a deep blush sweep over his face. "I meant the *solution*, not the problem."

"Oh," said Melanie contritely. Now why am I baiting this man? she wondered.

But Frankenthaler seemed only momentarily put off his stride, and picked up again with his sales pitch.

"I've got a marvelous postdoc from Stanford who has been working in my lab on the role of nitric oxide in vasodilation. It occurred to me that if we experimented with the smooth muscle of the corpus cavernosum — "

Melanie, feeling she didn't need an explanation of penile anatomy and the erectile tissue of the two corpora cavernosa from Felix Frankenthaler, cut him off. "You relax the smooth muscle, blood pours in and . . . ," to her surprise, she found herself flipping the bird with her middle finger. The ensuing laughter relaxed them both.

"Renu Krishnan — that's my postdoc — is working on NO-synthase, the enzyme responsible for production of nitric oxide in vivo, and on NO-releasing substrates. Initially, that was all basic research, but then we were wondering about possible clinical applications, and treatment of impotence may be one. That's why I am here."

"But Felix, persuading me to give you twenty-five thousand dollars out of my director's kitty in return for taking me to the opera," she waved his protestation away good-naturedly, "will hardly get you very far. In fact, what will 25K do for you?"

"Send Renu to Israel for a few months — maybe three."

"But why to Israel?"

Felix Frankenthaler had begun to explain why the Hadassah Medical Center in Jerusalem would be the ideal venue for exploratory clinical studies when once again Melanie interrupted.

"All right," she said. "Let's send him to Jerusalem."

Startled by the speed of the decision, all Felix could think of to say was, "Renu Krishnan is a her, not a him."

"Even better. I always thought a clever woman was all you needed to treat male impotence. By the way, I'm not sure whether impotence of the heart is not a more serious malady and even less curable."

———

Since neither one had seen the Janáček before, they postponed the opera kibitzing for dessert and coffee after the performance. "Tell me more about your Kirchberg Conference," Frankenthaler asked at dinner. "What sort of people did you meet? And what did you talk about?"

"I talked about birth control: what else? Specifically, the need for more scientific research on fundamentally new approaches — not the sort of piddling improvements the pharmaceutical companies seem to be indulging in these days."

"And did they all jump up and ask for REPCON grant application forms?"

"No, they didn't. But I hadn't expected that, considering the composition of the group. They weren't basic or even applied scientists in reproductive biology, although judging from your response this morning, they may not have been tempted by my bait. Most were concerned with population *policy* issues: demographic implications of environmental degradation; economic development; food production . . . and others were there to mouth their particular government or quango line. 'Population' can cover a lot of ground. Still, I imagine that most went home having learned something new."

"So what did you learn?"

Melanie leaned back in her chair. "The sort of thing I don't run across in the grant applications coming to REPCON. For instance, did you know that metro-agro complexes where intense agricultural and urban-industrial activity cluster together are responsible for three-fourths of the world's energy and fertilizer consumption? And for nearly two-thirds of food production and export?"

Frankenthaler had been drawing lines with his fingers on the condensation of his ice-cold water glass. Now he looked up. "Are you really interested in those issues or was this just some intellectual one-night stand?"

"Don't knock one-night stands."

"My, my! I never expected such words from Dr. Laidlaw."

"Come now, Felix." She made a dismissive gesture. "Don't be a prude. Even one-night stands can have long-lasting consequences." She laughed somewhat self-consciously. "You better not quote me out of context."

"I better not quote you at all," he laughed back. "But what were the people like? Where were they from?"

"From all over," Melanie said eagerly. "A fair number from Eastern European socialist countries. Some were apparatchiks, for whom these annual trips were important perks and who didn't deviate from the party line. Our population group attracted some of those. But there were some interesting mavericks, at least in private, and especially in the Middle East debates."

"You went to these?" Frankenthaler was astounded.

"Yes. I met a fascinating Israeli, who decided that my background needed broadening. And a Frenchman," she added quickly, "who spoke charmingly fractured English, smoked continuously, and was called *le gourou*."

"Was the Israeli from Jerusalem? Should my postdoc look him up?"

Melanie shook her head. "He's from Ben-Gurion University in the Negev. A nuclear engineer."

"What else did you people do there aside from meetings? I have to admit that this question comes from a born city slicker, but what, in fact, can you do in a small Austrian village besides talking about metro-agro complexes?" Frankenthaler barely attempted to hide his disdain.

Melanie smiled. "Felix, you'd be surprised what can be done even in the smallest village — provided you keep an open mind, that is. Furthermore, I also went to Vienna."

"All by yourself?"

"No, the Israeli came along."

10

"You said Vienna. But where, precisely, are we going?" Menachem had asked Tuesday night as Melanie got ready to leave his room.

"You'll see." She tousled his hair. "Leave it to me."

"And how are we going? By bus or — "

"American organizational talent has already taken care of that. I've rented a car, but I'll let you drive it."

"I don't drive."

Under ordinary circumstances, Melanie would have pursued this nugget of autobiography, so surprising for a male hawk from the Middle East. But the postcoital ambiance had muffled her natural sense of curiosity. "In that case, I'll be the chauffeur," she said and kissed him, with a lot of tongue, one last time.

The buses for the tour of the *Bucklige Welt* — the area around Kirchberg named so appositely "hunchbacked world" — followed by a banquet that evening at the Semmering, a nearby mountain resort, were lined up in front of the *Volksschule* as Melanie drove by in her red Volkswagen rental. It was Wednesday, the day traditionally declared time off at Kirchberg Conferences from serious deliberations in order to entertain the official participants and all *impedimenta*: spouses, significant others (though hardly ever from the prudish Communist countries), observers, student assistants, and the odd journalist who manages to get admitted even though officially everything but the final session is supposed to be off-record. Menachem had asked her to pick him up by the pond, and she had assumed that he'd suggested that spot out of a sense of discretion. She was only partly right. As she drove up, she discovered that the discretion was meant for someone else: the chemist from Tunis who was not a Tunisian. Melanie caught sight of him as he turned from Menachem and headed back to the village center.

"I thought you wanted me to pick you up here for sentimental reasons," she said jokingly, "but I notice you had another date."

"Yes," he said. "But I'll deny it."

"Are you certain no one saw you?"

"Who cares? Today, I just didn't want to be overheard. And I'm sure some people saw us last night when we had dinner at a small place down the road. I even offered to pay, but he turned me down." He paused momentarily, looking out his side of the window.

"I liked that he insisted paying for his meal. 'No indebtedness,' the man said, 'not even the slightest.' He even had a sense of humor. 'Not unless you are willing to deduct it from your income tax for entertaining a member of the PLO,' he said. But Melanie, here at Kirchberg, everyone is expected to be able to talk to everyone — off the record that is. During the height of the Nigerian civil war, at a Kirchberg Conference in the Soviet Union, of all places, I saw two of the key Ibos from Biafra meet with their Hausa counterparts. Everyone noticed and was pleased about it, but I'm sure both sides would disavow that they'd ever met."

He reached for the handle underneath his seat to push himself back as far as possible. Melanie wished he had not done so. It moved him out of her peripheral vision, whereas he, as the nondriver, could eye her at leisure. "That's why I'm in Kirchberg, of course — to talk in private. You saw what went on at our session yesterday afternoon. You'd have to be a masochist to come here solely to defend your country's position in front of people who have already judged you guilty."

"You exaggerate, Menachem. There were people in that room whom you impressed."

"Hmm. Just name one."

"Easy. Yours truly."

Menachem reached over and patted her hand on the steering wheel. "Thanks. That made it worthwhile."

"There were others. Maybe not the Brit, whatever his name was. But I could tell that one of the Indians, Kapoor, was almost nodding in agreement as you spoke about NWFZ. Then the German, von Mützenbecher — "

"Really?" Menachem sounded surprised. "How do you know?"

"I could tell by the way they paid attention to you. I don't know how many you *convinced*, but you certainly *impressed* some. Don't be such a typically Jewish paranoiac." Melanie turned and threw him a quick, affectionate glance. She wasn't sure how he would take that.

"Tsk, tsk. What a Waspish diagnosis," he replied in the same bantering tone. "In my position, paranoia is a luxury I can't afford. I call it realism. Not Jewish realism, but the Israeli variety: when we say the political situation in the Middle East is about average, we mean it is worse than last year, but better than the next."

"So who *is* this Tunisian?" she asked.

"I told you he isn't a Tunisian. He's a Palestinian who lives in Tunis. Or maybe he just buys his plane tickets in Tunis. But I guessed right: he is a chemist." Menachem sounded self-satisfied. "I'm interested in him."

"Because he's a chemist?"

Menachem shrugged. "He seems smart, and, even more importantly, a realist. El-Gammal, the Egyptian, just talks. Like the Brit, he lives in some fantasy world; and like so many Egyptians who studied in British universities, he has a complicated love-hate relationship. They all idolize Oxbridge, but usually only get into a red-brick university or some polytechnic where they are treated as second-class citizens. When they return to Cairo, they brag about their British education and pay the English back by incessant carping, especially since the Suez Canal fiasco, but at the same time they despise the PLO. Like many Egyptians, El-Gammal uses the Pal-

estinian issue for his own purposes. À la Thucydides." He chuckled briefly, recollecting the Austrian chairman's pompous introduction, before turning again serious.

"Ahmed Saleh is different. In a way, he reminds me of the Zionists thirty years ago. Some of us were terrorists, but we were also
realists. Our form of terrorism was a means, not an end." For a long
moment, he let the scenery along the narrow, winding road glide past
his eyes.

"Of course, there are many in the PLO, who are nothing but terrorists. Our official line is that they're all terrorists and that's why
we refuse to have any contact with them. Or they with us," he added
with another shrug. "Ahmed Saleh is part of the PLO but different.
And so am I: an Israeli hawk, as *le gourou* would say. But a different subspecies."

Melanie could sense his glance focused on her. And then he
touched her arm. "You understand, of course, that I'll deny I ever
said that."

"Of course," Melanie said. "How did you know he was different?
At first, I mean."

Menachem laughed. "A sauna is a marvelous place for initial
meetings. That's where we both first talked."

"You mean you *intended* to meet there? In the sauna?"

"Why not? A sauna is a good place to find out what a person looks
like. It can even lead to unexpected consequences."

"As if I didn't know." They had entered the main highway
near Gloggnitz where Melanie could afford more frequent side
glances. This one was playful. "But you said he was different. He
didn't look particularly different to me." On the contrary, she wanted
to add, he looked like the typical man ogling a bare-breasted
woman.

"We also talked."

"That was in Arabic."

"So? It was a convenient language, given the rather crowded
setting. Also, it showed that I was willing to meet him on his own
grounds, so to speak."

"That was hardly the message I heard from him yesterday afternoon just before the coffee break."

"That was different. Some of it was not addressed to me, but rather to El-Gammal and even other Arabs who were not there but would eventually hear what was said. Of course," he momentarily raised his hand, "he also meant Israel as a state."

"But not you, as an individual Israeli?" she persisted.

I don't think so, because why did he agree to meet last evening? Or this morning? And why do I take Ahmed to be a realist? During yesterday's coffee break, I argued about Israel's indispensable need for a nuclear option. I still follow Ben-Gurion's line: in public, never use the word bomb; *always say* nuclear *option; never promise not to build* a bomb — *just talk about not* introducing *one.*

"Okay," Ahmed agreed. "Let's have some hypothetical scenarios." So I gave him one: a massive, successful Arab military invasion of the populated areas of Israel with the ostensible objective of driving us into the sea.

"You mean if the Yom Kippur War just four years ago had gone differently, you would have exercised that option?" he asked.

"Maybe," I said.

"So you do admit you have some bombs?" he countered. Of course, I ignored that question to which he really didn't expect an answer. I just asked whether he wanted any more scenarios. "Okay," he said, "a couple more."

"Destruction of our air force."

He just laughed. "You mean when you are left with just a couple of planes, you'll use them to drop the bomb? Be serious," he said. "I'd love to see your air force destroyed, but that won't happen. Not within the time during which I want to see an independent Palestinian state. A separate independent state," he added. "You will live within your pre-'67 borders and we — "

"Wait a moment," I interrupted, "is this the new official PLO line? No destruction of the Zionist entity? Recognition of Israel?"

He just looked at me, but he wasn't smiling. "Aren't we just talking about hypothetical scenarios, you and I? Let's hear your third," he challenged me.

"Massive chemical or biological attacks on Israel," I replied, "or nuclear ones." Ahmed stared at me, somewhat differently from the

way he had earlier. We both knew that this time we were approaching plausibility.

"And who would drop these bombs — chemical, biological, nuclear? The PLO?"

"What about Iraq?" I asked.

"Just a few minutes earlier, I heard you say you won't be second," *he said.*

"Precisely," I replied, and that's when we agreed to meet again. He and I alone.

"Who really knows?" said Menachem.

"You were pretty adamant yesterday about the necessity for Israel to have a nuclear arms capability," remarked Melanie.

"Did you hear me say that?"

"Well, not in so many words — "

"I am relieved." His voice was full of irony.

Melanie was not going to let him off the hook that easily. "You certainly meant it. Suppose you had the bomb. Under what conditions could you even conceive using it?"

"Off the record?" he said jokingly.

"Cross my heart."

"That doesn't carry much weight with a Jew, but it will do. At least this afternoon. By the way, what *are* we going to do in Vienna? Last night — "

"That secret can wait. We still have nearly an hour before we reach Vienna. You were going to answer something off the record."

"Melanie," he said, the banter gone. "Do you realize that in a sense everything about the two of us is off the record?"

"Of course." She knew what he meant. Besides, to whom would she disclose her affair with Menachem? "You were saying?"

Why not? Menachem thought. What I'll tell her isn't news. At least not to the people who count in this business. "Our problem isn't really any different from NATO's in Germany: Is there *ever* a right moment for atomic or nuclear arms to contain a massive enemy attack based solely on conventional weapons? When the enemy has already deeply penetrated your territory? We are so small that dropping an atomic bomb would affect our own civilians. Use such a bomb as a *preemptive* weapon on Arab armies? It would be too early and cause unacceptable political damage to Israel."

Melanie was amazed. "But what you are saying is that the bomb is useless. Exactly the opposite of what you said yesterday."

"I'm doing nothing of the sort." Menachem found himself enjoying this dialog. For once, he was not arguing with an enemy; he was indulging in an intellectual discussion with a lover. He had not done that for almost twenty years, not since. . . . He slumped back in his seat, out of Melanie's vision.

"For argument's sake, let's accept that Israel cannot resort without advance warning to nuclear arms in the middle of a war. But what if we remain on the very edge of a ready nuclear capability and that we see to it — through rumors, innuendos, scuttlebutt — that our enemies are aware of it? Not as open deterrents, as with the Americans or Russians, or even the French or Chinese, but as hidden ones."

"And yet not acknowledge that you possess nuclear weapons?"

"Exactly," replied Menachem. "The point is that their knowledge, or at least their serious concern, should prevent our enemies from embarking on military adventures of the type that even they would recognize as triggers for a nuclear response. And to validate our nuclear deterrent, we must have the technical means to demonstrate our nuclear capability on very short notice."

"But Israel has not had any open tests of nuclear explosions, like the Indians, for instance."

"The days are passed when you need to do this," he said firmly. "Do you know that in the very early 1960s some American scientists, waiting for clearance at Los Alamos, occupied their time by designing a nuclear bomb from the open technical literature? All we need to do is demonstrating an effective delivery system. We can do so within minutes. But enough of regional conflicts. Remember, Wednesday is supposed to be the Kirchberg Sabbath."

But Melanie couldn't let go of the topic. "Sabbath, snabbath! Aren't you a secular Jew? Besides, you started me out on the Middle East conflict. I would never have come to your group yesterday, if you hadn't dragged me there. You talk about *indirect* deterrents, about *implying* Israeli nuclear capability, about *options* rather than bombs. But most people in the States, and certainly our newspapers, suspect that you have built some bombs. *Le gourou* is certain you have some."

"I see." Menachem's voice had again turned toward irony, even sarcasm. "So we're back with your French source. Did you really only meet a couple of days ago? You seem to be great friends."

"I met Luc here in Kirchberg, some fifteen minutes before coming over to ask you about the queen of Sheba. So far, we are acquaintances. I'd probably enjoy becoming friends with him — I might even rediscover the little French I'd learned in high school." She took her eyes off the road for a long moment, and caught his gaze. "I don't think you and I are as yet friends."

"Oh come on — " he protested.

"Recent lovers? Yes. But friends?" Melanie thought of Justin and his triple fancy: friend, lover, companion. She'd never speculated before about the optimum order.

"And why not also friends?" Menachem leaned forward so that she could see him with only a slight turn of her head. By now they were traveling on the main autobahn connecting Graz with Vienna; their Volkswagen was virtually on autopilot.

"It depends on your definition of 'friend.' To me, it involves a degree of confidence. . . . I mean in the sense of confiding . . . that we have not yet reached. Perhaps we won't reach it, because circumstances may not permit it."

But he surprised her. "Go on," he said, reclining back into his private space. "You were telling me about Luc Morand."

"It was 'Morad,' he told me, when he met you." Exploring Menachem's history suddenly seemed of greater interest to Melanie than pursuing Israel's nuclear capabilities.

"Well, well," he said, "you two have covered quite a bit of ground." He made no effort to conceal his surprise. "But he was Luc Morand when we first met. He only became Morad in Beersheba."

"Actually he did say that you first met in the Sahara. And that you were there because of your French."

"Well hardly that alone," Menachem laughed. "There are plenty of French-speaking Israelis. I am also a nuclear engineer by training. But it's true: my first language was French, because I was born in the Congo and I spent my childhood there. Of course, I also learned Lingala, the lingua franca of the Congo with its hundreds of dialects."

Melanie thought of Luc's heavy accent. "You don't have a French accent."

"I went to boarding school in South Africa. Any remaining accent disappeared in the RAF."

Melanie felt as if she were assembling tesserae for a mosaic.

"But we were talking about *le gourou*," Menachem said. "Not me."

"Why do they call him *le gourou?*"

"I gave it to him. When he came to Beersheba in the very early 1960s — by now everyone knows that the French helped us with our nuclear center at Dimona even after De Gaulle had ordered them to discontinue official cooperation — he was the nuclear guru of the French contingent. He hardly learned any Hebrew and his English was even worse than it is now. He and I, of course, had no language problem, so I gave him a French sobriquet and it stuck. Especially in Kirchberg circles, where, incidentally, he became so obsessed with non-proliferation issues, he metamorphosed into a dove. It's one of his two faults."

"What is the other."

"Graphology."

Her laugh was explosive. "Menachem, you can't be serious."

"I don't think he knows much about graphology — he just believes in it. As do many French, particularly in business. If it were up to Luc, he'd ask every job applicant to the national atomic research center at Saclay to submit a résumé in his own handwriting. I used to argue with him about it, but it's like an astronomer trying to dissuade an astrologer. I was even prepared to concede that handwriting is a form of self-presentation, but so is the way you make your bed in the morning or squeeze your toothpaste. To think that the slant and size of your letters or the way you cross your *T*s is supposed to tell you something about the person's qualities or even more significantly, their blemishes! *Nom de Dieu!*" He rolled his eyes.

His outburst astonished Melanie. "What's come over you? It sounds amusing, even charming — "

"Amusing? Maybe. But charming? I think it's idiotic, especially since Luc even wanted to carry it over to security clearance. He bragged — not seriously, I hope — that he'd never slept with a woman until he'd first received a handwritten letter from her. Next thing, they'll diagnose syphilis by graphology." He snorted with derision.

"Yet otherwise, Luc is such a curious and intelligent man. Even now, when we meet — mostly to argue — he comes up with surprising insights. Last year, when I accused the French of speaking with forked tongues, he asked me to define forked tongues. The French don't use that expression. They simply say *mentir* — to lie. I was getting irritated and said something like, 'Wait a second, the point is to describe your government's behavior, not to define an expression.' But he challenged me, 'Then describe a second.' To get him off that track, I replied, 'How about one-sixtieth of a minute?' But he continued, 'In that case, what is a minute?' When I said, 'One-sixtieth of an hour' and he continued, by asking me to describe an hour, I stopped him. 'What are you driving at?'

"And now comes the interesting point. He asked why I didn't define a second on its own terms, because once you do, all subsequent questions are taken care of. In other words, don't define the thing — in this instance, France's supposedly appalling behavior — by reference to the undefined forked tongues."

Melanie, who had been wondering where the conversation was leading, started to laugh. "Okay," she said. "So what is a second?"

"A good question, that only a physicist — not any physicist, but some physicist — can answer. A second is the duration of 9,192,631,770 periods of the radiation corresponding to the transition between the two hyperfine levels of the ground state of the cesium-133 atom."

She looked open-mouthed. "How on earth do you know that? And how can you remember such an enormous number?"

Menachem chuckled. "When Luc mentioned it, I looked it up, and he was right. So I memorized it as a tour de force to argue with physicists and to impress all others. In the process, I also looked up the definition of one meter. It is 1/299,792,458 of the distance traveled by light in a second. And don't forget, we have already defined a second."

"How many more of these do you know?"

"That's all. If I can't dazzle someone with a second and a meter — "

"Enough!" exclaimed Melanie. "You were talking about Luc."

"Yes, Luc and me. During most of his Dimona days, we used to enjoy conversational Ping-Pong, each wanting to get the ball over the net, with only an occasional slam. All in French, of course. It reminded him of home, and me of my youth. When our Ping-Pong became mostly slams, I knew it was ending. It was mostly de Gaulle's fault, not ours." He stopped, his eyes on the distant foothills, as if the physical landscape had finally taken precedence over the mental one. But then he continued. "I can't really stay angry with Luc, yet the present French position is inexcusable. It was bad enough when they refused to sell us uranium. But a few years later, they turned around and started to supply the Iraqis, of all people, with nuclear fuel and equipment. When it comes to Iraq and Saddam Hussein, they are playing with more than just fire. . . ."

Sooner or later, all conversations turn toward Iraq, toward Osirak. That makes sense, most of the time. It made sense this morning with Ahmed, but not now, with Melanie.

"Did you know that Iraqis have never come to these conferences?" I asked him.

"So what?" Ahmed smirked. "All you people do here is talk."

"True," I admitted, "but it depends who talks to whom."

"All right," he said, "talk."

I talked. I talked about the signs of Iraqi preparation for biological and chemical warfare our Mossad had started to pick up.

Ahmed stopped me. "Why are you telling me all this?"

I reminded him where we had ended last night. "This isn't hypothetical. When Saddam Hussein is ready, he'll deploy these arms. And what makes you think that they will hit only Tel Aviv and not Hebron or Gaza?"

"Go on," he said.

"When Iraqi nuclear missiles are aimed at Israel, not a single Palestinian in Israel will be safer than we Jews. Or are you prepared to write off all your compatriots in Israel just so the Zionist entity is destroyed? Once that happens, what will you have to get back to?"

"Get to the point," he prodded me.

When I finished, he nearly exploded. "You want me to help you? Are you crazy? What is there in it for me — for us? And don't dare offer me some shekels!"

"The Iraqis will never be your saviors," I said. "You should make better choices among Israel's enemies."

"We can't afford that luxury," he said bitterly. "Your enemies are our — "

"Don't say 'friends,'" I interrupted him. "You're too intelligent to accept that uncritically. In the end, there must be an accommodation between Israelis and Palestinians, even between the state of Israel and the PLO. Many in Israel and in your PLO do not believe that, but I do and I think you do. If that is the case, then your association with Jordan, Egypt, the Saudis . . . is acceptable, but not Iraq."

When he countered, "I don't see Libya on your list," I knew he was listening.

"For the time being, they're too far away, and Qaddafi is too crazy," I told him.

"Go on," he said. "What do you want? What do you offer?"

That's when I saw how useful the Kirchberg forum is. All I had to do was to raise again yesterday's discussion of confidence building — through measures based on survival rather than good will. But this morning, the debate was between two relevant parties and not some Oxford Union sparring proxies. Israel must know what is going on in Osirak, I insisted. The Mossad had picked up plenty of evidence that this was not just a nuclear power reactor twelve miles southeast of Baghdad. Why had they negotiated in 1976 with the French for an Osiris-type research reactor with a power output of seventy megawatts thermal? That's not what they need for peaceful power purposes.

And instead of 20 percent enriched uranium, why are the Iraqis insisting on 93 percent enriched uranium-235? That's weapons-grade stuff! According to our estimates, with an annual consumption of ten tons of such uranium, the Osirak reactor could produce nearly ten kilograms of plutonium!

If Ahmed was surprised, he didn't let on. "But Iraq signed the Nuclear Non-Proliferation Treaty and you did not," he countered.

"Sure," I laughed. "And they agreed to have IAEA inspectors from Vienna look at what they'll permit them to see. How long do you think it would take the Iraqis to cancel such agreements if it suited them?" But we needed harder evidence, I pointed out: nuclear reprocessing, plutonium accumulation, probable date of critical start-up. . . . And what precisely are the French companies contributing to Osirak? Is all the Iraqi uranium coming only from France? Do the Iraqis have other sources? What about the rumors of a 350 megawatt Cirene-type reactor from the Italians, one that might have an annual capacity of one hundred kilograms of weapons-grade plutonium? Some of our questions are complicated, others are easier. "What kind of a chemist are you?" I asked.

Ahmed looked surprised and then laughed — the first open laugh between the two of us — when he learned how I'd guessed.

"Inorganic and also analytical," he volunteered.

"Excellent," I said. "And what do you expect in return for your help?" I asked. "I know it's not money that builds confidence. It's too cheap."

Ahmed nodded. "You mean, in theory?"

"Sure," I said, "so far, everything is theoretical."

"Release of our prisoners," he said, "high level contacts with your government. . . ."

I almost wished that yesterday's Brit were here — the man who was so skeptical about confidence building. We'll do it in driblets, I offered, just speaking theoretically. Some French intelligence tidbits for some prisoners, nuclear reprocessing data for a whole bunch of prisoners, plutonium evidence for substantive discussions with the PLO. . . .

"I'll think it over," he said just before Melanie appeared in her red beetle. We agreed that if contact were to be maintained, it would have

to be at Kirchberg-sponsored events. In addition to the annual meet-
ings, there were always smaller specialized group meetings — mostly
in Europe — dealing with topics for which our presence would raise
no suspicion.

He'd almost turned to go when he stopped. "Suppose Osirak is more
than just a nuclear power reactor? You Israelis always claim you
won't be the first to drop an atomic bomb in the Middle East, but you
won't be second either. How will you accomplish that if Iraq is build-
ing atomic bombs at Osirak?"

"With the right information at the right time," I told Ahmed, "we
can avoid being second without breaking our promise that we won't
be first."

"Enough about all that," Menachem said, throwing his hands up
as though scattering chaff to the winds. "The French and the Iraqis can go to hell without any help from me. Why waste our time
on them? We have so little time. Three more days."

"You're right." Her hand reached out for his. "Enough about
arms. Or at least that kind."

"So what's planned for Vienna?"

"Do you go to the opera?" she asked.

"Opera?" Menachem let out a guffaw. "Can you imagine how
much opera there was during my childhood in the central Congo?
Or in the British army? Or in Dimona? No, no opera. Never."

"Good," Melanie said. "Very good. I'd hoped you'd say that."

11

Melanie pointed to the *Makropoulos Case* program by her side.
"Would you want to live that long? Like this three-hundred-year-
old opera singer, still sexually alluring, who has run out of her longevity potion?" She was playing with her post-opera cheesecake,
which she had ordered out of habit. Tonight she had no appetite for
it. Jet lag, she told herself.

"Probably not. But then, I've never fancied Ponce de León." Felix Frankenthaler sounded distant, as he usually did when he wanted to change the subject. "You know what interested me?" His chin had been propped in his hand, but now he straightened. "All it says in this program is that 'Baron Prus, who died apparently childless in 1827, was in fact the father of Ferdinand Gregor, whose mother was the famous singer Ellian MacGregor.' That's about as uninformative as one can get, considering that proof of that illegitimate progeny is one of the key issues of the opera."

"And why does that bother you?"

"I have the feeling that Prus never knew he had a child by Ellian. I don't think Ellian ever told him."

Melanie finally swallowed the cheesecake morsel she'd been playing with. "Maybe she's a version of a modern single mother."

"Do you approve of single mothers?"

She glanced up at him. Was he serious? "I don't think it's really a question of approval. Many single mothers have no choice."

"I know that," he said impatiently. "But take someone like Ellian," he stabbed the open program with his index finger. "Financially independent, her own career, beautiful — "

"Stop!" Melanie interrupted. "Beauty has nothing to do with it. But under the first two conditions? Sure," she said more forcefully, "I could understand not telling the father."

Frankenthaler made no attempt to hide his surprise. "You can't be serious."

"Why? Just because Janáček has it end tragically?" She tapped her forehead. "You're too easily brainwashed, Felix. I don't even want to discuss it with you until you've had a chance to see an opera that goes about it from a different point of view."

"Such as?" Felix looked puzzled, a little frustrated. Melanie could see him racking his brain for a specific opera.

"You'll never come up with the one I'm thinking of," she laughed. "But just think of the Amazons."

———

"Are we going to the opera? In these clothes?" Menachem sounded worried, almost shocked.

"I often wear pants to the opera. Just feel the material." Melanie reached over to lead his left hand to her lavender raw silk pants with little slits in the bottom of the trousers. "And look at my shoes." She pointed to the gas pedal. "Jourdan T-straps. Not exactly hiking boots."

"But look at me." Menachem fingered his open shirt collar. "I don't even have a tie."

"Stay close to me and don't worry. This evening is on me, from beginning to end."

Masturbation and fantasy: for most people, I suppose it's hard to imagine one without the other. Why wasn't it that way for me? Oh, there were fantasies, early on, modeled after a coffee-table book on the erotic friezes of South Indian temples. God only knows how I came across that, but it didn't take me long afterward to seek out a copy of the Kamasutra. But all of the perverse imagination I spent in my teens — on this position, on that — all of it paled in the weeks and months following my first time in that darkroom at Columbia. From that day on, it was mostly variety in locations that I wanted for my fantasy life: on a table, under a table, in a church pew, on a dentist's chair, against a giant Henry Moore reclining bronze woman, in the opera. . . . The first three fantasies I actually consummated with my sexy TA, but by the time my imagination had reached dental chairs and bronzes, I was with Justin. I could sense that he'd have thought such notions kinky. The dental chair and Moore sculpture I realized on my own in my post-Kegel, autoerotic marital phase, but once I had ticked them off, so to speak, the novelty was gone.

Not so with opera. Music that speaks to the soul penetrates the mind at a certain pitch, just as perfectly destined sexual contact or deep erotic feeling awakens the senses. They enter the mind and body in similar fashion — as effortlessly as a favorite finger or a lover's phallus enters the ardent woman. Not only could I pleasure myself à la Kegel in public at the opera, but I did not even have to hide any auditory evidence of sexual pleasure. All I needed was some advance knowledge of the opera, anticipate when the audience would collectively scream bravo, and I could let myself go with an abandon hitherto reserved only for the most soundproof recesses of my home.

Even such operatic intuition, mostly in works by Verdi, Puccini, and Donizzeti, I learned soon, was not indispensable. There are operas, say those by Janáček, which are interrupted only occasionally by applause. In those operas, and especially in the Wagnerian marathons, I soon learned a subtler strategy. The masturbatory tempo had to be fitted to the music — an observation that led to a great deal of advance homework on my part. But that was not all. One evening at the Met during my ecstatically drawn-out accompaniment to the immolation scene in Walküre, I had produced such copious honey that I was afraid it had spotted my dress. It had not, but out of my worry I suddenly realized that opera, with its sartorial and social exhibitionism, rendered much of my subtlety — even Dr. Kegel's exercises themselves — unnecessary. Initially, I draped a shawl or jacket over my lap during the performance in order to screen my hand, but eventually even that became superfluous through a remarkably simple sartorial innovation of mine.

I would be lying if I denied that on occasion I had dreamt of enlisting an accomplice, but that's where it always began and ended: in a dream. Tonight will be different. Tonight Menachem, who has already erased years of inhibition, will become my unwitting agent for converting dream into reality. Everything is perfect. Even the choice of performance.

Back in New York, as soon as I had decided to attend the Kirchberg Conference, I contacted the local Austrian Tourist Office to find out about opera schedules in Vienna. The options for this September Wednesday, the only day off at Kirchberg, were Don Giovanni at the Staatsoper, Die Fledermaus at the Volksoper, and a concert performance of Handel's Thalestris and Alexander in the Jugendstiltheater, a venue I'd never heard of before. The choice had been obvious, even weeks before I'd met Menachem.

Ever since the Frankenthalers had converted me into an opera aficionado, I had joined a loose opera-going coterie, consisting mostly of other couples and some single women. We'd meet for an early dinner at Fiorello's or at The Ginger Man near the Met to indulge in anticipatory opera schmooze or else for post-operatic critique over coffee and dessert at O'Neal's across the street from Lincoln Center. Everyone knows that serious opera buffs are elitist, assertive, deeply biased, and, when assembled, incapable of resisting one-upmanship.

In such company, picking Die Fledermaus, *in spite of its quint-
essentially Viennese character, would have been stigmatized as tour-
istic gaucherie. Going to a Mozart opera at the Vienna Staatsoper,
was, of course, beyond reproach, though certainly no supreme statement of one's sophistication. But Handel? Handel had written more
than thirty operas but except for* Semele *and one performance of*
Giulo Cesare *at the Met, I'd only heard recordings, and those had
been limited to occasional excerpts from* Alcina, Agrippina, *and*
Orlando. *Even better, I'd never come across an opera — by Handel
or anyone else — entitled* Thalestris and Alexander. *No Handel bi-
ography or any logical compendium like the* Grove Dictionary of
Opera *listed such an opera. This made me curious, so I kept looking — and my research led me all the way back to Plutarch's and
to Quintus Curtius's accounts of Alexander the Great — to discover
that Thalestris was a mythological queen of the Amazons, who had
supposedly proposed to Alexander to lie with her for thirteen days,
promising to hand over to him any male child resulting from such a
sexual union, but keeping any female offspring in the Amazon manner to perpetuate their race.*

*All of which was very interesting, of course. But how come there
was no written record of that opera? I got the telephone number of
the ticket office in Vienna, called them, and asked that they mail me
a program. For an additional exorbitant fee, they offered a copy of
the libretto, which naturally I accepted. I could hardly wait to tell
Felix Frankenthaler and the rest of my opera cronies about this pa-
tently insane coup, but then I decided to wait until my return from
Europe.*

*And then the theater scoop! . . . so much easier to discover than
the Handel opera details, because there were plenty of books on
Vienna's Jugendstil period. Every one featured the famous Steinhof
Psychiatric Hospital in Vienna's Fourteenth District with its archi-
tectural masterpiece, Otto Wagner's church inside the insane asylum
compound. To show how modern Vienna's psychiatric care was
around the turn of the century, Wagner had also been commissioned
to design a theater for the benefit of patients and staff. Space restric-
tions during the First World War had led to its conversion into clinical wards, but lately it had been restored to its original purpose as a*

*theater, apparently even including the original Thonet Jugendstil
furniture. Of course, I decided to pick the Handel performance for
my single free Vienna evening. Who could resist seeing the world
premiere of an opera in a nuthouse?*

Unlike the early curtain times of performances at the Staatsoper,
the concert version of the Handel was not scheduled to start until
eight in the evening; they had time for dinner at a restaurant that
Melanie had picked, primarily for its name: Restaurant Papageno.
It was her private apology to Mozart for not attending one of his
operas.

"It's the first time this week that we can actually choose what to
eat," remarked Menachem as they studied the menu. "Back at
Kirchberg, it's been like boarding school. You eat what's put in front
of you. What are you having?"

Melanie had picked *Beuschl mit Knödel* — a typical Austrian
peasant dish. "When I travel, I like to try things I can't have back
home."

"Are you referring only to food?" he asked.

Melanie was opening her napkin. Now she looked up. "As of last
Monday, the answer would have been 'yes.'" She grinned. "Tomorrow, I may well change it to 'most certainly not.' What about you?"

"Right now, I can think only of food. I haven't had any lunch.
What exactly is *Beuschl?*"

"It's lungs — generally veal. Prepared like beef Stroganoff."

"No lungs," he said firmly. "Let's see what else they have."

"Are you squeamish about meat in general or just organs?"

Menachem put down the menu. "If you knew what meat I ate in
my youth, you wouldn't ask such a question."

"So tell me. What did you eat?"

"Buffalo — "

"Big deal," she interrupted.

"Let me finish." He counted with his fingers. "Buffalo, chicken,
and corned beef were standard fare, but the delicacies were mon-
key, porcupine . . . ," Menachem paused for a moment to relish
the change in Melanie's expression, "and the real delicacy, *inkuta*,
with its totally white meat."

"What's *inkuta?*" she asked suspiciously.

"Diving antelope."

"Come on, Menachem. You're pulling my leg. *Diving* antelopes?"

He nodded. "You heard right. They eat plants under water. But since there are no diving antelopes in Austria nor porcupine *mit Knödel*, I'll have the *Forelle mit Gurkensalat.* I like trout."

"Fine. But this is the last decision you can make tonight on your own," she announced playfully. "For the rest of this evening, everything else is up to me. And since you're my guest, let me tell you about tonight's opera."

The explanation for the absence of any prior written information on Thalestris and Alexander was all provided in the lengthy introduction to the libretto that had reached Melanie prior to her departure from New York. According to the notes, Handel's last operatic composition had only recently been discovered in manuscript form at the Trinity College Library in Dublin, where it had lain misfiled and apparently also unread for more than two hundred years.

His last few operas, ending with *Deidamia*, had been flops in London. He'd been encouraged by managers, impresarios, and even some librettists to switch from Italian to English texts for his music — advice that he followed in his subsequent oratorios, notably *Messiah*, which had its world premiere in Dublin in 1742. Its enthusiastic reception, even surpassing that of *Alexander's Feast*, with its English text based on Dryden's poem, must have convinced him to stick henceforth to the vernacular.

Handel had brought along to Dublin his first English opera, *Thalestris and Alexander*, the libretto of which was based loosely on a 1667 play by John Weston, entitled *The Amazon Queen; or, The Amours of Thalestris to Alexander the Great.* The play had never been performed, but it had been published by Henry Heringman, the copyright holder of Shakespeare's plays — a provenance sufficiently weighty to convince Handel's regular librettist, Charles Jennens, of the play's merit for adaptation. Dublin, unburdened by the thirty-odd Italian-style Handel operas with which his London audiences had become satiated, seemed just the right venue to launch Handel's English-language career.

Arrangements were well underway for an oratorio-style presentation, without scenery or action, at the *New Musick-Hall* in Fishamble Street, when Jonathan Swift — then dean of St. Patrick's Cathedral — learned of the Jennens libretto, which in Swift's view condoned undisguised adultery between the brazen Amazon queen and the happily married Alexander. In 1742, Swift had already gone off his rocker, but he was still dean of the cathedral, and his disapproval nixed any possible opening that year. Handel departed from Dublin on August 13, 1742, never to return to Ireland nor to see his first and last English-language opera performed.

Menachem had listened to Melanie's tale attentively, all the while continuing to eat his trout. But now he stopped her.

"How on earth did you learn all that?" he asked, dumbfounded. "Surely, you can't be doing such homework before every opera? And when did you find the time in Kirchberg? It certainly couldn't have been during the last two nights. . . ."

"Ah," she said and proceeded to tell him what had transpired in New York. "But most of it is right here, in this program." She reached down by the side of her seat and opened her shoulder bag. "Even the sophisticated audiences going to the *Theater am Steinhof* here in Vienna could not have known anything about Handel's *Thalestris*. So they produced this program," she held up a slim volume, the size of a modest paperback novel, its glossy cover showing the benign face of Handel, double chinned and heavily wigged. "I read it on the plane from New York, so let me tell you the actual story of the opera. It's not very complicated, but I want you to know something about Thalestris." She paused, and struggled again with the flush mounting in her cheeks. "And especially about the moment when she starts her first aria."

"Go ahead," he nodded good-naturedly. "But do you think I'm such a neophyte that I won't even know when she starts singing?"

"Of course not. But in this opera your timing is . . . essential."

"*My* timing? I'm just going to sit back and let it all happen."

"No you won't," she said, perhaps more emphatically than she'd intended. "I told you this is *my* evening. You are coming as my guest and you will do as you are told."

"Yes Ma'am!" He touched the side of his forehead in a military salute. "Understood."

"First, some brief background about baroque opera. Just enough," she said, as calmly as possible, "for you to understand the operational setting."

"This is starting to sound like the military."

"Perhaps it is," she laughed. "But remember, among the Amazons, the queen also leads the troops. And Thalestris was queen. Now pay close attention. A baroque opera has a series of recitatives, conversations spoken in a form of sing-song, with a continuo background created by the harpsichord, because in Handel's time they didn't yet have pianos. But interspersed will be arias by the main characters, in which they elaborate on their feelings and emotions. That's when you get the real music and the participation of other instruments."

"No chorus?"

"I'm talking about *baroque* opera: as it matured, there was less and less choral intervention. Still, the one we will hear tonight has a chorus of Amazons. But all you need to know for tonight's performance is that most of the musical action is during the arias and not the recitative. And when the first aria starts, that of Thalestris, queen of the Amazons, you will put your hand into my left pants pocket."

"Why left?"

For a moment, Melanie was taken aback. She had expected some other question — at least an expression of surprise or amusement — but not such a practical one. But then she caught his laughing eyes.

"Because you are right-handed, which is also the reason why you will sit to my left, Lieutenant Dvir."

"Understood."

She raised a warning index finger. "But not during the recitative, remember."

12

Once Melanie's hunting instinct had tuned in on the Amazon Queen Thalestris, she had sniffed beyond the Handel libretto to its literary source, the Weston text of 1667, which she had managed to track down in the Lowe Library of Columbia University. Though charmed by what she read in the fifty-six photocopied manuscript pages, she couldn't help but be disappointed by the play's ending. As usual, the man wins, but at least, she reflected gratefully, Handel's librettist, Charles Jennens, decided to pursue a more feminist line in his adaptation.

In John Weston's seventeenth-century text, now completely forgotten, the emphasis is on Alexander — handsome, virile, and, as the play opens, horny. He is burning to marry the beautiful, virginal Statira, daughter of the recently conquered and deceased Persian King Darius. Although clearly smitten by Alexander, parental and patriotic love cause Statira to turn down Alexander's entreaties. Piqued and priapic, he decides to marry that very night another woman, Roxanna, who, unbeknownst to Alexander, is neither amorously inexperienced nor monogamously inclined. Statira, in spite of having just rejected Alexander, is shocked to hear the news of Alexander's impending wedding. "Can he so soon forget his vows to me, / to love me best into eternity?" she whines to her attendant, who realistically explains, "No Madam, he's but to another fountain gone, / To seek relief when you afforded none."

But then, one of Alexander's commanders announces the impending approach of Thalestris, queen of the Amazons:

> We have beheld a Queen fair, fierce, and gay
> Who will make good what fame does of her say:
> Her women too, an Army brave and bold,
> Look as they ne'er had been by foe control'd;

Their discipline exact, they keep their ranks,
Else we had been assaulted with love pranks.
For at this time of year, to procreate,
They seek out Males, whose Governments they hate:
For they not long endure to live with men,
But send them their male children back again.

In Weston's rhyming couplets, as soon as Alexander hears Thalestris's desire to have a child by him, he agrees: "You fill my soul with wonder and delight / Madam, we'll marry if you please this night." Thalestris, a stickler for unequivocal terminology, does not buy such a rash offer ("You use me ill to talk of marriage, / I scorn to be your tame bird in a cage"), especially when she learns that Alexander is also enamored of Statira, whom he eventually marries after dumping Roxanna ("The truth is, she is but a woman now, / But was divine before I her did know"). Amazons, as a matter of principle, insist on complete fidelity during their brief mating season:

Yes, we too now will give a strict parol,
To be a year all one body and soul.
If in that time I chance to have a Boy,
Let it command that world which you enjoy:
But if a Girl, then a Queen shall be
Of all the female Heroes that are free.
And I will scorn till then any new flame,
So you will be engag'd unto the same.

Alexander cannot see himself making such a commitment, not even for the single month Thalestris proposes as a trial ("Let me but have you for one month alone, / Then trust to proofs who you most dote upon"), whereupon she turns him down permanently: "Since you have so inslav'd your noblest part, / I shall not give you my unconquer'd heart. / And let your Slave [Roxanna] possess your person too, / I scorn to have with half a man to do." Thalestris leaves Alexander's encampment:

And therefore to avoid temptation,
We take the surest way, to live alone,
And that we think is more security,
Then your wives give you, though they are less free.

though still enamored of Alexander and humbled:

Nature and justice give all love to him,
But his defects with scorn I disesteem.
So that I shall for him a Virgin die,
Which on your lives conceal as infamy:
For with my people great will be the stain,
That with this Macedon I have not lain.

Melanie had deemed it superfluous, even contraindicated, to burden Menachem with the literary antecedents of the operatic performance they were to witness that evening. All he heard in the restaurant was a summary of the Jennens rendition that Handel had set to music, but which Dean Jonathan Swift had considered much too tendentiously licentious for an eighteenth-century Dublin audience.

———

"As a Shebaist," she started, throwing him an affectionate glance, "you've probably also studied classical mythology."

"Try me."

"How did the Amazons avoid dying out after one generation?"

Menachem didn't even falter or ruminate. "Periodically, they went on warpaths, caught some men, violated them — "

"Spare me!" Melanie's sarcastic interruption, though brief, was sufficient to stop his tale.

"What's there to 'spare me' about? Or should I have said, 'they made love to them?' Unless I'm mistaken, they killed them once they got inseminated and even murdered any male children."

"All right, all right." She raised her palms in a pacifying gesture. "That's one version — the male historian's. The one we'll see tonight is more charming and certainly less brutal. Instead of fighting Alexander the Great, Thalestris, accompanied by three hundred of her Amazon warriors, visited him during his campaign against the Persians, leaped down from her horse with two spears in her right hand, strode forward and fearlessly inspected him. Apparently she liked what she saw, because the next thing she did was announce that she'd come to copulate with him for thirteen days — "

"Why thirteen?"

"Who knows?" She dismissed the question with a flick of her hand. "But here is the point that seems to have bothered Swift so much. Thalestris obviously must have known that Alexander was married, be it first to Roxanna or later to Statira. Yet without alluding to that fact or at least unconcerned about his marital status, she propositioned him. A rather modern woman, this Thalestris, don't you think so?"

"And what did Alexander say?"

"It depends whether you follow the original play or the opera. I prefer the version we'll see tonight." Melanie quoted from the open program by her side. " 'The passion of the woman, being, as she was, more keen for love than the king, compelled him to concede. Thirteen days were spent in satisfying her desire. Then she went to her kingdom, and Alexander to Parthienê.' "

Menachem stroked his chin as if he were thinking of a weighty problem. "Is Alexander's wife one of the characters."

"Statira? Yes. Why do you ask?"

"What did she think of her husband sleeping with another woman for thirteen days?"

"Maybe Alexander didn't tell her."

"But she must have heard about it."

This is extraordinary, Melanie thought to herself. Menachem is asking the question one would expect from a woman, whereas I present Thalestris as the heroine. "Maybe Statira is back home in Macedonia. He could have decided not to write her about it."

———

"Soon!" she whispered. Melanie had caressed Menachem's right hand throughout the recitative following the first aria, sung by a mezzo-soprano in the trouser role of Alexander; now the *coro* of five Amazons announced the impending arrival of their queen, Thalestris. The orchestration was uncommonly lush compared to the modest size of most Handelian opera orchestras consisting of perhaps a dozen strings, frequently without violas, a couple of oboes, and harpsichord continuo. But this time, the all-male orchestra was right below the stage, at the level of the audience, thus making Handel's unexpected largesse visually as well as auditorily evident: an expanded string ensemble, including cello and double bass, accompanied by oboes, bassoons, and paired recorders as well as extra brass and timpani for some of the choral accompaniment. For a change, the continuo support was not provided solely by the harpsichord, but also by a harp and a theorbo, with double bass and cello additionally contributing during some of the recitatives. Most strikingly were two chalumeaux which the players raised to their mouths just as Thalestris, sung by a countertenor in tails, stepped forward. During the orchestral tune-up before the lights were dimmed, Melanie had commented upon the gender assignment of the main roles: "I wonder whether this was Handel's intention or a Freudian reading by the director?"

Melanie had managed to get excellent tickets in the orchestra, just below the shimmering, circular glass chandelier that illuminated the golden, stylized frieze around the edges of the white ceiling. But the unaltered Thonet chairs, to which her earlier research had called so much attention, were unexpectedly harsh. Even in sentimental Vienna, many a theater devotee probably would have preferred padding over authenticity by gladly trading some of the *Jugendstil* severity of the highly polished, dark brown wood construction for some upholstery. To Melanie, however, the original Thonet design of the side arms more than made up for any deficiency on the comfort front. The wooden armrest ended in a graceful curve attached to the seat, but otherwise presented no barrier between neighbors: a hand could equally well slip over as well as under the arm rest into an adjacent lap.

Menachem sat on the aisle, with Melanie to his right, and the male partner of a stiff, formally dressed older couple to her right. "Now!" she whispered once more, this time with greater urgency, and led Menachem's hand to her left pants pocket before releasing it. "Now enter," she commanded as the first tones of the chalumeaux reverberated through the auditorium. Melanie had slouched back, her thighs spread slightly apart. "Try following the music," she murmured — a message that never reached Menachem's consciousness. It was not so much the opening words of Thalestris's aria — "That appetite we get by fasts, / Requires prompt relief at last" — that had masked Melanie's request, as the startling tactile sensation of his finger tips from their first contact with her naked flesh through the bogus pocket. A quick glance at Melanie revealed nothing. Her head was reclining against the high and slightly arched splat of her seat, her body semi-recumbent. Like a fig leaf, the open program rested on her lap. Melanie's eyes were closed, but so were those of her neighbor to her right. Many a purist at concerts concentrates on the music in such fashion and *Thalestris*, after all, was a concert performance and not an action-filled, staged opera.

Menachem's hand, though warm, was temporarily frozen into immobility. Discreetly, he turned his gaze beyond his seemingly slumbering companion to the other persons in their row. All were focused on the stage or at some interior picture of their own. Staring at Thalestris, as if he were trying to catch and then fix her eyes, his right hand crept sideways over Melanie's naked belly until his little finger reached her belly button. Menachem's digital probing halted while his peripheral vision strained to the right. Reassured that no head had moved, not even Melanie's, his pinkie circumnavigated the outer rim of her navel, moistened ever so slightly by her perspiration. Menachem had explored that part of Melanie's anatomy only once — with his tongue, an instrument incapable of measuring nuances of dampness. Using his pinkie as combined pivot and brake, he rotated his hand until his stretched thumb pointed straight south, whereupon the digital brake was withdrawn from Melanie's navel to allow resumed downward exploration of his palm, the guiding thumb moving cautiously back and forth like a slowly flickering tongue. Just when Menachem had reached the startling conclusion that Melanie was naked under her trousers, his flickering thumb encountered the waistband of her bikini, cut so low that the tips of her upper pubic hair tickled the skin of his wandering thumb. In the same solicitous manner he had used earlier at dinner to lift the upper fillet of his trout with the knife blade, Menachem's thumb now slid underneath the waistband until he felt it pass over his wrist.

It was time to rest. He had reached, patiently but surely, the intended objective: Melanie's mons veneris. The time had come to spread the fingers of his right hand like the tentacles of an amorous octopus until they covered all of her pubic hair — a movement that produced the first overt quiver in Melanie as well as an instantaneous, almost painful tumescence in Menachem. Hastily, he glanced down to reassure himself that his erection was not scandalously obvious. Only then did his gaze return to Thalestris, this time to her wide open mouth, because her eyes seemed to be studying him, making it impossible for him to maintain eye contact. With indolent slowness, Menachem's pinkie crept forward until the continuously applied, slight pressure caused it to dip. Just as the little finger's tip felt the first viscous moisture of vaginal honey, Melanie spread her thighs some more, simultaneously pressing with her open right palm down onto the program, which now shielded Menachem's hand in its entirety.

If it had been up to her, she would have settled for gentle, methodical strokes of her clitoris by his pinkie — a finger she never used herself. But tonight's operatic arousal was not within her control; perhaps she did not even desire it to be subject to her cues. Menachem's finger, with its gentle but inexorable pressure, had found little resistance between her labia. Soon, it had entered her so deeply that the web at the base of his pinkie had turned slippery. For Menachem, the rest of the sexual play gradually turned more active, more rapid, more penetrative . . . more male. His little finger withdrew, to be replaced by its longer, thicker neighbor. When the ring finger had sunk into her to its limit, he pulled it out, to insert the longest digital masturbatory instrument of them all, Melanie's favorite: the middle finger. But Menachem had no favorites. All four fingers acted like surrogate penises, each in turn entering and withdrawing, entering and withdrawing. Melanie, who had dreamed of slow masturbation accompanying Handel's music, had become subject to a totally different tempo that, she sensed, was rushing toward an uncontrollable crescendo.

"Stop!" she panted under her breath, simultaneously grasping his wrist and squeezing her thighs so firmly that Menachem's middle finger was immobilized on the spot. She turned to him until her tongue brushed his ear. "Please, Menachem," she whispered in a gasping voice while reducing slightly the pressure of her thighed vise. "Please. All the way. Out of the pocket."

———

At intermission, the crowd pushed through the main foyer — with its white patterned tile floor, interspersed with green floral designs — past the officious no-smoking signs (*Rauchen behördlich verboten*) to reach the outer small smoking sanctuary. On their way in, Melanie and Menachem had stopped to read the large marble tablet marking the October 8, 1907, opening by the emperor: *erbaut unter der glorreichen Regierung Seiner kaiserl. und königl. Apostopolischen Majestät FRANZ JOSEPH I, Kaiser von Oesterreich, König von Ungarn u.u.u.* They had felt as if they were entering another era. Where else, but then, and only in Vienna, could such tasteful and yet stuffily deferential attention have been paid to what was basically a spectacular insane asylum with a theater.

But now, with Menachem shuffling behind Melanie, their thoughts were elsewhere as her hand brushed inadvertently against the bulge in his crotch. "Is that how you respond to opera?" she asked, turning back to him.

"To Thalestris, yes. Just sniff my hand." His right hand moved past her ear to touch her cheek. "And now tell me how you expect me to wait until we get back to Kirchberg," he whispered.

"You won't have to," she whispered back. "I've made reservations for tonight in a hotel with a big *Doppelbett*."

Menachem turned to her, a sheepish look on his face. "We can't register under my name."

"You don't have to." She squeezed his hand. "I made the reservation in the name of Mr. and Mrs. Laidlaw."

"What sort of passport will I show them?"

"They may not even ask. But if they do, you'll say you forgot yours in Kirchberg. I brought mine — just in case."

———

Something, she wasn't quite sure what, had roused her from deep sleep. Melanie squinted at the early morning light filtering around the edges of the thick drapes. Turning over to see whether Menachem was still asleep, she found his side of the bed empty.

Now fully awake, she heard his low voice in the dressing alcove. Melanie jumped up, nearly tripping over the telephone cord that reached around the corner, to find Menachem crouched on the floor, cradling the telephone in his lap. He was speaking rapidly in an urgent tone in a language she took to be Hebrew.

"Menachem, what happened?" she called out.

"Shh," he whirled around, covering the mouthpiece. "Quiet," he hissed.

"But who are you talking to?" she whispered, suspecting an emergency.

"My wife," he replied.

13

"Isn't the whole Amazon mythology a paean on single motherhood?" asserted Melanie after regaling her opera companion with the story of the long-forgotten Handel score and the world premiere of *Thalestris and Alexander* in the *Jugendstiltheater*.

"Of a rather peculiar kind," Frankenthaler interjected. "But there are plenty of other examples of single mothers. Why look for them in mythology — look at nature. Have you ever heard of the brown antechinuses?"

In response to her baffled expression he spelled the word. "It's pretty late, so I'll make it short. I'll skip some of the juicier aspects of their reproductive behavior other than to inform you that their copulation lasts for more than five hours." He stopped, waiting for Melanie's response.

"Not bad," she said coolly. "Who does most of the work?"

"You're looking at it too anthropomorphically. The male, of course, enters from the rear, and the pair remains firmly locked together — "

"Humans are known to do that," Melanie observed, "though not for five hours."

"This is not what I wanted to talk about, but I see that I must. They alternate between an active phase of ten seconds and a quiescent one of four minutes."

"Tell me about the ten seconds."

"It will certainly take longer to describe it than to do it." Frankenthaler was willing enough to take the thing in the spirit Melanie seemed to have adopted — but he had a sense, as he did so, that he was on somewhat thin social ice. Sexual esoterica — in contrast to technical details of reproductive biology — had never been part of their earlier post-opera conversation. "The male antechinus braces his feet against the female's butt end and gives one powerful coital thrust — "

"Just one?" she asked miming disenchantment.

"One only," he said firmly. "But so forceful, that both animals roll over to one side, still connected, and then they return to their former position. After four minutes, another — "

"I get the picture. But what really got you started on this tale?"

Frankenthaler looked at his watch. "It's not easy to be concise about the reproductive behavior of female antechinuses without skipping the interesting parts."

"You mean there's more?"

"Sure," he nodded. "Then there's the post-copulatory phase. These mammals breed within a very short period of time, and as expected, the progeny is evenly distributed between the two sexes. Yet a few months later, not a single male can be found!" He looked expectantly at Melanie.

"So what happens?"

"It's connected with 'lekking,' a behavioral pattern common among some birds: the males congregate solely for the purpose of mating in places frequented by females. But it's very rare among mammals. Antechinuses are an exception. What happens is that once a female has mated, she leaves the area, whereas the males continue running around in a frenzy looking for other females. Within a few days they all die from gastrointestinal ulcers and other conditions associated with extreme stress." He leaned forward, as if it were important to get the point across. "So you see, operationally a female antechinus ends up as a single mother. And what is even more interesting, they resemble your Amazons, because while the daughters remain with or near their mothers, the sons are kicked out by their mothers as soon as they are weaned."

Melanie shook her head. "That's quite a story, but I'd draw a different conclusion. The only similarity I see to the Amazons is that your female antechinuses also favor their daughters. They're single mothers, because the biological fathers died lekking. There are plenty of such instances in the animal kingdom, including *Homo sapiens*." Melanie displayed a disarming grin. "Let me reciprocate by telling you a story about animal sexual behavior of female adders — an example that would be closer to the Amazons. Felix, what do you know about the sexual conduct of snakes?"

Frankenthaler raised his hands in mock horror. "I'm terrified of snakes. How do you know anything about them?"

"A Swedish group has applied to REPCON for support of research aimed to determine why these female snakes indulge in multiple matings with different partners. In most species, promiscuity in *males* has an obvious biological rationale: the more females they inseminate, the more offspring they will produce. We could consider it a reproductive lottery in which the males simply buy more tickets to win. But females? Once inseminated, they have no real reason for further matings."

Frankenthaler's eyebrows rose in feigned astonishment. "Surely you aren't extending this generalization to *Homo sapiens*?"

"Let's stick to snakes, for now. In many species sexual courtship always has an element of competition and exploitation. Males compete for females, but between the sexes, there's also a competition: to see which can use the other as a vehicle for passing on its genes. Given the way these things are usually set up, it's generally up to the female to accept or reject a mate — if she's given the choice. Usually, and certainly among humans, we consider successful rejection a victory for the female, and acceptance a victory for the male. But is there a way the female can take a more active role? Like the Amazons? Take her fate more into her own hands? In *Vipera berus*, they seem to have found a way: multiple mating."

"But I don't see the point — " Frankenthaler began.

"That's because you don't know the trick," Melanie said, looking a bit smug, "whereas these adders do. That's the research we're now supporting," she added quickly.

"My, my." Frankenthaler could not repress a salacious grin. "REPCON spending its valuable money to determine the benefits of female promiscuity? You're lucky you're not heading some governmental funding agency. I can just see the headlines about your wasting the taxpayer's dollar. But go on. I'm starting to regret my neglect of herpetology."

"Before giving you the punch line, you need to know two aspects of life among the snakes. First, the males provide neither nuptial gifts nor parental care — "

"Come now, Melanie. That's not even uncommon among us humans — "

"As if I didn't know that," she interrupted him. "But in addition, the female adders are able to store sperm within their body for months prior to ovulation. It represents a form of genetic bet-hedging. Or at least that's what our Swedish grantees are trying to find out."

"Bet-hedging?"

"Precisely. By repeated mating with *different* males, the female greatly increases the genetic diversity of her stored sperm."

"And then she decides which sperm is optimal for fertilization?" Frankenthaler made no attempt to hide his skepticism.

"That's exactly what the Swedes are trying to find out. In humans, of course, a woman can do that by simply picking the right man — "

"Or going to a sperm bank."

"Whatever," Melanie agreed airily. "But a snake has her own sperm bank. The question is whether female snakes have some special biological mechanism that allows them to pick the best sperm among the various stored samples, or whether such multiple mating is just a general strategy to allow sperm from a genetically superior male to triumph over the ejaculate of his competitors."

Melanie stopped. For a few seconds, neither of them had much to say. "What exactly got us going on this path?" she finally asked.

Frankenthaler shrugged. "The character of Ellian MacGregor in the *Makropoulos Case* and the loaded words 'single mother.'"

"Ah yes," exclaimed Melanie. "I was working up to something. Take a professionally and financially independent single woman, whose biological clock is ticking. Or maybe the alarm has already started to ring. Let's assume she has all the attributes of a good mother, but she hasn't found the right mate for matrimony. Does that mean she cannot be allowed to have a child unless she's willing to run out and commit herself to someone she wouldn't otherwise consider? Or what if she's found the right man, but he isn't available for family commitments? Let's say he's married. And can't get divorced," she added, seemingly as an afterthought.

"That's a pretty precise scenario you've outlined here. You mean you just made it up?"

"That's neither here nor there," Melanie said.

"Whether you did or did not, surely that doesn't mean that she has to behave like your Thalestris — "

"Not *mine*. Handel's Thalestris."

"Anyone's Thalestris. Why can't your professionally single woman," Frankenthaler barely masked his disapproval, "go to a sperm bank? In fact, behave like a snake in terms of your bet-hedging, but do it by artificial insemination. Why does she have to commit adultery?"

"Who's talking about adultery?"

"You said the man was married."

Melanie flushed. "I suppose I did say that. But in my scenario, he'd be serving solely as a sperm donor — not as a true father. He need not even know that his semen was used for fertilization."

"How on earth would she pull that off? Some version of Ellian MacGregor in the *Makropoulos Case*? No: don't tell me: you've thought of this too, haven't you?"

"Have I?" Melanie responded, and for a moment her look went distant. "I suppose I have. Theoretically."

———

"It's getting late." Frankenthaler gestured to the passing waiter for the check by scribbling with his finger in the air. "Before we part, let me thank you once more for agreeing so promptly to support Renu's stay in Jerusalem. I'm sure it will pay off."

Melanie nodded absentmindedly. "And when does she plan to go?"

"In the early spring. She still needs to prepare some material for the clinical studies — some special types of NO-releasers — really the key to our project." He looked at Melanie. "Who knows? Israel is such a small country and all the academics seem to know each other. Maybe she'll bump into your Israeli from the Kirchberg Conference. Do you plan to stay in touch with him?"

"Who knows?"

That's what Menachem asked me in the car on our way back to Kirchberg. "Shall we see each other again?" but then he corrected himself. "Do you want to see me again?" he asked, "now that you know a lot more about me?" "I think so," I said.

And why not? Even before I surprised him on the telephone, I was almost certain that he was married. Except for the banter during our first few minutes together, each had refrained from volunteering many biographical details. Although excruciatingly short, or perhaps because of its brevity, my encounter with Menachem had become almost all-encompassingly sexual. But sexual in a purely erotic context, without any plans beyond Austria. I am not a widow of opportunity, and I've never been one. For Menachem, as I learned as soon as he'd put down the telephone, it had not been quite so free of self-reproach. And as he explained on the way back to Kirchberg that morning, I understood why Luc Morand had not wanted to pursue the question of Menachem's second wife.

During the late 1950s, when Menachem spent a few months at Saclay, the French atomic research center outside Paris, one of the Israeli technicians who had arrived there earlier was seconded to him. According to Menachem, it started out as an affair between two married people far from home. But as the affair deepened — or was it already a liaison? — Shulamit's husband learned of it. Refusing to wear the horns of a cuckolded spouse quietly, he not only ditched Shulamit but also informed the first Mrs. Dvir about what was going on in Paris. The brief story of the subsequent divorces and Menachem's and Shulamit's marriage barely registered in my mind after I heard the biblical punishment, which is how I interpreted Menachem's rationalization of the subsequent events: the car accident in the desert before their first anniversary, which had permanently paralyzed Shulamit from the waist down. Since that day, Menachem had refused to sit in the driver's seat of a car. And he promised Shulamit to telephone her every morning whenever travels would take him from home — a promise he said he'd kept now for nearly twenty years.

Our last two days in Kirchberg were different — less sexually charged, but in some respects more intimate. Was it the knowledge that there could be no future that set us free to dwell on our respective pasts? Or that both of us had decided to be grateful for the physical pleasure we had given each other without imposing other demands? "Until the next Kirchberg Conference," Menachem whispered when we said good-bye. "No sooner?" I whispered, but he may not have heard me, because I was sobbing.

I wish I had a friend to whom I could talk about Menachem, but I can't. We both pledged total discretion, but he promised to get a post office box to which I could write. Would talking to a shrink count as a violation of that pledge? But I have never had the urge for such a psychic crutch and I still don't. Talking to Felix would be interesting. What would a Jewish, seemingly monogamous, long-married family man think of all this?

14

"Dr. Dvir," the woman's voice said. "One moment. Professor Yehuda Davidson wishes to talk to you."

She had gone off the line so quickly that he could not interpose his usual "*Mr.* Dvir." Menachem Dvir was proudly arrogant about the absence of any doctorate from his CV — very much like British surgeons, who insist on being mistered rather than doctored. But this time, he actually wanted to say something else: "Why can't he dial the phone by himself?" Menachem had made it a fetish never to use a surrogate for phoning, even during his tenure as director of the nuclear center in Dimona.

"Menachem? *Shalom.*" The warmth of Davidson's *shalom* punctured the small balloon of Menachem's irritation. "I'm calling to ask for a favor."

"What? No foreplay from the distinguished urologist?" Davidson and Dvir had first met during their common military service; banter was their usual style of conversation.

"Foreplay? I should have thought of that, considering the subject of my request."

"Oh?" Dvir's interest was piqued. A fugitive image of Melanie flashed through his thoughts, distracting him.

"We have an Indian investigator here from America in our reproductive biology unit who would like — "

"Well, well," interrupted Menachem. "So now you're even getting American Indians at Hadassah? Don't tell me he's a Jewish Navaho. Or is it a Sioux?"

"Very funny," Davidson said through Menachem's laughter. "You're wrong on all fronts. *She* happens to be an Indian from India on the staff of Brandeis University. She is spending a short research leave here with us. But here is the point of my call. She's one of the top researchers in the nitric oxide field — "

"I haven't had much chemistry," Menachem interjected, "and most of that was decades ago. But nitric oxide in the medical school?"

"I was coming to that when you interrupted. She is working on nitric oxide at the cellular level — endogenously produced nitric oxide. It's quite a new field and very exciting. Until just recently, nobody thought NO played an important role as a signal transducer."

"'Transducer.' I love it when you biological types use physical terms. As if you clinicians knew anything about piezoelectricity. But go on. What does your Indian lady want to transduce?"

"Menachem," Davidson complained. "You haven't changed a bit. You demand foreplay, but then you don't give me a chance. What Dr. Krishnan — that's her name — is interested in . . . ," he delayed the punch line for a few seconds, "is penile erection."

Dvir's end of the line fell briefly silent. "Did you say 'penile'?"

"I did. It is also a topic that has interested me for a long time, because impotence in men can be a terrible problem. A quarter of diabetics may suffer from it." Yehuda Davidson felt that the most effective way to change the tone of the conversation was to turn clinical.

"So what can I do for you?"

"You have a new man, Dr. Jephtah Cohn, doing bioengineering — "

"Cohn," Dvir interrupted. "He works with an interdisciplinary team in mechanical and electrical engineering."

"You know him?" Davidson sounded impressed.

"Listen, Yehuda. Here at Ben-Gurion, I'm vice president in charge of skinning cats. Which means that I'm supposed to know who needs money or who can bring some in. Mostly, it's the former. And for that, I need to know where people are working."

"That's exactly why I'm calling you. *My* Dr. Krishnan may wish to collaborate with *your* Dr. Cohn. Her present grant just supports her stay here for the next couple of months — until the middle of July. It doesn't even cover local overhead. I agreed to cover it on our side, but for the work at Ben-Gurion — "

"From whom is your Dr. Krishnan getting her grant? Why don't you ask them for supplemental funds."

"I thought of that. But I think it would be wiser if they could do some preliminary work first, to see whether our idea actually has merit. If it does, then we could ask for considerably more money. For both of our institutions."

"You're probably right. But since you're talking about medical applications, why don't you call Moshe Prywes. He's the dean — "

"As if I didn't know that," grunted Davidson. "He was at Hadassah for years. He didn't leave in exactly a good mood. And once he went to Beersheba, feelings here weren't much better. You've got to give the man credit for what he has accomplished, but quite honestly, I was not one of the ones who favored the idea of another medical school in Israel. We don't have enough money — "

"Stop it Yehuda." Dvir's brief laugh sounded sardonic. "My heart is bleeding. The last time I was at Mount Scopus, I was green with envy or whatever the color of envy is. And it was not just the view from your windows. We won't be able to beat that, but I'm learning about skinning cats. And you people at Hadassah are masters at it."

"Listen, Menachem." Davidson didn't know what had gotten into Dvir, but whatever it was, he didn't want him to continue on this path. But Dvir was not finished.

"Have you ever bothered to read all the plaques you have in your hallways? Every few meters, another one. 'Three-bed patient room given by so-and-so.' 'Infant transport incubator in memory of the late so-and-so.' 'Respirator for the cardiology department given by so-and-so.' Even just 'A piece of equipment donated by so-and-so.' Was that just a stapler?" He snorted and then fell silent.

"What's gotten into you?" Davidson asked.

"Don't plead poverty to me," Dvir grumbled. "If you want to learn about academic poverty, come down here and learn what it takes to start a new university. But I shouldn't get pissed off at you. I understand why you don't want to go to Prywes for a financial favor, and I'll take your word that if this project looks promising, we could apply for *real* money. Only remember that we expect our cut. 'Penile erection,' you say. A catchy subject, although I don't believe that you'd be prepared to acknowledge such a grant on one of your plaques. By the way, who is supporting the work of your Indian doctor?"

"A private foundation in New York. I doubt you've ever heard of them. They're very specialized."

"You're probably right. Still — try me."

"It's called the REPCON Foundation."

———

"Renu," Frankenthaler had said after her return from her three-month stay in Jerusalem, "you have convinced me that the project is worth pursuing in Israel. But if you want to go back that soon, getting money from the NIH is out of the question. In fact, I don't know anyone who will consider a grant application that quickly.

Even private foundations have their rules and bureaucracy. You are talking about a fair amount of money: between funding your stay for a year — "

"It may take longer than that," she interposed. "Better make it two."

Frankenthaler cocked an eyebrow. "That long? Even more expensive then. But even for the first year — between you, Hadassah, and the man at Ben-Gurion — "

"His name is Jephtah Cohn."

He shrugged. "Whatever. You're talking at least 100K. And then there is our cut for the Rosenstiel here at Brandeis and travel . . . better think of close to 150K."

"So what do you suggest?"

"Let's go to New York," the Prof offered. "You and I. Melanie Laidlaw ought to meet you. She should hear from your mouth what you think could be done with your series of nitric oxide releasers and why Israel would be the optimum place for doing this work. She wants to see more women active in reproductive biology . . . so let's demonstrate to her that her discretionary money was well spent. Now if she could give us 150K. . . ." His eyes rolled heavenward as if he were praying to some God of Reproductive Funding. "One can always dream," he laughed.

———

"Greetings, Felix," Laidlaw said as she shook Frankenthaler's hand. "And *shalom* to you, Dr. Krishnan. I am Melanie Laidlaw." She motioned her visitors to the sofa while she sat in an armchair facing them across the wide coffee table.

"Shoot," Laidlaw said without further ado. "But before you tell me what you plan to do, I'm curious to hear what you accomplished in three months in Israel. And whether this work could not have been done closer by." She waved her hand in a manner that could have encompassed the entire United States.

When it came to discussing her own research results, Renu, like most postdocs, needed little prompting. That's what they did all the time at the Frankenthaler group seminars, and she saw no reason to behave differently at REPCON. After all, Dr. Laidlaw was a scientist.

"Very good." Laidlaw was starting to become impatient. She had been impressed by the young woman's self-assurance, the organization of her material, the absence of the deferential mannerisms she encountered so often when potential grant applicants appeared in her office, but this was starting to take too long. Melanie Laidlaw knew perfectly well why Felix Frankenthaler and his postdoc were here. It was not to justify how well the earlier twenty-five-thousand-dollar grant had been spent — after all, that money was gone for good — but to get more. How much more, the cagey Frankenthaler did not want to disclose until he had first presented the potential goodies. She knew all that and she was pleased that he had let his young collaborator carry the ball. But none of this was getting at her real question: why the continuing Israel connection? When Felix had called about the appointment, he had made it plain that they wanted to continue that collaboration.

If this young woman wasn't going to answer the question herself, it was time for her to ask it. "I also know why Professor Frankenthaler wanted to send you to Jerusalem for the first few months, at least: he didn't have any personal connections with clinical urologists in the Boston area interested in the problem, and he knew Professor Davidson in Jerusalem. You people were anxious to conduct some preliminary feasibility studies quickly. REPCON was delighted to fund that, but since your report indicates sufficient promise, why not continue the research here? There are plenty of qualified people in the States who have spent years working on the corpus cavernosum."

The sudden forward move from his relaxed position, together with the audible clearing of Felix Frankenthaler's throat, indicated that he was about to take over. But Renu wanted one more opportunity.

"You are completely right, Dr. Laidlaw," she started, following Frankenthaler's often proclaimed advice that if you want to disagree with your sparring partner, you first disarm the person with a compliment. "But we're past the corpus cavernosum stage. That's why I went to Jerusalem, but that's not why I want to return there. In fact, I want to expand my operations to Beersheba."

"Beersheba?" Laidlaw leaned forward, her surprise evident. "Beersheba?" she repeated. "Why would you want to go there?"

Renu was taken aback by the effect her mention of Beersheba seemed to have produced on Melanie Laidlaw. She glanced at Frankenthaler, but he seemed equally nonplused.

"I mean Ben-Gurion University, specifically the biomechanics group in their new medical school."

"Have you been there?"

"Yes," Renu replied. "And let me tell you why."

"Go on," said Laidlaw, still leaning forward.

Renu proceeded in persuasive sequence. How unpublished work from Davidson's laboratory had shown that absorption of vasodilators through the urethral mucosa seemed to be much more effective than direct injection into the corpus cavernosum. . . . She didn't need to finish the sentence, because Laidlaw waved her right along.

So she turned to the interesting, but also time-consuming problem. How does one consistently and conveniently apply carefully quantified amounts of the vasodilating agent into the urethra?

"And this is where the bioengineering unit in Beersheba enters," concluded Renu. "There's a man there, Dr. Jephtah Cohn, who specializes in this type of work. There aren't many people who are experts in that field. Professor Davidson encouraged me to discuss our project with him, so I went to Beersheba for a couple of days."

"And?"

"We both agreed that a collaboration might be productive, but it's time-consuming work. . . ."

"Go on," Laidlaw prompted her, deadpan.

"Their department — in fact Ben-Gurion University all together — is strapped for funds. Dr. Cohn took me to meet someone in their administration to explore how we might proceed. One of the vice presidents, Dr. Menachem Dvir — "

Melanie Laidlaw rose so rapidly that Renu stopped cold. She watched as Laidlaw walked over to the window. With her back turned toward her guests, she said, "It's *Mr.* Dvir."

Renu, not knowing how to proceed, turned to Frankenthaler, but his warning finger stopped her. "Wait," he mouthed silently.

After an awkward interval, Laidlaw returned to her seat. "So what happened?"

"We talked about a possible budget, how a tripartite collaboration could be instituted. . . ."

That was the point where Frankenthaler finally took over. "Davidson and Renu called me from Israel. After some discussion, we concluded that it would be simplest all around if we wrote up a research grant from Brandeis, with Hadassah and Ben-Gurion as subcontractors, so to speak. It should simplify correspondence, logistics, financial reporting — "

"And increase the overhead," Laidlaw observed dryly.

"I thought REPCON didn't cover overhead," countered Frankenthaler.

"Not if you call it overhead. But I'm sure an expert like you, Felix, knows how to direct an appropriate amount toward Brandeis." She waved away any impending riposte. "How much money are you thinking of?"

"Oh . . . ," Frankenthaler began. "Something in the six figures."

"Felix, Felix." Laidlaw could not repress a grin as she wagged her finger. "I'm sure, it's not $100,001. So how much is it?"

"Around 125K," he responded without meeting Renu's surprised look at the sudden erasure of $25,000. From which kitty had the Prof taken those funds? she wondered.

"And when do you want to start?"

"Right away," exclaimed Renu.

"Dr. Krishnan . . . or may I call you Renu?" Seeing the expected nod, Laidlaw continued. "A grant of that magnitude cannot be handled out of my office. You have to follow our standard procedure, although I could arrange for expedited scrutiny. When can you people have an application in our office?"

"How about the end of September?" offered Frankenthaler.

Laidlaw walked over to her desk to look at her appointment book. "Can you make it earlier? Say by September 14? I'm leaving the following day for Europe. I wouldn't mind taking a copy along."

"Is that another one of your Kirchberg Conferences?"

Laidlaw turned away before answering. "No. I'm going to Brussels. On business. Reproductive biology business."

15

Fucking in London,
Joining incognito.
The idea discreet
Sown.

If pressed, Melanie would have admitted that her poem was not
original. Nor was it completely plagiarized. Three of the words —
fucking, *London*, and *joining* — were her own. But in the end, she
didn't mail it. The crude directness of the first word had appealed
to her, but on further reflection she wasn't sure how appropriate such
bluntness was after a year's separation. *Coupling*, with its romantic ambiguity, seemed closer to the mark, and *Coupling in London*
became the first line of the version that she appended to her letter.

My dear Menachem,
    I continue to be surprised by the intensity of
my desire for you, and I am stunned by its
persistence after such a long hiatus. A bridge
connects, but it also separates--as does sexual
pleasure. I have prided myself that what we had
wasn't simply a one-night stand, but now I
realize that a four-night stand is not much
longer. Does the persistence of my desire--almost
a year now--add to those days? Does it make this a
334-night stand? And can desire alone make
something substantial out of what we did? Not
mine alone, certainly. But if it were ours? Our
desire?
    But that raises so many other questions,
questions that I'm not sure I want to face--or
that you do, either (obviously: otherwise, why a

four-night stand in the first place?). Can it do
either of us--or those around us--any good to
continue this? I hope we do--continue this, I
mean. I think we have earned it, both of us. Do
people have to earn their happiness?
All these questions. I suppose we have earned
them as well. Or can't ignore them, anyway.
Whatever our relationship is, it's so far outside
social norms we can't take anything for granted.
We have to think about everything. Damn it.
Ami exquis; exquis amant. After our first night
in Kirchberg, my first night in bed with a
stranger, I thought: making love with a stranger
is best because there is no riddle and there is
no test. But the last night in Kirchberg, when
you were not a stranger anymore, showed that I
was wrong.
Let me know if Kirchberg in England is in the
cards.
Musingly,
Melanie

Melanie mailed the letter and the poem inside a larger envelope to
Menachem's Beersheba post office box — the private one he'd
opened after his return from Austria. That outer envelope contained
the announcement Melanie had received of the next Kirchberg conference, to be held in Oxford in September 1978. Among the list
of working groups was one entitled "Nuclear Terrorism." Melanie
had circled it with a line to the margin and the words, "Are you
going?"

————

"I know I'm waking you up, Melanie." Menachem's voice sounded
contrite. "I couldn't call until now."

"What time is it?" Melanie had groped for the telephone without switching on the light.

"Lunchtime . . . but in Israel. Will you forgive me? It's the only
time I can call today."

111

Melanie flicked on the light. She was now fully awake. "I forgive you. I would forgive you even more if you were here in person."

"Are you naked?" he asked quickly.

"Yes, of course," she said. "I always sleep naked."

"Always? Even in winter?"

"Always," she said firmly. "Body heat has the most BTUs — even if you sleep alone. Provided you swaddle yourself efficiently with your blanket. But that's not why you called. Are you going to Oxford?"

"Naturally. Somebody from Israel has to be there to be sure the Arabs don't blame nuclear terrorism on Israel — the way they'd manipulated the UN into making Zionism a synonym for racism." His tone had turned sarcastic. "Of course, if they really stick to the subject of nuclear terrorism, Israel for a change may not be in a minority of one. But what about you? I saw no working group on population."

"There isn't one, but I have something to do for REPCON in Belgium. So I decided to time it around the Oxford Conference — just in case. Can you come to London early? The weekend before?" she asked eagerly. "Can you make up a reason?"

"Sure," he said. "If you travel, you lie."

Melanie laughed, but not comfortably. She never lied when she traveled. But then she thought of the forthcoming trip to Belgium. Not a lie, but a string of half-truths: to her secretary, to the Belgians, to Menachem. . . .

But Menachem, seemingly following his own thoughts, was still speaking in her ear. "If a woman and a man want each other; if there is no lie or duress between them; no pressure other than their mutual desire — "

"Yes," she murmured. "You're right."

But he wasn't finished. "But most importantly, if they accept that such intense coupling can't last and needs to be savored now — "

"What does your 'but' mean?" interrupted Melanie.

"Who ever explains a 'but'?" replied Menachem. He had said that once before, toward the end of their Kirchberg encounter, when

112

she had teased him about another *but*: "But if we keep seeing each other I'm likely to erode you."

His use of the word *erode* had charmed her. "I'll chance it," she had replied almost flippantly. "I've never been eroded before. Just so you do it gently."

It was one of those seemingly trivial banters people exchange without much reflection — remarks that somehow settle in the sub-conscious to surface when least expected. Today it had surfaced.

———

The Brandeis-Hadassah-Ben-Gurion grant application arrived in time to be included in Melanie's airplane reading on the way to London. She scanned it with more attention than she usually dedicated to grant perusals. She realized that she wanted it to succeed. Yet an application of this order of magnitude was way beyond the director's discretionary budget — it had to be approved by her board, which based its decisions mostly on reports from outside experts. This was the point in the process where she could still exert influence by seeing to it that potentially sympathetic referees were picked.

She found herself spending much more time on the proposal than she had expected, in part because she did not know much about male impotence — or "erectile dysfunction," as the condition was so delicately called by the authors. The three sexual partners in her life had not suffered from any dysfunction along these lines nor could she recall, offhand, any earlier application to REPCON that had dealt with male impotence. That certainly ought to be in their favor. And then there was Renu Krishnan.

Melanie had never hid the fact at REPCON board meetings that, like their founder, she favored greater involvement by women in reproductive biology research. A woman dealing with male impotence seemed only right. And an Indian researcher picking Israel? That certainly wouldn't hurt; there were plenty of Jews on REPCON's list of outside experts — somehow, reproductive biology appeared to attract Jews.

But even as she turned the pages of the proposal and assembled a list of referees, Melanie's thoughts kept turning to the question of Menachem's involvement. How much did Menachem know about this application? How important was it to him? How would it affect a relationship that — at least in part — had started because he had never heard of REPCON; because he had not been on the make for money?

These questions had preoccupied her ever since Felix Frankenthaler and Renu Krishnan had left her office last month. It had been that meeting, she realized, that had finally spurred her to write, that had brought Menachem's predawn phone call, that had moved their affair dead center into . . . some other, more ambiguous terrain. While preparing for this trip, with all its complicated agenda, she had given a great deal of thought to their London meeting. This time, she was determined, there would be no flickering shadows; she wanted real flames. She had even gone so far as to dig around in her bathroom for a package of oral contraceptive pills. She hadn't used any since Justin's death, no longer had a valid prescription. But she found a blister pack with a 1977 expiration date. It will do, she decided. I'm not using it for birth control, but simply to postpone my period. And then, there came the question of a convenient location — discreet and romantic. Except for the opera in Vienna, their meeting in Austria had been completely spontaneous. The place, the rooms, even the beds had been already there, seemingly waiting for them. Things had just happened.

But this weekend in London wouldn't be like that: it was undeniably a tryst with all the associated excitement — and worries. What if . . . ? In Austria, Melanie had not posed that question once; not to herself, and not to her lover.

My dearest Menachem,

    I just wanted to warn you (if you need a warning, after Vienna) that I have taken over the logistic details for our London coupling. I am arriving a day earlier, on Thursday morning, because I don't want to be jet-lagged when you arrive. I have made a reservation in my name for an enchanting double room--specifically room 17 in the Colonnade Hotel on 2 Warrington Crescent, in

the Little Venice area of London. I have stayed
there before.

I presume that you will be taking a cab from
Heathrow, but one of the problems of such a
preorganized encounter is that one tries to
anticipate every eventuality, so if you should
take the Underground, the hotel is just half a
block from the Warwick Avenue tube station on the
Bakerloo Line. The number 6 bus from the center
of London stops at the same place.

Don't be misled by the Church of Saint Saviour,
which will stare you in the face as you emerge
from the Underground. It is a church, even though
it has no cross on its tinny steeple, and is a
color best described as filthy caput mortuum.
Knowing your curiosity, I expect that you either
know what that color is or you will have looked
it up prior to your arrival. But don't let that
church discourage you. The moment you have passed
it, you will be on a wonderfully homogenous
crescent of white stucco houses, all four stories
high, all of them built in the 1860s. One of the
most attractive is No. 2--an asymmetrical double
structure with gracefully curved sides and
balconies on the first floor, which is also our
floor. I won't tell you anything about room 17
because I want to leave some surprises. But I
cannot resist telling you (before the historical
markers on the front of the building give it
away) that it was the birthplace of Alan Turing,
the great British mathematician who broke the
German code during the war, and that Sigmund
Freud first stayed there when he emigrated to
England. And if you cross the street and walk
where the red brick houses on Warrington Crescent
start, you will find another blue historical

marker affixed to No. 75. Your own David Ben-
Gurion once lived there!

And one last teaser. The area is called "Little
Venice" because it abuts the Grand Union Canal.
On one of our evenings, we will walk arm in arm
all the way to Regent's Park along one of the
quays lined with houseboats. We'll behave openly
like lovers, because I cannot imagine that anyone
knowing you or me would be walking there. Or we
can take a boat. But the canal will have to wait
until after we have coupled in No. 17.

Fervently,

Melanie

They were sitting on one of the benches under a huge lime tree in
Rembrandt Garden, a small jewel of superbly maintained public
horticulture, at the confluence of two canals, looking at the houseboats lining the bank. The nearest was ablaze with flowers, its decks
given over to pots, half-barrels, window-boxes, and crates of luxuriant bloom. Melanie leaned on Menachem's shoulder. "Do you
suppose it's possible to rent one?" she asked. "We could meet here
the next time. . . ."

Menachem looked across the long reflection of the tree rippling
in the water. "Think about now — not next time. Whenever that
might be. Besides, what boat could handle your room seventeen?"

It was true. How could a room, perhaps twenty by twenty-five feet,
with tall bay windows, and most strikingly, on three levels, fit into
one of the narrow houseboats anchored along the canal? When
Menachem first walked through the double doors into the room, he
could only gape. The large double bed on an interior gallery, ac-
cessible up some steep steps, was dominated by a voile canopy that
hung from the ceiling in the shape of a mogul tent. The champagne
colored sheer fabric gave it a pruriently bridal touch.

Their first embrace on the bed had been intense, rushed, yet
deeply satisfying. Afterward, as Menachem picked up his trousers
and shirt from the floor, he asked, "Is there no bathroom in this
bridal chamber?" Only then did he discover that from the living

room, steps descended to a third level with carefully camouflaged doors on each side. "My God," Melanie heard his muffled call, "what luxury." He had come upon the huge bathtub that they proceeded to share.

"Where did you find all this?" he asked as they toweled each other dry.

"I stayed here once before — "

"Alone?" He eyed her curiously.

"Yes," she said firmly. "Alone. Before I met you. But I promised myself that if I ever returned to London with a man, we'd stay here. And here we are."

_____

The evening was mild, so mild that the hotel had set up some dining tables in the outside garden. Melanie and Menachem picked a table under a towering lumpen acacia — at least that's what Melanie had called it mirthfully when the maître d' had identified the tree with a whispered, "*Robinia pseudacacia*, ma'am." The dinner was unhurried, the conversation free, and yet the evening was touched by a vague feeling of unease. Melanie felt it partway through the main dish — the typical British summer fare of poached salmon garnished with scales of transparently thin, sliced cucumbers and served with boiled new potatoes. She'd been updating Menachem about her past year, but now she'd reached the summer — in fact early August. Should she relate the Frankenthaler-Krishnan meeting? And if she did, where would this lead? To a discussion of the grant . . . allusions to institutional poverty of the fledgling university . . . implied assurances of funding? Not on their first evening together, she concluded.

"But enough about me. What about you? What have you been doing in Beersheba?" It just slipped out. Although the question sounded innocuous, Melanie was fully conscious of the freight her question carried — and that Menachem might feel it as well. But her curiosity had the better of her. She knew nothing about Menachem's current home life. She tried to imagine him with a partly paralyzed wife, but her imagination was hampered by her awareness that everything she knew about the two of them was two decades old. What was their life like now? What was the nature of

_____

117

their current relationship, sexually and emotionally? Melanie could imagine the former. But the other?

She was certain that Menachem, like she herself, had rationalized his adultery as the private affair of two consenting adults, who had been careful not to hurt a third party. And had he not said that their affair couldn't last and therefore had to be relished now? Actually he hadn't used the word *affair* — not that time, not any time.

Melanie wasn't sure if it was disappointment or relief she felt when Menachem chose to respond to her question as if it had been a professional one. Was he ducking? Or was it simply that his profession was his life now? As he spoke, his voice was full of enthusiasm, excitement, even pride. Carried along by its impulse, for a while, Melanie forgot about Shulamit Dvir.

"No more than 10 percent of Israel's Jews live in the Negev, but you only need a map of our country to see that the future must lie in the empty southern half. If we don't develop the Negev, eventually we'll end up paving the triangle between Tel Aviv, Haifa, and Jerusalem. Just imagine what would happen if we ever had another major immigration? For instance, if the Soviet Union really would open up," he laughed. "One can dream, can't one? Ben-Gurion certainly did. Which reminds me. If there is to be a future in the Negev, then we also need a university here. A full-fledged one — with emphasis on technology and medicine." He leaned forward. "Take our nuclear center in Dimona. Its presence — the presence of so many scientists and technicians — made the quick birth of an institution of higher learning in the desert possible. It was precisely in the technical areas — chemistry, physics, engineering, some biology — that we started. Of course now, we cover all of the other disciplines. But excuse me," he sounded embarrassed. "Here we are, 'joining incognito' as you wrote in the only poem I ever received . . . and all I do is talk about my university."

"No. Don't stop," Melanie exclaimed. And she meant it. She realized that until now, most of Menachem's discourses about Israel had been rhetorical, defending the country, justifying its policies, its very existence. Now, as he leaned forward across the table, talking about the future, his eyes flashing with a disarmingly ingenuous, pioneer's enthusiasm, she wanted to hear more. It was another side of her lover, a contemporary side, which had opened up. There was nothing erotic about it, but still, it was exciting. "Tell me more. We have another day together — "

"And two more nights." He squeezed her hand. "All right," he said, "*lama lo* — 'Why not?' But I must warn you!" He grinned as he raised a monitory finger. "Stories of Ben-Gurion university are hard to stop." Melanie smiled, and settled herself to listen as Menachem, without seeming to draw breath, launched a virtual non-stop conversational caravan out of the Negev.

"You've got to understand," he began, "what life was like in Beersheba just a decade ago during the first birth pangs of our university. I don't think a New Yorker — or any American — can really imagine it. Take our social life . . . so much depended — and still depends — on family, on long-established connections, that if you had no access," he frowned momentarily, "it would be terrible to be alone in Beersheba."

"What about movies, concerts — "

"You see?" Menachem exclaimed triumphantly. "A typical question from someone who is accustomed to a post-industrial standard of living. Just listen to Beersheban realities. For many years, we had *one*, I repeat, *one* large auditorium — the 'Keren.' But with no air-conditioning, no heat — and remember, this is the desert, where you need both, one during the day, the other when the sun is gone, especially in the winter. I remember one concert of the Israel Philharmonic on a cold winter night when the pianist for the Tchaikovsky piano concerto had an old kerosene heater next to him to stay warm enough to play." Menachem rubbed his hands as if the remembered cold had stiffened them.

"And the acoustics! It's been ten years now, and I don't think the Israel Philharmonic has ever come back. But the 'Keren' was our Carnegie Hall compared to the four or five neighborhood 'cinemas.'" Menachem grimaced while drawing quotation marks in the air. "Wooden seats, cement floors — they'd roll the empty pop bottles along it, which created quite a racket. Not that it made much difference, because people were talking all the time."

"Talking?" Melanie asked incredulously.

Menachem shrugged. "It made no difference to most people,

because they were reading the Hebrew subtitles. Some of them even read them aloud. That's not all," he added, with a martyr's relish. "*You* eat popcorn, but *our* audiences were cracking sunflower seeds, and of course spitting out the shells, which would hit you in the neck. Or you could later comb them out of your hair. I know this sounds corny, but there was also something touching about it. This was the time between the Six-day War of 1967 and the Yom Kippur War of 1973: the audience included lots of soldiers, lots of new immigrants: North Africans, Romanians, the first small groups of Russians, South Americans . . . some of them having no idea how to behave in a cinema. And this same audience, this was also the student population of our first university classes."

Menachem suddenly turned serious. "I don't think I'll ever forget our first graduation . . . I think it was 1971. These students had been taught in temporary quarters all over town — converted stores, former hotels, and the like. And since we didn't have as yet a proper auditorium, graduation was held in one of the movie houses. No one had caps and gowns — not even the faculty. Most of the students were dressed in scraps of military uniforms, and — need I add? — also without ties. I was already a vice president — I'd left Dimona before the Six-day War — so I was sitting on the stage. Suddenly, up on the ceiling, I noticed a whole slew of pigeons who must have entered through some openings in or near the roof. I kept thinking that at some critical moment, one of the pigeons would let go with some droppings on the very first diplomas we were handing out."

Melanie clapped her hand over her mouth. "But they didn't, did they?"

"I don't think so," replied Menachem. But he didn't smile. His eyes were fixed beyond Melanie. "One thing really struck me about the students. They were all of military age and of course in the active reserve. Some never came back after 1973. Don't forget," his eyes focused back on Melanie, "our students are at least three years older than yours, because of Israel's obligatory military service at age eighteen. And yet they behaved like typical students. Once they got their diplomas, they danced around, yelled, waved to the audience. . . . It was touching, looking at those families. Many of them were very simple, poor-looking North African Jews, and this was a big event in their lives. It was a very . . . ," he searched the air for a word, grabbing at it half-consciously with one hand, "leavening experience — like the Friday afternoons: where we would hold small open houses in the temporary university buildings all over town with soft drinks and cakes. Everybody showed up — what else was there to do? — but everybody: the people doing menial jobs, like guards and clean-up personnel, and the students and faculty. And they all mingled, all of them talking together, regardless of education or rank or age or where they came from."

Melanie reached over to touch Menachem's hand, moved by some impulse she barely understood — perhaps simply the desire to share in the reminiscent joy that radiated from his entire being. He registered her touch, abstractedly, as the talk continued to stream from him like the overflowing of a fountain.

"And the faculty." Menachem leaned back, a wan smile playing around his lips. "The faculty," he sighed. "That, as you can imagine, was the most difficult problem in the Beersheba of the sixties — a sort of Dodge City of the desert with Bedouins rather than cowboys." He gave Melanie a sidelong look. "Am I right? 'Dodge City?' I don't even know where it is. But it sounds like a cowboy town."

"It's in Kansas," laughed Melanie. "Now tell me about these cow town professors."

"Yes, the professors. Our advantage . . . and our problem. Our first university, the Hebrew University in Jerusalem, was based on the traditional European model. Almost all the professors came from Europe. . . . After the war, we had many Americans, and many of our advanced students went to your country rather than Europe for further training. Then we had a couple of universities in Tel Aviv and the Technion in Haifa — our MIT or Caltech — and, of course, the Weizmann Institute in Rehovoth, which in its way is a graduate university. Many of the faculty and much of the research were world-class. Better than anything else in this part of the world. That was our strength. How else, I ask you, could we have established our nuclear center in Dimona? Of course, initially we had assistance from the French — *that* certainly is no secret any more — but all the people *inside* the Dimona complex were Israelis. You wouldn't guess what our first problem was at Dimona. We had the necessary scientists and engineers, but we didn't have enough technicians. We had to develop courses for them, special training. . . . I think that may have been one of the seeds of our eventual university. Many of the initial staff members from Dimona also served as part-time teachers here in what we called the Institute of Higher Education. And then we brought other faculty down from Jerusalem, and Haifa, and Tel Aviv. Most of them first-rate."

"So what was the problem?"

Menachem laughed. "Academics are the same everywhere, basically snobs who look down at universities at the bottom of the totem pole. Initially, the first group of professors — other than the Dimona staff — came from sophisticated centers. They were accustomed to concerts, to theaters, to bookstores. . . . I told you what Beersheba was like. In fact, what it still is to a large extent. Many of them didn't even bring their families down. They held two jobs — the one up north for family and children's education, for security, prestige. . . . But how do you run a university with divided loyalties? In the final analysis, you need a swim-or-sink mentality."

"And how did you foster that atmosphere?"

Menachem eyed her with a twinkle. "It wasn't easy. People in Israel — and especially senior academics — are accustomed to connections," Menachem produced a simulated cough, "and to special under-the-table deals. I'm not talking about illegal arrangements, but fringe benefits, dual jobs — the sort of thing that's so common in a country with lousy academic salaries. So we simply imported some senior American professors — mostly idealistic Zionists, who were not part of the system, and hence novices in matters Levantine." He shrugged again, miming modesty. "We made some of them chairmen and asked them to staff the departments with full-time, younger people, hungry ones, many of them trained abroad. It's working."

"I've heard of one of your younger staff," Melanie said musingly.

"You have?" Menachem angled his head as if for a different perspective. "What's his name? I probably know him."

"I don't recall his name," Melanie said quickly. "But continue. What's your highest priority right now?"

"Our building program and raising money. Or really, the reverse, because just as we got going, the Yom Kippur War broke out. It completely wrecked our budget. We haven't recovered yet. Now I spend much of my time helping with the new medical school we started in '72. But that's another story."

16

"So what are your plans?" Menachem was stretched out shoeless on the turquoise sofa, the remnants of the London *Sunday Times* strewn around the no-man's-land between his sofa and Melanie's armchair in their room number seventeen.

"Waiting for you to come back on Wednesday — on your day off from Kirchberg," replied Melanie from the depth of her chair.

"I know." He blew a kiss across the newspaper detritus. "But in between? For instance tomorrow?"

"I'll go to the National Portrait Gallery to see the Holbein exhibition and maybe also to the Tate."

"I'm not much of a museumgoer, but aren't museums usually closed on Mondays?"

"This, my dear, is London, where museums are open seven days a week. I may even take in a play, while you solve the problems of nuclear terrorism at Oxford. And visit a couple of REPCON grantees in London and Cambridge."

Menachem looked at her curiously. "Do you keep track of all the groups your foundation supports?"

"I try to," replied Melanie.

"What about applications?"

"As many as I can. Why do you ask?"

Menachem stalled. "That must be terribly time-consuming."

"It's manageable. REPCON is not that large a foundation. We have no fixed deadlines, so the applications come in dribs and drabs."

"One of these days," he said slowly, "you'll be getting one from Israel."

"I already got it," she replied, her eyes suddenly focused on the newspaper page that had been lying in her lap. "I brought it with me to read on the plane."

"You have it here?" Menachem rose halfway from his sofa. "Here?" He looked around as if he were searching for an intruder. "Why didn't you mention it earlier?"

"Probably for the same reason you didn't: it wasn't germane to 'joining' or 'coupling.'"

"I think I know what you mean."

Melanie dropped the paper on the floor and sat up, facing Menachem. "Ever since I became director of REPCON, most of the men I meet want something from me. Oh, they're all polite — even deferential. Many are even subtle. But I've become very conscious of the underlying fund-raising motive, probably too conscious." Her tone turned reflective. "It was so different when we first met. You had no clue of REPCON or of my position. You didn't even pay attention to what I wore. Remember what you said when I asked whether you could describe the clothes I'd been wearing at our first meeting?"

"Sure," grinned Menachem. "I said that if you recall exactly what a woman wears, she can't be very striking. It's like focusing on the base of a sculpture. Furthermore, if it's too ornate or complicated, it detracts from the sculpture."

Melanie nodded. "It's a nice compliment . . . or were you just being clever? Like Solomon with the queen of Sheba?"

"Who knows? Maybe a bit of both."

Both fell silent — so long that the stillness turned awkward. Menachem was the first to break it. "And now with this request for money," he waved his hand around the room as if the application's pages were surrounding them, "surely, you don't think that I've become like all the others."

"Menachem!" Melanie walked quickly to the sofa and lifted his left arm to make some space for her to sit by his side. "Of course not."

"I really had very little to do with that application."

"I know." She patted his hand. "I got the whole story from Renu

Krishnan and Felix Frankenthaler when they came to my office. But Ben-Gurion University is in on it, which to me means only one thing: it's Menachem's grant. I can't help it. It's not your fault."

"What about Frankenthaler?" asked Menachem. "Is he a friend?

"Yes."

"Well," he remonstrated. "He's the principal investigator. Has it affected your relationship?"

"Not really," she said slowly. "But he's different. He's a social friend from way back. We go to the opera together — "

"Just like us." Menachem's tone was ironic.

"Stop!" Melanie struck his hand in mock rebuke. "He *and his wife* were the ones who introduced me to opera. We go together as a group and there are no hands in my pockets" — other than mine, Melanie silently added. "At times, he's even a sort of confessor. . . . No," she added quickly. "Not confessor, but advisor . . . or maybe just a foil."

"And he's never been your lover?" Menachem asked quietly.

"No." Melanie's voice was firm and unequivocal. "He's married."

"So am I."

"I know." Melanie had been sitting against the curve of Menachem's reclining lap; now she turned to look at the mirror above the marble mantelpiece, only to find Menachem's reflection studying her. "But it's different. . . . I've known Shelly all along."

"And if you'd known my wife?" For a long moment the two of them stared at the mirror, each locked on the other's eyes. It was Menachem who turned away first. "No," he said firmly. "I take it back. First, it's a stupid 'what if?' question. And second, it's my problem, not yours. But Melanie," he took her face in his hands so that their eyes met again, directly now, no mirror as an intermediary, "it would not have happened with anyone else. It probably would not have happened even with you if it had been somewhere else at some other time." He released her face. "Anyway, I'm glad Frankenthaler is married, and that you know his wife, and that she comes along with you to the opera."

"Felix is not my type." Melanie thought of his plump frame, his large ears, his receding hairline partly offset by longish sideburns, his searching eyes behind the professorial mien, his store of esoteric tales. "He's a wonderful companion, but simply not my physical type. Besides, he's too old." The last words were delivered as if they'd settled the issue once and for all.

"How old?" asked Menachem.

"I'd guess, he's pushing sixty."

"I see." Menachem could not restrain a snicker. "An elderly man. Not like this strapping fifty-six-year-old youth." He struck his strong chest with his fist. "But enough of other men. Let's return to you. Why do you really read all these applications?" This time, Menachem's hand just waved dismissively. "I don't mean *our* application; I mean, in general. You're not making these decisions by yourself, are you?"

"Of course not," said Melanie. "Except for some small ones, which I can handle out of my discretionary budget, it's our board that finally approves funding requests."

"So why do you read them?" Menachem persisted.

"I want to know what's going on in reproductive biology in general . . . and I like to see our referee's comments. I like to observe their manners."

"Meaning?"

"Meaning who hates whom; who scratches whose back; who is disciplined, judicious, and constructive. . . . I've been a researcher in my time, which gave me plenty of opportunity to observe the deterioration of good manners in competitive fields. So I particularly appreciate referees who are generous with their time and fair with their comments. But what I like best is to pay site visits to our grantees; to meet them personally; to see where they're working; and in clinical projects, to see how they interact with their patients."

"Does that mean you'll come to Beersheba?"

"I don't know — I don't go to all of them." She laughed self-consciously. "The grant hasn't been awarded yet. Besides, judging from the budget, the bulk of the money seems to go to Brandeis and Hadassah. I admit that I'm very curious about Beersheba." She rose to step to the bay window. "Curious . . . but also afraid. It could become very complicated. What do you think?" Melanie turned around to look at Menachem on the sofa.

His hands were linked behind his head, resting against the side pillow. "Probably," he said, looking straight at the ceiling.

———

The weekend weather had been uncharacteristically balmy. Menachem and Melanie had returned for one last time to their favorite spot in the Rembrandt Garden, the bench by the side of the canal. The whole setting — even the quaint sign, *Dead Slow Past Moored Boats* — bucolic though it was, had not diverted Menachem from his earlier curiosity. He started to wonder whether it was the grant, minimal as his involvement was, or mere interest in Melanie's professional life that had piqued his curiosity.

"Your grantees . . . you said you enjoyed visiting them. Whom will you see here?"

Melanie looked at him reflectively. "Are you really in a mood to hear about scientific research?"

"Sure," Menachem said cheerfully. "I'm a curious man — at least as long as the subject interests me. So what's REPCON spending its money on over here?"

Melanie gazed at two gulls floating past them in the water. "I wonder whether they're related to our Western gulls."

"Now what makes you ask that question?"

Melanie continued to gaze at the water. "I'm thinking of the effects of DDT on the endocrine system. Did you know that DDT and its principal breakdown product, DDE, mimic some of the biological actions of the estrogens?"

Menachem mimed ignorance, astonishment, doing his best to draw her out without interrupting.

"At the end of World War II, thousands upon thousands of people — for instance, the whole population of Naples — were sprayed with DDT against the threat of epidemics. It saved lots of lives. Later on, malaria control with DDT preserved millions of lives. But it also exposed millions of people to DDT levels that are now considered unacceptable." She turned pensive. "Who knows? Could those exposures have exerted estrogenic effects on developing males that only became apparent years later?" Melanie continued to stare after the drifting gulls.

"Did you — " Menachem started to say, but Melanie wasn't yet finished.

She turned to him, tilting her head to the departing birds. "Just a few years ago, Michael Fry, at the University of California, found that the sex ratio between males and females among Western gulls is now heavily skewed toward females. And that many of the male gulls have become sterile."

"Did REPCON fund that work in California?"

Melanie shook her head, and turned again toward the distant gulls. "No. But there may be a relation between that research and what our two English groups are studying: the decline in sperm quantity and quality since the end of World War II . . . that is, not in gulls, but in humans."

For a moment she did not continue. She was not sure how to proceed. Melanie had never forgotten their first truly carnal moment on her bed back in Kirchberg, when the absence of a condom had caused her to learn of Menachem's infertility — a topic that neither one had raised again. Was it indifference — or inordinate sensitivity — that caused him never to broach the subject? But to Melanie, the topic had become increasingly relevant. Ever since her discussion about single motherhood with Felix Frankenthaler at the Met last year, she had started to think about Menachem's 'infertile' status. Her interest had taken a quantum jump upward when the latest report from REPCON's Belgian grantees arrived on her desk — a report claiming extraordinary success with their ICSI procedure. The Belgian work had not yet appeared in the open literature, but even if it had, she'd have felt obliged to see the results with her own eyes. As director of REPCON, it had not been necessary to make up any excuse for visiting André Van Steirteghem and his group in Brussels. But to Menachem?

In the end, Melanie decided on a compromise. In her recital of REPCON's research support, she would remain on this side of the Channel. The gulls of London's Little Venice had appeared as if by providence.

"It seems that since the end of the war, which roughly corresponds with the widespread introduction of DDT, there has been a gradual decline in male fertility all over the world. No," she corrected herself, "that's too strong. What has been documented by

British and Danish researchers is the gradual decrease in sperm count during the last few decades — "

"How much?" interrupted Menachem.

"By nearly 50 percent."

Menachem let out a low whistle. "I didn't know that."

"And a possible doubling in the incidence of disorders of the male reproductive tract."

"Go on."

"Let me backtrack," said Melanie. "The reason I withdrew the statement about apparent reduction in male *fertility*, as compared to reduction in *number* of sperm is that many knowledgeable people in the field feel that sperm concentration, per se, is not the chief determinant of male fertility. Of course you need a lot of sperm. If a hundred million are ejaculated in a woman's vagina, only one-tenth make it through the cervical mucus. One-tenth of those reach the upper uterine tract, and when they finally make it to the fallopian tube containing an egg, less than one hundred thousand are left. That, of course, explains why if a man's sperm count falls to just a few million sperm, say three rather than one hundred million, it makes him, for all practical purposes, infertile."

"As if I didn't know that," Menachem murmured.

Melanie looked up quickly, but Menachem waved her on. "Sorry," he said, "I didn't mean to interrupt you."

"The point I wanted to make is that a fall of one hundred million to fifty million may not yet manifest itself in actual fertility reduction, unless there is also a concomitant deterioration in the *quality* of the sperm. For instance, inability to undergo the acrosome reaction — "

"Now you've lost me," interjected Menachem.

Strange, she thought. I'd expect someone suffering from male infertility to know more. "Let me explain, but stop me — "

"I won't stop you, Melanie," he said. "It's the first time I've heard you lecturing and I love it." He leaned over and kissed her cheek.

"Another kiss, then, before I go on . . . but on my lips, please," she replied, offering her mouth.

"Now that my lecturing ability has been restored, let me continue and be brief. The zona pellucida is the outer layer of the egg. The sperm must penetrate the zona," Melanie pushed her right index finger into her clenched left fist. "It does that with the help of enzymes contained in the so-called acrosome — a kind of cap on the head — of the sperm. That's what we mean by 'acrosomal reactivity,' and that's one of the qualities a sperm must possess. And motility, of course. If the sperm can't swim up to the egg, no supply of acrosomal enzymes will help. But once the acrosomal reaction has caused it to penetrate the zona pellucida, that single spermatozoon can now go to the true barrier, the vitelline membrane, and eventually enter the cytoplasm of the egg. Which is where fertilization really happens."

"So that's it?"

"I'm afraid not. I need to go back one step. There are many thousands of sperm heading for that egg. Only one will bind to the zona, and once that sperm has penetrated, changes occur in the zona to prevent any further penetration by other sperm. It's basically a race, winner take all, because then the door of opportunity slams shut." She laughed. "What else is new in life?"

Menachem had become intrigued. "How does that single sperm bind to the egg?"

"Ah," Melanie said, "now you're getting to the heart of a lot of current research. The zona pellucida contains various glycoproteins, called ZP1, ZP2, and so on. The ZP3 protein is the principal component of the zona responsible for the binding and activation of the sperm. It has even been separated and purified. You can put some of that ZP3 on a glass bead in a petri dish; if you now add some sperm, they'll be fooled: they'll head for the bead and bind to it, thinking it's an egg."

"I'll be damned," exclaimed Menachem. "But how is this related to the work here in England?"

"Oh, all that was just a crash course — and a greatly simplified one, I must emphasize — on fertilization. The groups we are supporting are focusing on large-scale studies, basically retrospective epidemiological ones, that point to quantitative and possibly also qualitative deterioration of human sperm over the last few decades. They want to find out which factor, or probably *factors*," Melanie practically hissed the last letter, "are responsible. To really deter-

mine how all this affects human fertility, and not just sperm numbers, we shall eventually have to carry out *prospective* studies; meaning carefully selecting subjects to eliminate the many uncertainties one encounters in retrospective studies — "

"What kind of uncertainties?" Menachem interrupted.

"You've got to understand that the present tentative conclusions
are based in part on some fifty or more earlier sperm collections and
measurements, performed by different investigators over many years
with close to fifteen thousand men. But they ranged in age from
seventeen to sixty-four years; their duration of abstinence prior to
collecting the ejaculate was often not recorded; there were no really good controls. . . . So you see, there are lots of problems."

By now Menachem could not let go. "And what are some of the
suspected factors?"

Melanie pointed to the gulls, which had drifted back and settled
on the opposite side of the canal, under a magnificent weeping wil-
low leaning over the water. "DDT and related pesticides are certainly suspect, because we now know that they mimic some of the
biological effects of natural estrogens. We also know that these substances were first released into the environment in the 1940s. And
estrogens most certainly can inhibit sperm production and growth
of the testes. By the way," she pointed to Menachem, "how extensive is or was the use of DDT in Israel?"

*Who cares? That was not my problem. Mine requires no prospective
scrutiny, either, because I was already scrutinized. The present generation, perhaps even I, tend to forget what the fifties and early sixties were like — those heady days of the start of the Dimona project.
The Hiroshima and Nagasaki bombings did not offer reliable data
about the effects of lower-level radiation on the fertility of technical
personnel. All the countries with atomic and nuclear projects faced
that problem, but ours may have been more acute, because our people
at Dimona were on the whole younger. The Americans — the only
ones whose work we knew anything about — were attacking the problem by controlled irradiation of "volunteers" — prisoners in Washington and Oregon. Supposedly, they were all non-Catholics and had
agreed to undergo vasectomies at the end of the experiment.*

But Israel was not, and is not, the United States. They used prisoners; we used true volunteers, which meant secular Jews of the Dimona project. And just as officers in our army lead in any attack, so at Dimona many of the volunteers came from our upper echelons. To study the effect of possible ionizing radiation accidents, subjects' testes were exposed to increasing doses of X rays. The goal of the tests was straightforward: they wanted to know which dose caused reduced sperm count, oligospermia; *which would lead to* azoospermia *or total absence of sperm; and whether any resulting sterility was temporary or permanent.*

To this day, I remember their conclusion: in general, man appears to be highly radiosensitive in regard to temporary sterility, but quite radioresistant with respect to permanent sterility. Most of the men were exposed to fifty roentgens or less, some to one hundred roentgens, and a few to four hundred. Even in the top dose, sterility lasted for less than two years. And then, they asked for someone willing to expose himself to six hundred roentgens.

As usual, any conclusion starting with the words, in general, means that there are some exceptions. At Dimona, there were two: one of the four-hundred-roentgen volunteers and the single six-hundred-roentgen guinea pig, Menachem Dvir.

"I have no idea," replied Menachem. "Why do you ask?"

"Just curious," she said quickly. "But there are other explanations, beyond DDT, kepone, and other pesticides. Some knowledgeable people claim that humans now live in a 'virtual sea of estrogens.'"

"Come on, Melanie," he shook his head dismissively. "Or as they would say here, 'Surely you jest, madam.'"

Melanie raised both hands. "Don't blame me! First, I'm only reporting. Second, they're simply dramatizing a number of other postwar trends. Shall I list some?"

He shrugged. "Sure. Go ahead."

"One possibility is the postwar increase in body fat, which is known to convert other steroids in our body into estrogens. Or dietary changes such as increased consumption of plant products. Many of them are known to contain weak estrogens, so-called phytoestrogens — soya being one of the richest. Or the increased consumption of cow's milk — "

"Stop," he exclaimed. "I don't want to hear any more."

"One more possible culprit — a nonchemical one." She smiled. "Take the postwar fashion for tight pants. Prolonged driving or sitting in tight pants might raise the temperature of the scrotum and adversely affect sperm production."

"How Anglo-Saxon," laughed Menachem, "to blame Italian fashions instead of organic chemistry. But enough science or fashion for today."

"Then kiss me," she replied, "before we walk back to the Colonnade."

———

They had an early breakfast in their room — in time for Menachem to catch the 7:48 from Paddington Station to Oxford. "You're looking forward to this Kirchberg, aren't you?" asked Melanie. "I can see it in your face."

"What you're seeing right now is my pleasure with these eggs." He motioned with his fork bearing a mouthful of fried egg topped by a morsel of banger. "You know," he smiled, "for me the ultimate example of American technology is your fried eggs. Here you ask for fried eggs and you get fried eggs. In your country, you have a complete vocabulary — 'over easy,' 'sunny-side up,' and God knows what else — for a cook in front of a big metal rectangle rather than an ordinary skillet. But it's strange," ruminated Menachem. "The government of the most scientifically advanced country in the world pays the least attention to its scientists. Just take the present American Kirchberg group as an example. They brag about Henry Kissinger as one of their former Kirchbergers. But you don't find him mixing with these people, now that he's in power. He's of the breed that thinks science and scientists should be on tap, not on top." He swallowed. "Melanie, you people don't even have a national science policy. Is that your strength — that you can afford not to have one — or your Achilles heel?"

Another bite of banger-topped egg disappeared. "But you're right. I'm looking forward to the meetings . . . with a mixture of emotions. It's exciting to find scientists and even apparatchiks from all over the world discussing and debating important policy issues. I'll even admit that I enjoy defending my country's views, although it's somewhat lonely always to have to do so in a minority of one."

"Come now, Menachem. I remember last year. There were several who agreed with your position — at least silently."

"All right," chuckled Menachem. "I modify my statement: it's lonely to be in an *open* minority of one. Speaking of 'open,' what really interests me — why I continue to go to Kirchberg Conferences — are the *private* encounters, the ones you cannot easily have elsewhere." He reached across the table for Melanie's hand. "And I don't mean only you and me."

———

"Well, well," murmured Menachem during the coffee break of the opening plenary session. "Our eminent Tunisian chemist — "

"I'm not a Tunisian," interrupted Ahmed Saleh. "I was born in Hebron. So was my father and his father."

"Sorry," said Menachem. "What should I have said?"

"Palestinian will do nicely, thank you."

Menachem inclined his head, but said nothing. This was not the way to renew their acquaintance. "I didn't see your name on the list of participants."

"Are you surprised?" Saleh's irritation had not yet dissipated. "Palestinians in the diaspora — and especially representatives of the PLO — are not interested in announcing their travel plans. Too many things can go wrong."

"I understand," replied Menachem. "In any event, I'm glad you've come to Oxford. I've been looking forward to continuing our conversation from last year."

"Our *theoretical* conversation." Saleh's irony was palpable.

"Our conversation wasn't all theoretical." Menachem stuck to his quiet, measured tone. "Some of the scenarios were . . . but not all."

Saleh gave him a searching look. "Have you discussed our meeting with anybody?"

"Yes," Menachem nodded. "With two people who count. Who agreed that our conversation need not be all theoretical. By the way, are you joining the nuclear terrorism group this afternoon?"

"Yes," replied Saleh. "Wasn't that the subject of our *theoretical* conversation — your view of nuclear terrorism?"

"Have you mentioned our meeting to anyone?"

"Yes. One man."

Menachem waited for more, but Saleh remained silent. "Shall we meet for dinner tonight? Just the two of us? To distinguish between theory and fact?"

"Why not?" replied Saleh.

———

Menachem's pessimism about the direction of the nuclear terrorism debate proved to be well justified. As he'd expected, the Egyptian immediately expanded the definition of nuclear terrorism to national nuclear programs — specifically to Israel's. Menachem's attempt to deflect such reasoning by emphasizing that it would then also have to apply to the nuclear superpowers, carried no weight.

He attempted another line of argument. "Let's consider the 'ecological' and not just additive function of what most of us accept as the definition of nuclear terrorism." He tapped his pen on the table and waited until the Egyptian delegate stopped whispering into a colleague's ear.

"The existence of small, autonomous, terrorist groups with access to nuclear weapons isn't just additive. It changes everything — the entire political ecology. If you add a drop of red dye to a beaker of water, it doesn't just color one small spot. The entire beaker changes color. Therefore, the entire community of nations must find a means of combating this threat before it becomes unmanageable."

"Mr. Chairman." The interruption came from an unexpected source, the same Dutchman whose supposed objectivity had galled Menachem in Austria. "I accept Menachem's argument about the dangers of nuclear terrorism. I also appreciate his metaphor."

At least he calls me *Menachem*, reflected Menachem, rather than *Israeli colleague*. But his bubble of satisfaction was punctured promptly.

"I believe that this analogy applies with equal force to Israel's nuclear energy program."

"Thanks for calling it 'nuclear *energy*,'" Menachem interjected sarcastically.

"I misspoke," replied the Dutchman, not missing a beat. "I meant nuclear arms. And I see no way for you to introduce a nuclear capability in Israel and just expect it to remain there in your small corner of the political beaker. It perturbs all of the water — meaning the whole Middle East, in fact, the whole world." He turned to Menachem. "Don't you agree?"

"I do not!" replied Menachem. "The water you're referring to is not clear. It's already filthy, opaque, and exceedingly contaminated."

"So you are prepared to contaminate it further?" asked the Dutchman.

"Contamination is a subjective term. What you consider a further Israeli contamination of already filthy political water, I call a preservative — or perhaps even a disinfectant."

"Would our Israeli colleague enlighten us with an explanation of his use of the word 'disinfectant'?" Menachem abhorred the Egyptian's mannerism of addressing a speaker as if he were invisible; another way of not recognizing the right of Israel, or of an Israeli, to exist.

"I think we're starting to indulge in too much razzmatazz here," remarked Menachem.

"What is that supposed to mean?" El-Gammal asked suspiciously. For once, the Egyptian looked straight at Menachem.

"Look it up in the dictionary. I heard it from an American at a UN conference. I liked its sound; and after looking it up, I also appreciated its meaning." He looked at the chairman. "Isn't this a good time for our tea break?"

———

This Kirchberg Conference was held at Oxford's New College, which, despite its name, was founded in 1379. Menachem had learned this fact during registration for his meals and accommodations, along with another piece of historical esoterica. William Archibald Spooner had been warden of New College during the first couple of decades of this century — the same Spooner for whom the term "spoonerism" was coined. The small brochure accompanying Menachem's registration materials even contained one of Spooner's better-known gaffes — "Let me sew you to your sheet" for "Let me show you to your seat" — producing an epidemic of newly coined spoonerisms for the rest of the conference.

———

Ahmed Saleh had concurred with Menachem's suggestion that for the sake of privacy, they'd be better off meeting at an off-campus site — a small, second-floor Indian restaurant on High Street, across from Lincoln College. Now they sat facing each other, each sipping iced lassi the waiter had brought with the menus. Menachem had ordered his lassi sweet; Saleh took his salty.

"You certainly were quiet this afternoon," remarked Menachem. "What's your view — off the record, naturally — about our group's topic? You must be concerned about nuclear terrorism — any intelligent person would be."

"Thanks for the compliment," Saleh said curtly. "But why should I have said anything? Even the Dutchman was jumping on you, and he certainly didn't need my help." He smiled slightly. "Even your drop of red dye was used against you. By the way, did you pick red for blood or politics?"

Menachem eyed him with elbows on the table, chin in his hands. "Blood," he said quietly. "All of ours. So what's your view?"

"Mine? On blood?"

"No. On nuclear terrorism."

"Why should that matter?"

Saleh's bitterness did not escape Menachem. "What I'm about to say is not flattery: your opinion interests me more than anyone else's here."

Saleh had been playing with a poppadam. It bothered Menachem, the way Saleh broke the thin, crisp sheet, over and over again — without putting a smidgen into his mouth — until it had turned virtually into rubble. Now he picked up a fresh piece from the basket. "All right," he said, putting down the poppadam unbroken. "You'll probably be surprised to hear it, but I actually thought you had a point this afternoon. I'll offer you a nugget of information — worth the release from your jails of at least five of our prisoners. It's also a test of our *theoretical* scenario."

"Go on," said Menachem. Saleh leaned forward. His voice fell almost to a whisper. An observer across the room would have seen nothing on Menachem's face as, for the space of perhaps four minutes, Menachem listened intently.

"We'll see," he finally said. "If what you say checks out, we'll make it seven prisoners. Five for what you called your 'nugget of information' and two more to demonstrate our good faith."

"Not good will?" asked Saleh.

"Let's not rush matters, Ahmed." It was the first time that day Menachem had used the man's first name. "Even good faith between us is a step forward."

"I suppose so. By the way, Menachem, would you like to hear a spoonerism that might actually be apt for us?"

Based on his experience during the past three days, Menachem's inclination would have been to say no, but Saleh's use of his first name caused him to nod.

"Fighting a liar."

Menachem wrinkled his forehead. "I don't get it."

"Lighting a fire."

17

"I thought there is no work at Kirchberg Conferences on Wednesdays," said Melanie.

"I couldn't get away earlier," he mumbled.

"Meeting one of those persons you can't meet elsewhere?"

He shrugged. "More or less. But what have you got in mind for us on our last evening in London?"

"First, the National Portrait Gallery."

Menachem looked at his watch. "It's almost six o'clock!"

"Wednesday is special: they stay open until eight. And don't ask why I'm taking you there."

———

"'Hans Holbein the Younger and the Court of Henry VIII,'" he read out loud as they walked through the main entrance. "Is that what you're taking me to?" Seeing her nod, Menachem continued. "Anything particular, or do you just think I need cultural enlightenment?"

"Both," she said, "but especially the former." She took him by the hand. "Right through here and up the steps."

They entered a narrow, dimly lit gallery featuring a special exhibition from the Queen's collection of miniatures and small drawings — mostly in black and colored chalks — showing the faces of noblemen and ladies of King Henry's court. Menachem headed straight for the stunning portrait of William Warham, archbishop of Canterbury, in a black, ecclesiastical cap extending over his ears. During her visit on Monday, Melanie had been struck by the same portrait, finding it to bear some resemblance to Felix Frankenthaler: the same clean-shaven, incipient jowls, the same warmly penetrating eyes. But tonight, Melanie had another goal in mind.

"Come," she commanded. Again taking his hand, she led Menachem to the end of the room, to the only drawing not a portrait. "First this."

"Well, I'll be damned," Menachem exclaimed, bending down to read the descriptive label. He leaned so close to the small watercolor that one of the guards hurried over. "You *must* keep your distance, sir," he admonished in the guilt-inducing whisper usually reserved for libraries.

"Solomon and the queen of Sheba! I never knew." He studied the small drawing. "*Vicisti famam / Virtutibus tuis*," he slowly read the legend inscribed on the base of Solomon's throne.

Melanie pointed to the descriptive label. "Here's the translation: 'By your virtues you have exceeded your reputation.'"

"What a surprise," murmured Menachem, his eyes still fixed on the drawing. He squeezed her hand. "Thanks for bringing me here."

"How could I help it?" she replied. "After all, it was Solomon and the queen who brought us together. "But," she jabbed him playfully, "where is the fake pool? The goldfish? The raised hem? The hairy legs? It all looks so very — " she searched for the right expression, "regal, I would say. It's all about Solomon. You can't even see the queen's face."

"It's obviously based on the version in Chronicles and not on the Koran. But you're right," mused Menachem. "Such a lovely drawing, yet so asexual. That version would never have brought us together."

"Tell me." She looked at the drawing as if she were addressing

Holbein's figures rather than Menachem. "They did have sex, didn't they?"

For the first time Menachem turned away from the drawing to look at Melanie. "What a modern question," he chuckled. "But yes, the assumption is that they *knew* each other — biblically speaking. Why else go to the trouble of constructing a fake pool and prescribing a depilatory?"

"But is there any mention of an issue?" she persisted.

"Issue?"

"Issue of the union. I was trying to be decorous. Did the queen ever bear a child of Solomon's? After all, he wasn't infertile."

Menachem's eyes returned to the drawing, to Solomon enthroned with arms akimbo, legs spread open, his regal potency unmistakable. "Not that I know," he replied.

———

For once, none of the weather reports resorted to their standard summer repertoire: "sunny intervals with occasional showers" or "rain at first, sunny intervals developing." Even weather-wise Londoners left their umbrellas at home, finally persuaded that the splendid September weather was here to stay.

Melanie and Menachem walked from Trafalgar Square to the Victoria Embankment and then partway across the Thames. They stopped at one of the semicircular turnouts on the Hungerford Footbridge, and took a leisurely view of the magnificent London cityscape while pedestrians hurried past to Waterloo Station and the South Bank Theater complex. In an ebullient mood Menachem played the unabashed tourist, reading off the names of the various landmarks — starting with St. Paul's Cathedral and ending with Cleopatra's Needle — etched in silhouette on the large metal plaque affixed to the railing.

"Look at the boat," he gestured with his head toward the approaching vessel filled with sightseers while rummaging in his pockets. "There we are," he sounded pleased. "A paper clip." He reached over the railing to drop the clip just as the boat passed under the bridge. "Now what would you say if a paper clip had dropped on your head from the sky?" He grinned like a mischievous adolescent.

"Easy," she said without a moment's hesitation. "I'd take it as a sign from heaven to clip the last thought in my mind to my tongue."

For some seconds, Menachem seemed bemused, even startled. "That's a remarkably complicated answer," he finally said leaning against St. Paul's Cathedral. "What do you mean by that?"

"To actually mouth what I've been thinking about."

"Which is?"

"Come," she said, linking arms. "We can talk while we stroll back. Let's head for the Strand and catch a number six bus back to our hotel. It's our last night in London and we haven't even sat together in the first row of the upper deck like tourists."

———

"Menachem, have you ever wanted a child?" The question that had been clipped to Melanie's tongue for days was finally set free. They were still on the bridge, walking side by side. But just as she spoke, a train rattled by on the other side of the wire mesh separating the footpath from the rails.

"Have I ever wanted what?" he shouted over the rumble of the receding train.

"A child," she repeated.

He stopped; though if he was surprised, he did not indicate it. A raised eyebrow, perhaps. "Was that thought prompted by the Holbein painting?"

"No," she interrupted him. "Before. Quite some time before."

They were at the end of the bridge where the steps led down to the street level. "You asked, if I *ever* wanted a child. *Ever* is a complicated four-letter word, like 'love' or 'hate.' If you really mean *ever*, then the answer is probably 'yes' — or at least not 'no.'

"I was certainly not against the idea," he continued as they proceeded along Villiers Street to the Strand, "but it wasn't high on my list of priorities."

What about your wives' priorities? Melanie wanted to ask. But she didn't ask, because as Menachem told a rambling account of his career — his postwar studies in Manchester as an RAF veteran, his underground Hagana activities, the post-Independence days — with an emphasis on how little opportunity he had had to think about the question, he finally disclosed the one datum she had been so curious to learn. "I was in my thirties . . . when I suddenly became infertile. So the question of a child became moot. And I certainly was never interested in adoption."

"You mean you chose voluntarily to become infertile?" Melanie realized that her questions seemed precious — almost Victorian. Yet somehow, she couldn't get the word *vasectomy* to cross her lips.

"No," he said, "I chose nothing of the sort. But enough of me — "

"One more question," she interrupted. "What if somehow you could become fertile again? What if — "

It was his turn to interrupt. "It's too late for 'what if' scenarios."

"But Menachem, there are plenty of men in their fifties who become fathers."

"I'm not talking about my age," he said. "In my present circumstances, it would be too difficult. Impossibly difficult. What about you?" He turned to look her in the eyes. "Do you want any children?"

"Do I want any children?" Repeating a question, instead of answering it, was not one of Melanie's traits. She disliked this in other people, especially in women, and she rarely indulged in such mannerisms unless she wanted time to consider her response. Now she had deliberately used that conversational trick. Time? Time was exactly her problem.

"Yes," she said quietly. "I do."

———

"Menachem," she whispered into his ear. "I must confess something." She was lying naked in his arms beneath the tented canopy. "Remember when we made love for the first time?"

"How could I forget?" he murmured back.

"When you were about to enter me and I stopped you? Because you had no condom?"

"Yes," he said under his breath. "But in the end you let me."

"I did. And every other time. But not tonight." Her mouth was so close to his ear that her breath made him shiver.

He had been on the verge of arousal; now he drew back to catch her eyes. The only illumination came from the streetlight shining through the bay windows. "What?" he exclaimed. "On our last night?"

"I've had a vaginal discharge for the past couple of days," she murmured, hiding her face against his shoulder. "It's probably a yeast infection, but I don't want you to catch anything. Let's use a condom."

"But I haven't got one." Menachem made no attempt to mask the exasperation in his voice. "Why didn't you tell me earlier?"

"Because I brought one." She started to massage his penis, gently and persistently. "Stop talking . . . it's time for coupling."

The moment she felt his swelling erection, Melanie reached quickly to the night table by her side where she had placed the Milex seminal pouch made out of medical-grade plastic — the type of material least likely to alter sperm. She had bought several in New York, and had even practiced slipping one onto an unpeeled banana with one hand. The first try had convinced her that she would have little difficulty since, unlike a conventional condom, the Milex pouch was both wider and looser. The next step, however, had bothered her — the one for which banana practice was useless. It depended on the man's awareness.

Place supplied elastic over glans of penis (see illustration). Elastic will not constrict penis and performs double function of preventing pouch from slipping off and containing all of ejaculate in lower end, the instructions on the wrapping had read. The banana in New York had proved docile, but not Menachem.

"What are you doing?" he exclaimed, trying to rise from his supine position.

"Relax," Melanie panted, immobilizing him by squatting over his knees. Stretching the band with the first three fingers of her left hand, she deftly managed with her right hand to slip it over his plastic-sheathed glans, silently thankful for the circumcision that prevented the elastic from slipping. She relied on haste rather than subtlety to carry the moment.

"Now," she mock-moaned, clutching his detumescent penis in one hand and his balls in the other, "please . . . please. . . ." She inserted the tip of his glans into her vagina while straddling him until she felt the rubber band passing her labia. "And now let me fuck you," she exulted as she felt his once-again tumescent penis enter her fully. Nothing but Menachem's ejaculation had become her focus. She rode him relentlessly, her small breasts bouncing up and down, until, with several loud, spent groans, he pulled her toward his chest. Only then did Melanie allow herself to cry out convincingly, while heaving aerobically against his neck. She had never before faked an orgasm with Menachem.

"Wait," she commanded as soon as his heavy breathing had slowed. With clinical care, she slipped the pouch off his penis — anxious to accomplish the task before postcoital limpness and reality had taken over. She had not forgotten the printed instructions: *After removal, concentrate semen in tip of pouch. Tightly wind elastic over pouch after it is folded in two.* "Wait," she repeated, "I'll be back in a flash."

Upon her return from the bathroom, she found Menachem sitting part upright, his back propped against a couple of pillows. "I haven't used rubbers for a couple of decades," he announced, "but a rubber band? Is this something new?"

"Yes," she nuzzled him while improvising. "The friction feels good to me. It will also keep any infection from reaching this precious tip." She touched his flaccid but still moist penis.

"Rubbers and rubber *bands,*" he renewed his lament, "on our last night?"

"Hush, my dear," she said, drawing his head to her breast and rocking him in her arms, her nipples brushing his nose, lips, and cheeks. "No more rubbers this night."

That September evening in London proved to be a double first for Melanie: in addition to her faked orgasm with Menachem, she had never before fellated a man all the way through ejaculation. The taste of his semen, though slightly acerbic, was not unpleasant.

Melanie was all packed, waiting for the taxi to take her to Heathrow Airport. "So you're leaving for Brussels," Menachem said. "When will you be back in New York?"

"Soon," she replied. "Probably before you return to Israel."

"By the way, what are these Belgians of yours working on?"

"ICSI," she said.

"Icksy? What's that?"

"I C S I," she spelled it. "It's an acronym for intracytoplasmic sperm injection."

"Oh?" He looked up. "What precisely does ICSI do?"

"It's too late to ask that, my dear," Melanie replied. "Here's my cab."

18

The day I saw the title of Van Steirteghem's grant proposal, "ICSI vs. SUZI," I was intrigued. It sounded like a lawsuit, or maybe a wrestling match. It was the first application REPCON had ever received from Belgium. By the time I'd put down the last page, I was certain of our board's approval.

I'm not a fan of acronyms, but ICSI and SUZI appealed to me — cute children's names. Especially SUZI, until I learned that it stood for subzonal insemination, a procedure for inserting sperm just below the zona pellucida, and then abandoning it to its own devices. *In the end, I favored ICSI. It wasn't because of its formal definition,* intracytoplasmic sperm injection, the direct injection of sperm into the egg's cytoplasm. *For successful fertilization, the spermatozoon has to get inside the cytoplasm of the oocyte. If you're going to do it, I thought, you might as well go* all the way. *What convinced me more than any other practical considerations was that ICSI offered the much more alluring mnemonic:* I can still inseminate. *Once I thought of it, it stuck. Besides, according to Van Steirteghem's proposal, when success rates were measured, ICSI won hands down.*

I'd never met André Van Steirteghem before, nor any other member of his team at the Center for Reproductive Medicine. But I'd seen a photograph. If I'd been asked to describe him succinctly, I would have been forced to use the word "average": middle-aged; average height; average weight, not too stout, not too thin; closely cropped, silver-gray hair, combed back without a part in the fashion I associate with French businessmen or politicians. Thin, horn-rimmed glasses framed his most striking feature: deep, wide open, scrutinizing eyes — serious even while his mouth was smiling. But the photograph didn't do them justice. When he picked me up at the Brussels airport and learned that I wanted to head straight to his laboratory because of the sensitive material I carried with me, his eyes grinned in synchrony with his mouth as he gave me a lesson in contemporary Belgian political reality.

"You do know that we are not part of the Université Libre de Bruxelles, *don't you? We belong to the Dutch-speaking* Vrije Universiteit Brussel, *so your sperm sample will be examined in a Flemish, not a Walloon laboratory." He laughed in a charmingly self-deprecating sort of way, but I just nodded politely. This morning, all I wanted to know was whether Menachem had any motile sperm — enough so that one could be injected into a receptive egg. Everything else was still hypothetical.*

On the short flight from London, I'd read the last Belgian progress report one more time. I had already marked some of the sentences with a yellow highlighter:

> *The ICSI procedure consists essentially of aspiration of a single spermatozoon from a droplet containing 10% polyvinylpyrrolidone in buffered Earle's medium. The eggs are held by a holding pipette on the heated stage of a Nikon Diaphot inverted microscope at x400 magnification while the injection pipette is pushed through the zona pellucida into the cytoplasm. . . . Even round-headed spermatozoa can be selected for ICSI, although normally they are unable to fertilize the egg owing to the lack of the acrosome.*

I thought of the lecture I'd given Menachem by the side of the canal in Little Venice: about the acrosome tip of the sperm containing a bundle of enzymes necessary to penetrate my zona pellucida. Of course, I had not said my *zona pellucida, enveloping* my *egg, but by then I'd already been thinking of mine. Menachem, I said to myself, apostrophizing the pouch in my handbag, I don't mind if you're missing a few acrosomal enzymes. ICSI can handle that. Only please be viable. One of you.*

I don't know how quickly the Walloons examine sperm samples, but the Flemish results were back within hours. That evening, when Van Steirteghem and the clinic's director, Paul Devroey, picked me up for dinner, he gave me the thumbs-up sign.

"It's possible," he said, "though by no means certain. There seem to be enough useful ones swimming around. Of course, we'd also have to examine the wife. Can she come to Brussels? Where does she live?"

I ignored his questions. I had read in detail what "the wife" would have to do: first, undergo ovarian super-stimulation with a combination of a hypothalamic-releasing hormone analog and gonadotrophins to produce a supply of eggs — a procedure she could do anywhere. Only then would she have to come to Brussels to have them washed out, and to have each injected under the microscope with a single spermatozoon. After that, it was mostly prayer. Praying that at least one, but preferably several, oocytes had been fertilized so that up to three of them could be reimplanted within forty-eight hours into the woman's uterus; and praying even harder that during the next ten days her chorionic gonadotrophin levels would rise. The rest — echographic confirmation of clinical pregnancy within seven weeks, subsequent amniocentesis and possible genetic counseling, and then waiting for at least half a year — all that could be done at home. So they were only talking of a couple of weeks in Brussels. I knew all that. I had read some of their case reports, I had learned of their success rate — on the order of one out of five — and of the number of healthy babies that had already been born as a result of ICSI. But there was one piece of crucial information missing. All their reports had dealt with fresh semen. I showed monumental self-discipline by waiting until the last course was served before I popped the question.

I masked my excitement by focusing on the maraschino cherry atop my dessert. I imagined the stem to be the spermatozoon desperately trying to penetrate my cherry's zona. "Have you ever tried frozen semen?" I finally asked while pushing the cherry by its stem into the whipped cream.

All I wanted was a 'yes' or 'no.' Instead, I got the après vous Monsieur *routine — or whatever the Flemish call this kind of back-and-*

forth deference between scientific colleagues. Finally Devroey, prompted by "You tell her, Paul," informed me that they had successfully used cryopreserved sperm with ICSI in a few testicular cancer patients rendered sterile by chemo- and radiotherapy. I didn't even bother to ask how old the sperm was. Under the circumstances described by Devroey, it would've had to have been weeks, if not months.

I asked whether I could watch an actual ICSI procedure performed in Flemish style the following day.

I watched on a color video monitor connected to the microscope. I will never forget the moment when Van Steirteghem himself — in homage to me as director of the foundation supporting his work — immobilized an egg on the petri dish, with its polar body in the twelve o'clock position. I held my breath as he pushed the capillary needle, containing a single spermatozoon — aspirated tail-first into the injection pipette — through the zona pellucida from the three o'clock side. The sudden spasm I sensed in my lower abdomen as the tip of the needle stopped to eject the solitary sperm deep inside the egg gave way to tears as the needle was withdrawn with infinite gentleness and the injected egg released. Of course, I'm romanticizing the event, but it seemed I had witnessed a solemn event, primordial in nature.

Even though it was not my egg, nor Menachem's sperm, I stayed in Brussels for the next couple of days. For ICSI, the eighteen hours following sperm injection are crucial: the incubating egg is examined for any damage that may have been caused by the micro-injection; if two pronuclei are found — the first evidence of cell division and fertilization — incubation is continued for another twenty-four hours to ensure that embryo formation had been achieved.

I didn't stay to watch the actual transfer of the new embryo into the woman's uterus. I didn't want to meet the woman. As spectator at the most intimate moment in a woman's life — a moment never witnessed by the billions of mothers of this world in pre-ICSI history — I had intruded in an undefinable but palpable way on her privacy. But even more importantly, as the capillary pushed through this stranger's zona pellucida, the pellucid thought of Menachem's presence filled me. From that moment on, I could only think of the day when Menachem's single sperm would penetrate my zona pellucida from the three o'clock direction.

148

*Before I left Brussels, I made an appointment with Van Steirt-
eghem. We decided on the first couple weeks of January. That would
give me ample time for the preparatory work with the endocrinolo-
gist in New York whom Van Steirteghem recommended.*

Melanie had finished telling Felix Frankenthaler about his resemblance to Holbein's portrait of Archbishop Warham of Canterbury.
Were there some Jewish genes in the archbishop? Felix had joked.
But it hadn't taken him long to switch to his favorite subject: satisfying his professional curiosity.

"But you were going to Belgium, I thought. What fancy research
is REPCON supporting there? Don't disclose trade secrets," he
grinned conspiratorially, "just tell me the real hot stuff."

After Melanie told what she had seen in Brussels, Frankenthaler
ruminated for a while, chin supported in his right hand.

"It's not my field," he said finally, "but I wonder how far this will
be taken? A Wild West of reproductive science? Or have you not
thought about it?"

"What do you have in mind?" Melanie's voice had a hard edge
Frankenthaler didn't miss.

"Relax." He momentarily touched her hand. "Couples with infertility problems are so desperate, they're willing to try almost
anything. I was wondering about the absence of any regulation, even
guidelines. What are the limits beyond which such methodology
should not be employed?"

Melanie looked down at her hands, folded as if she were praying. She remained silent.

"These days, why does every couple feel it must have a child?"
he continued. "Is motherhood all that attractive a profession?"

Melanie looked up sharply. "I must correct you. Since you're
talking about couples, you mean *parenthood*. That may well be over-
rated. What do you know about motherhood?"

Frankenthaler frowned. "But who wants to do it alone?"

"I imagine lots of women: those who haven't found the right partner or had a lousy one . . . or women who want a child before it's
too late."

Frankenthaler had not forgotten the argument they'd had after the *Makropoulos Case* performance at the Met. "I'm thinking about all those single women who are going to want to use this technology, that's all. You can't deny it's hard to raise a child alone. Those single mothers better have an adequate supply of maternal hormones."

"I presume you're not talking about progesterone or prolactin or — "

"No." He sounded almost as irritable as she did. "No steroids. No polypeptides. I'm talking about one the scientists haven't identified yet. But we know it exists. It's not inherited and has been known to disappear like this." His inflated cheeks collapsed with a puff. How Gallic, thought Melanie, like *le gourou*'s puffs, except that his usually contained real smoke.

"Very interesting," she said in an affected precious tone. "Do you think there are paternal hormones, Felix? And if they don't exist, then you have just made the endocrinological point in favor of single motherhood."

"*Paternal* hormones? Who knows? In any event, my supply was limited. Probably like that of most research scientists." He wagged a warning finger. "They're good providers though; and on the whole, good husbands. But to get back to you. Is it the maternal hormones and the ticking clock, or is it the supermom syndrome? Like the mythological Amazons, who tried to be both warriors and single mothers. Of daughters," he added as an afterthought.

"I'm not romanticizing my egg as a sleeping maiden waiting for the magic kiss by Prince Sperm," Melanie said sarcastically.

"Good God," exclaimed Frankenthaler, "I didn't realize what button I was pushing. And that you are such a collector of reproductive metaphors." He rearranged his silverware, trying to push the conversation into a less reactive course.

"I don't collect them. I make them up."

"Touché. So what happens now?"

Melanie wasn't so ready to let it go. "Let's continue the hypothetical scenario we explored at the Met a couple of months ago," Melanie said, her eyes now fixed on his. She leaned back. "Let's take a fertile woman who wants a child by a man who thinks he's infertile."

"*Thinks?*" he interrupted. "There are ways of finding out."

"All right, *she* thinks he's infertile. Wait," she raised a hand to stop his incoming question. "She can't find out because . . ." she shook her head impatiently, "because they aren't living together and it's not a question she can ask."

Frankenthaler didn't need to verbalize his skepticism. His eyebrows spoke for him.

"What I mean is, he doesn't know that she wants a child by him, so how can she ask?"

"Is this still hypothetical?" Frankenthaler had started to lean forward. He always did that when he became interested — with students, with dispensers of academic gossip, with purveyors of scientific tidbits. . . . But Melanie Laidlaw? She'd always kept her personal life to herself.

"More or less," she said sheepishly.

He nodded. "I understand." As far as he was concerned, her answer meant that it was true. "Go on."

"Earlier on," Melanie reminded him, "you asked if motherhood was such an attractive profession. I'm not so sure it has to be 'attractive'; for some people, I think it's an obsession."

"You're talking about the supermom syndrome," he declared flatly. "Or the super-supermom syndrome where there is no father?"

"Quite beguiling." She laughed. "Melanie Laidlaw, the super-supermom. You may be right. We ought to talk about that some more."

"All right, let's." Frankenthaler took it as a challenge. "Specifically, why don't you go to a sperm bank and get inseminated with clinically proven, fertile sperm? With a fertile woman the success rate is very high. As far as I recall, as high as in ordinary intercourse."

Though not as pleasurable. But that's the kind of trite response that has no place here. Of course, Felix is right . . . and yet he's wrong. I am not one of those women who believe that the moment of conception has to occur with an earthshaking orgasm — or even through intercourse. But I want to know the father of any child of mine. Not just have a visual image, but also a mental one. I'm not ignoring

*genetics nor physical traits, but, in the final analysis, for me it's an
undefinable feeling of the man's personality.*

*Justin, of course, would have fit the bill. In a way, Felix would
. . . as a biological father, at least. But since Justin's death, it's only
been Menachem who has convinced me that he would be the right
biological father. A good co-parent, too, but that's not possible.*

*Why Menachem? It all fell into place in Brussels at the moment
the needle penetrated that unknown woman's egg when I thought
about his presence, his eyes especially. It's not the color of his pupils
or the shape of his eyes nor the feminine long lashes in his very male
face, but their pellucid luminosity that transmits his true virility. True
virility. Although he has a strong, muscular body — a bit too hairy
if I could have made a choice — and he has pleased me sexually to
a depth that no other man in my limited experience had done before;
when I think of Menachem's virility I feel something else: virility in
character, in intelligence, in curiosity, in the absence of pretense.
These are all features I wish to see in my son. If I were to bear
Menachem's child, it would be bound to be a boy.*

"Because I can't go to a sperm bank — "

"You mean, 'I, Melanie Laidlaw'?" he interjected.

"Yes. If we're going to pursue the topic, let's not do it in the total abstract. I, personally, feel that I can't deal with an anonymous
sperm donor. I simply must know the biological father of my child."

"I see," he interrupted again, his irony showing. "And what, may
I ask, are you searching for in a biological father? Looks can be
deceiving. What about longevity, for instance? How will you check
that out?"

"I could make inquiries, but longevity is not that important to
me," she countered quickly. "I'd pay some attention to overall
health, even shape and physiognomy, but the overriding factor
would be intelligence — "

"Not wisdom or kindness?"

Are these rabbinical psychoplatitudes, she wondered, or does he
really mean it? "I don't know whether there are genes for them,"
she replied. "But yes — I would like them as well. Especially in a
parenting father — not just a sperm donor. Eventually I could see

myself looking for a parenting father. The wise and kind one may take longer to find, but I'd have more time for that search. The biological one, I need that right now."

"I gather you have found him," he said gently.

19

Frankenthaler's pleasure in receiving notification of the grant approval was barely diluted by having learned of it via the standard form letter under the signature of the REPCON board chairman. Still, he was surprised that Melanie had not called him personally. They had been friends for years. Friends are here for congratulations, he thought. He looked forward to some mock admonition at their next opera, *La Forza del Destino*.

But on the night of the opera, Melanie did not show up. At the last minute, with lights already dimming, Melanie's secretary slipped into her seat.

"Where is Dr. Laidlaw?" he hissed as the conductor's head rose over the rim of the pit.

"She doesn't feel well," the secretary whispered. A hushed moment, tapping from the pit, then the overture welled out.

"I hope it's nothing serious," Frankenthaler muttered.

"You look somewhat peaked, Melanie." Frankenthaler held her proffered hand in both of his as a gesture of warmth. "We missed you at the opera. I decided to stop by to see how you are, and also to thank you personally for the grant. After we've spent all of your money, erectile dysfunction will never be the same."

Melanie smiled wanly. "You know it's not *my* money, but I'm happy for all of you that the grant went through. And it's nice to see you." She waved him toward the sofa. "Sit down. What brings you here — other than gratitude for REPCON's munificence?"

"Concern for you. I don't remember your ever having missed an opera. I'm giving a lecture this afternoon at Columbia — actually at your alma mater, at P & S — so I thought I'd take an earlier shuttle and drop by. I'm glad you could squeeze me into your calendar on such short notice."

"No problem," she said. "I've been taking it easy the last few weeks. I'm on a reduced schedule."

"Anything wrong?" She was sitting by his side on the sofa, partly reclining against the corner. Frankenthaler leaned over and patted her hands, which were folded over her lap. "Tell me. After all, what else are friends for?"

"Yes," she hesitated for a moment. "Why not tell you? Especially since you look so worried."

She leaned over, recreating his gesture by patting his hand. "There is nothing wrong with me. On the contrary, there's something very right with me . . . it's just that I feel nauseated much of the time. I can't keep any food down. I seem to be living on soda crackers and water." She pointed to a dish on her desk bearing some English-style biscuits. "I'm not even offering you any — they're too boring."

"Stop stalling," he interrupted. "Forget about food for me and start talking."

"It's morning sickness — that's all." For the first time this morning, Melanie laughed loudly. She pointed to him with her right index finger, while supporting her belly with her other hand — as if she wanted to prevent it from shaking too much. "Felix," she exclaimed, "what a precious expression. I'm pregnant. That's all. I'm halfway through my third month. Another couple of weeks, and I'll be through the worst. I've just had a chorionic villus sampling and everything seems all right. At least as far as CVS can tell. Six more months to go and you'll be invited to the circumcision."

"It's a boy?" he stammered.

Melanie nodded. "I knew it from the moment of fertilization. Now, of course, I know it from the ultrasound exam. But as I saw the spermatozoon enter the oocyte, I knew — "

"You *saw* it?" His surprise, indeed crass skepticism, showed on his face. "Most couples are too busy — "

"Most *couples*," she interjected, "but not *this* woman. I was sitting in a chair watching three of my oocytes on a TV monitor, each being gently penetrated by a *single* spermatozoon."

Felix's disbelief expanded hugely before bursting into a laugh. "Is that why you were gone in January? I remember Shelly mentioning your spending a couple of weeks in Belgium. You never told her why. So it was ICSI? Congratulations. But isn't this carrying your directorial responsibilities a bit far? Sorry," he said quickly. "That was in bad taste. I couldn't resist. What if someone at REPCON is tempted to do that with the research you're funding with us?"

"Never mind. It wasn't such a bad crack." She gazed at him reflectively. "You aren't totally surprised, are you?"

"No," he said quietly. "You did give me indirect notice. Tell me," he said, looking at the floor, "does the father know?"

"What do you think?" Her tone was sharp, her voice unexpectedly firm for a woman suffering from morning sickness.

"He doesn't." Frankenthaler's gaze remained fixed on the carpet.

"Felix, cheer up. And don't look so disappointed. You are the only person in whom I have confided. May I assume that this information — I'm referring to the question of paternity, not to my pregnancy — will stay private between the two of us? Not to be shared even with Shelly?"

He nodded, whereupon she continued. "Now that I have shared this secret with a trusted friend," for the second time she patted his hand, "I would like to consult you on another topic. But not here." She motioned around her office. "Are you staying in town this evening?"

"I'm having dinner with my Columbia hosts after the seminar — early enough to catch the last shuttle to Boston."

"Could you stay overnight at my place? In my guest room?" Seeing him hesitate, she rushed on. "I'll call Shelly. I'll even provide a fresh toothbrush."

———

"Thanks. No sherry. No port . . . in fact, no alcohol." Frankenthaler raised his hand to deflect the offered bottle. "I had wine at dinner and I always get sleepy when I have too much to drink. Is that all you had?" He motioned with his head toward the partially eaten banana and broken zwieback by her side.

Wincing, Melanie drew the throw covering her knees up to her lap. "That and some water. Another few weeks, though, and I prom-

155

ise to invite you for a real meal — or at the very least, a real breakfast. I'm afraid I don't even have eggs in the kitchen."

"Never mind," he smiled good-naturedly. "Tonight I'm here as
friend, confessor, advisor — whatever you wish. You said this morning that you wanted to discuss another matter." He leaned back in
the easy chair, a fond look in his eyes as he faced Melanie reclining on the sofa.

For a long moment, neither one spoke. Only then did
Frankenthaler notice the low tones of a cello emanating from the
hi-fi in the corner. "What are you playing? It sounds familiar."

"Bloch," she said. "*Schelomo.*"

"Of course. I should have listened a bit longer. I didn't know you
were interested in Hebrew themes."

"I am now," she said, straightening up. "That's what I want to
talk to you about. Can you introduce me to a rabbi?"

Frankenthaler had been sitting relaxed, legs crossed. Now he
leaned forward, both feet on the ground, as if he were ready to
pounce. "Rabbi? Did you say rabbi?"

"Yes," she appeared amused by his reaction. "A rabbi. Is that
such an unusual request?"

"Coming from you, I would say yes. I don't remember ever having spoken to you about rabbis or, for that matter, about religion.
Are you religious?"

"No."

"But you have decided now to become religious?"

"I didn't say that." She wavered. "But I'm considering converting."

Frankenthaler shook his head, amazed. "A subtle distinction, but
pregnant with meaning. But in any case I'm afraid I can't help you.
I haven't been to a synagogue in years. Like you, I'm not religious,
but I'm Jewish because I was born a Jew. But why do *you* want to
become Jewish — only some three decades after the Holocaust —
if not for the sake of religion?"

Melanie reached for the half-empty glass of water. She took a few
sips, then continued swirling it, clasping it with both her hands, her
eyes focused on the glass. "Guilt, I think — "

She put down the glass and looked at Felix. "I want my son to be born a Jew, and for that, I gather, the mother must be Jewish."

"So the father, who does not know he's becoming a father, is a Jew? And you think by turning into a Jewess," he hissed the word, "you are making up for keeping his son's existence a secret?"

Melanie made no reply. Her eyes were focused on her lap.

"I guess you do need a rabbi," he sighed. "There's a line in one of Wallace Stevens' poems: 'It was a rabbi's question. Let the rabbis reply.' I can't advise you because you know how I feel: the father has the right to know. It was *his* sperm you saw on the monitor. Didn't he know *that*?"

"No, he didn't." Again, she lifted the glass to give it a few swirls. Instead of drinking, she put it down. "He thinks he's infertile. As a matter of fact, *functionally*, he *is* infertile."

"But — "

"Felix, let me finish. He cannot get a woman pregnant. Not by any ordinary means. *He* did not get me pregnant. Even though we . . ." She fell silent.

"Are you finished?"

"Yes."

"All right." He sounded like a professor at an examination. "Question number one: how did you get a sperm sample without his knowledge?"

"A subterfuge. I used a condom."

"Conclusion: you stole his seed!"

"Felix, please. 'Seed.' It sounds so biblical. And you sound so judgmental . . . and unforgiving. How can I steal something that the owner considers worthless? That he has discarded hundreds of times?"

"Melanie!" He stopped her. "In law, there is no difference between the goods stolen and the value of the goods. Theft is an absolute term, like pregnancy."

For the first time, Melanie had become agitated. "Another biblical judgment! But he *knows* he's infertile. He never uses condoms, and he's never been a father."

"I'm sorry," he said curtly. "The question about rabbis got me into that mode. But tell me: if he's never been a father — could not

157

become a father — were you not concerned about the quality of that single sperm you 'misappropriated'? About genetic damage? No!" He raised his hand. "Ignore that question. It's off-base. It's none of my business and I should not complicate matters even further. Let's stick to the ethics of the issue."

"Don't tell me you're one of those persons who believes that life begins at conception."

"Suppose the rabbi does."

"All right, let's. If my egg is put in a petri dish and ICSId by a sperm, are you going to tell me that I am now pregnant? Or that life has now begun? Of course not. The egg has to be reintroduced and it must implant in *my* uterus. Only then can we discuss the question of life. In others words, fertilization and pregnancy are not synonymous. I am now speaking as a pregnant woman." Her gaze had risen from the glass and confronted him boldly now, daring him to challenge her on her turf. "But let me return to your last question about potentially damaged sperm and answer it as an *informed* pregnant woman. I told you I had a chorionic villus sampling, including state of the art genetic testing. Much more than most couples do. And I did it early enough for a first-trimester abortion in case of serious problems. By the way, the father told me that whatever had caused his infertility had only occurred when he was in his thirties. So it must have been something acute — perhaps exposure to radiation or chemotherapy. And we know that such patients slowly recover fertility without unusual complications. Does that answer it?"

Frankenthaler rose. He paced around the room, finally stopping in front of the sofa. "Melanie, you know I'm your friend. And I do feel for you. But you don't want me to pretend that I agree with you — it wouldn't do either one of us any good. I cannot help you."

He returned to his seat. "About your rabbi question: I don't know any, although I could get you the name of someone in Boston. But New York must be crawling with rabbis. Look in the phone book."

"Under 'rabbi'?" she asked mockingly. "In the Yellow Pages?"

For the first time that evening, their mutual laughter was open. It turned even louder when they discovered that the relevant entry in the Yellow Pages was under *clergy*, without any denominational subdivisions. The inquirer would have to guess which names sounded Jewish.

"I can't call a synagogue blindly," she said after they had recovered from their slightly hysterical interlude. "I first want to know something about the rabbi. That's why I tried you."

"I know the solution," he exclaimed. "Try JTS."

20

"Jewish Theological Seminary. May I help you?" The voice seemed warm, even unhurried. Perhaps their phone doesn't ring all the time, thought Melanie.

"I'd like to speak to a rabbi."

"In person or over the telephone?"

"You mean I can do it over the phone?" Melanie sounded surprised.

A pause. "May I ask what you're calling about?"

Melanie turned cautious as well. "I would like some advice . . . and some information."

"What kind of a rabbi do you wish?"

For a moment, Melanie was stumped. Kind of rabbi? A sympathetic, non-inquisitional, woman rabbi, she wanted to say, but she wasn't even sure whether there were women rabbis. "How do you mean?" she stammered.

"Orthodox? Conservative? Reform?" Melanie could sense the touch of impatience in the woman's voice.

"It doesn't matter," she said quickly. "I want to ask some questions on the phone about conversion . . . on behalf of a friend, that is." The last few words just slipped out.

"But it does matter," the woman replied. "Conversion practices differ greatly."

"Yes, of course," Melanie said quickly. What I want is something quick, simple, and liberal, she thought. "Preferably not Orthodox," she said.

"This is Rabbi Tannenbaum. How can I help you?"

For the past hour, Melanie had sat by the telephone, scribbling questions on a slip of paper. She wanted to be succinct. She didn't know how much time the rabbi would allow her over the phone, but there was an even louder clock ticking at her inner ear: if she wanted to become a Jew before the birth of her son, she had half a year at best. How do you ask a rabbi which form of Judaism was fastest? The lines from Wallace Stevens that Felix Frankenthaler had quoted to her had stuck in her mind. Was speed of conversion "a rabbi's question"? Would a rabbi even reply?

"I'm calling for a friend of mine who is considering converting to Judaism."

"From what religion?"

Melanie was taken aback. That was not a question she had considered. "None," she said quickly. "She isn't religious."

"Your friend was not born in any religion?" The rabbi's voice was deep and resonant, a cantorial voice, but also firm.

"Born in a religion?" Melanie wasn't sure she'd ever posed such a question to herself. "Christian, I guess. But not Catholic," she added quickly. "But is that relevant? Maybe I should have said that she wants to *become* Jewish rather than to convert."

"You seem to have Talmudic talents." He permitted himself a quick rabbinical chuckle. "But why does your friend need an intermediary?"

That was precisely the question Melanie had anticipated. "She is embarrassed — "

"Religion and embarrassment are mutually exclusive terms," the rabbi interjected. "At least, they should be."

"Perhaps," Melanie conceded, "but religion itself is not the source of her embarrassment." White lie number two, Melanie admitted to herself: "Let me tell you something about her," she rushed on, hoping that he would not interrupt with questions that might lead to other half-truths or worse: half-lies.

"So I ask," Melanie concluded, after having sketched her friend's widowhood, impending first childbirth, and related circumstances, "is her desire to bear a Jewish child, a sufficient justification for conversion?"

"Based on what you told me, I ought to inform you — or your friend," to her surprise, Melanie found herself flushing, as if the rabbi were looking at and through her subterfuge, "that I never convert someone for someone else. If the mother wants to convert solely because she wants her child to be *formally* Jewish, I will ask, 'Is the child going to be Jewish? Will it be brought up in a Jewish household?' If the answer is 'no,' then I will say, 'Bring the child to me when it is old enough to make up its own mind.' *Then* I will convert the child, but not the mother."

Melanie felt her heart sink. She hadn't anticipated such a difficulty. As if sensing her dismay, the rabbi continued, his voice taking on a less Talmudic tone. "You must realize that you are speaking to *one* rabbi, Rabbi Tannenbaum, who is Conservative. You may find other Conservative rabbis who will act differently — although I doubt it — or you might talk to some Reform rabbis who are more likely to make exceptions. Outside the strictly Orthodox, you will find the rabbinate to be quite diverse."

He stopped, long enough for Melanie to wonder whether they had reached the end of their conversation. She stared helplessly at the list of unanswered questions in her hand — a list headed by the words, *minimum conditions for conversion.*

"I may have been too precipitous," he suddenly said. "I was only thinking of your pregnant friend. What about the father? That may change circumstances. If the father is Jewish and desires a Jewish child, *and* the mother, though not Jewish, is willing to learn how to provide a Jewish home, I would convert the child upon birth."

"But not the mother?"

"Not for the reason you advanced."

Melanie let out a sigh. "As I told you, the mother is single. Suppose she knew that she will not be allowed to convert only for the sake of bearing a Jewish child? What if she . . . ?"

"Lies?"

"No!" Melanie's denial was brusque. "She simply states that she wants to become Jewish. What then?"

"There is no simple answer to such a question."

Ah, Melanie thought. Progress.

"Every rabbi might answer it differently, because it would depend on the rest of their conversation — *face-to-face* conversation."

"Of course." Melanie responded as if the words were the first response of a conversion ritual.

"If she appeared to me to be sincere, responsible, and mature, I would be prepared to admit her to our regular course of study — "

"Could she complete that in half a year?"

"I doubt it. Certainly not in our congregation. We would expect her to have experienced at least one Jewish year."

"But *could* she?" Melanie persisted. "If she really applied herself?"

"Perhaps." She could sense the rabbi's reluctance. "Certainly more likely if it were in a Reform congregation."

"What would she have to do?" Melanie had picked up the pencil by her phone.

"Again it depends." The rabbi's chuckle started to sound familiar to Melanie. "Most rabbis are prone to flexible answers."

"How flexible?" Melanie could not help interrupting.

"Again, it depends." The chuckle wasn't audible this time, but Melanie could hear the smile. "Even with the Orthodox. Here is a story of Orthodox flexibility for . . . your friend.

"According to Jewish law, condoms cannot be used for the same reason that masturbation is prohibited — the useless spilling of seed, called *zera levatala*. So what can you do in case of infertility, when the collection of semen is required for artificial insemination?"

Melanie felt herself turn crimson. This can't be real, she thought. This rabbi cannot know my story. "I'm talking between husband and wife," she heard the rabbi say. Unconsciously, she moved the mouthpiece away lest the rabbi heard the pounding of her heartbeat. "Not so long ago, Rabbi Goren, one of the chief Orthodox rabbis in Israel, solved the problem by poking a small hole in the condom with a needle. Because of the hole, there is a direct connection between the husband's ejaculate and the woman's vagina, yet most of the semen is retained in the condom, which can then be used for artificial insemination. Rather brilliant compromise, don't you think so?"

Melanie's thoughts were already elsewhere. "So artificial insemination is acceptable according to Jewish law?"

"It is, in the context of fulfilling the duty of begetting children — if that has been shown to be impossible by ordinary sexual intercourse."

Melanie's list had not included any questions bearing on her use of Menachem's sperm, but the rabbi's story had created an opening that she could not resist following. Their dialogue offered an anonymous way to equip herself with background that might prove invaluable in any eventual personal confrontation with a rabbi who would affirm her conversion.

"And if the man thinks he's infertile, the woman could then go to a sperm bank and get artificially inseminated — "

"Just a moment!" interjected the rabbi. "You are making an unacceptable jump for an Orthodox rabbi as well as for many Conservative ones. First, the collection of such samples would almost certainly involve masturbation rather than intercourse. But much more importantly, if the woman became pregnant through insemination with an *anonymous* donor's sperm, there is always the danger of incest, which is totally forbidden — no matter how small that likelihood may be."

"Incest?"

"That's right. Incest." The judgment sounded beyond appeal. "Suppose she bore a daughter, and some other woman, who also went to the same sperm bank, a son. It is not inconceivable that unbeknownst to all of them, some day these two siblings might meet, marry, and procreate."

"And what is the Reform position on that issue?"

"I suspect that some would condone such use. But we're getting off on a tangent. After all, that's not a problem for your friend."

From the rabbi's responses, Melanie had concluded that the Reform route was the way for her. Quickly, she scanned her list for any remaining questions, but the rabbi misinterpreted her silence.

"Or is it?"

Melanie was taken by surprise. "An unknown sperm donor? No," she shook her head vigorously as if the rabbi were looking at her. "That's not her problem."

"Does your friend have any other questions?"

"Let me see," Melanie said, "she gave me a list. . . ."

"While you are looking for it," the rabbi said, "could you answer one question for me?"

"Of course."

"Is the prospective father Jewish?"

"Yes."

"How do you know?"

"I just know. I'm 100 percent certain that he's 100 percent Jewish."

"A practicing Jew?"

Melanie hesitated. "That I'm not sure. Besides, I do not know your definition of 'practicing.' For instance, he doesn't seem to follow kosher dietary rules."

"Then he is not a practicing Jew. At least not by my standards, although he might still be to a Reform rabbi."

"What *is* Reform Judaism?"

"To truly understand this, you need to know what Orthodox Judaism stands for: insistence that tradition — everything that was revealed on Sinai or implied in that revelation — remains constant and unchanging; that nothing may be added or removed from that law. Reform Judaism allows a choice for obeying many of the ritual laws, or as they put it, 'to lighten the burden and not to aggravate it.'" His tone bordered on the dismissive. "The Reform movement accepts modern biblical criticism, which Orthodox Judaism denies. Services in Reform synagogues are held partially in the vernacular, and finally, they assume the complete equality of men and women."

"To me, this would be the most persuasive advantage," exclaimed Melanie. "I probably would have listed that first."

"I was answering your original question," the rabbi said tersely. "I am not trying to sell you or your friend on the merits of the Reform movement. Remember, we at the Jewish Theological Seminary are Conservative. Right now, I'm providing you with general information, but personally, I do not approve of the disregard of dietary laws, nor of the virtual loss of Hebrew, to mention just two examples. But I deliberately listed equality between the sexes last, because historically it came last. It's only in the early seventies that the first Reform women rabbis were appointed — "

"You have no women rabbis in Conservative congregations?"

"Not yet." His tone did not encourage Melanie to pursue that tack, but he didn't even give her the chance. "We were talking about the father. So he is Jewish, though apparently not very much of a practicing Jew. Anything more that may be relevant?"

"He lives in Israel."

"Oh," he said.

"Does that make a difference?"

"It could. Here in the States, custody questions often are complicated when spouses are of different religious affiliations. Suppose the father were a practicing Catholic, who might object to conversion of his child."

"Just a moment, rabbi." Melanie started to get agitated. He kept raising issues that weren't part of her agenda. "I was discussing the possible conversion of the mother prior to delivery."

"True," the rabbi replied. "And I am addressing the question of conversion of the child at birth or even later, because I wasn't prepared to go along with the mother's conversion — at least not on the basis of what you told me."

"Second," Melanie was not prepared to be diverted, "there is no question of custody. The father does not even know that my friend is pregnant."

"And she does not plan to inform him?" The rabbi's surprise was clear.

"She can't."

"I'm sorry." His tone had instantly turned remorseful. "I didn't realize he was dead."

"He isn't," she replied calmly. "He's married. And divorce is not in the cards."

"I see." His remorse had turned to prim reserve. "You are talking about too complicated a case for a telephone consultation, which, incidentally, has taken much longer than I had expected. I think your friend should meet a rabbi in person — even if conversion is not feasible. There seem to be other issues where a rabbi's advice might be in order."

"Could you recommend one to me — " Melanie quickly corrected herself. "I mean to my friend. A Reform rabbi."

21

"You've certainly changed, Melanie." Frankenthaler held her at a distance by her shoulders. His arms were stretched straight. "You're just . . . *blooming*," he announced. "And so . . ." He stepped back, his hands shaping an imaginary belly.

"Yes," she laughed. "I'm swelling. I'm starting to count the weeks to delivery. Come, let me show you something."

They went through her living room down a short corridor. "Look," she said, "Adam's room."

"Adam?" He looked past her through the open door. "A nursery! And you've already picked the name. Adam," he said again, slowly, as if he were tasting each letter. "Nice. What made you pick it?"

"Lots of reasons. You can't maltreat it; no nicknames; easily pronounced in other languages — and as you said, it sounds nice: Adam Laidlaw. No middle name. Short and to the point. Also, it could easily be Jewish."

"Ah, yes," Frankenthaler said, letting the words trail off.

"I thought I should get everything ready in plenty of time," she added hastily, brushing aside the implied question. "I've even lined up an au pair from Sweden. She'll start a couple of weeks before I go into the hospital."

"Why are you in such a hurry?"

"You probably don't know it, but I was an only child, so Adam has no aunts or uncles. And since my parents are dead, he has no grandparents — "

"You mean maternal ones," he corrected her.

Melanie ignored the interruption. "I wanted to have everything ready in plenty of time. With no close relatives, I thought that I better have some live-in help around. Now, let's go back into the living room. I'd like to hear about your trip to Israel."

———

"Of course, you also went to Beersheba to meet your collaborators there?"

Frankenthaler felt his way carefully here. "The key man there is Jephtah Cohn, the developer of the actual delivery vehicle. He came to Jerusalem, where we held all our meetings. Most of the people on the project work at Hadassah or the Hebrew University; besides it's too damn hot in Beersheba in the summer. But I was there briefly to talk about administrative details."

"So you met Menachem Dvir."

For some time now, Frankenthaler had wondered whether she would ask about Dvir. But when it came, it turned out to be a statement of fact.

"Yes. An interesting man." He looked at her appraisingly. "I gather you know him."

She nodded. "How is he?"

"He seemed well enough. By the way, he asked about you. I mentioned you were expecting."

"I know."

My dear Melanie,

   As you know all too well, I am not a good
letter writer. I have too little practice. Long
emphasis on secrecy in my work and even in my
life makes me reluctant to put much on paper. But
as you can read in the Psalms (45:1), "My tongue
is the pen of a ready writer." In other words, I
don't write, but at times I can tell good
stories.

   I had not heard from you since your New Year's
greeting. I imagined various reasons for your
silence, but frankly I did not guess the real
reason, which I learned, quite inadvertently,
from Professor Frankenthaler of Brandeis

University, who visited us recently. Let me start out by congratulating you. I know how important the birth of a child is for you. After all, how could I forget our conversation in London?

I have to admit to some pangs of jealousy when I heard about your pregnancy, although I have obviously no claims whatsoever other than emotional ones. If the circumstances of my life were different, I know I would have wished to have been your child's father--if I had never worked in Dimona. Would I have had any problem persuading you that "our" child should be brought up a Jew? I realize now that religion was never a topic between us. The closest we got was Solomon and the queen of Sheba.

But the clock of life cannot be restarted. In this life, I managed to rationalize my adultery with you--if adultery can ever truly be rationalized. Traditional Judaism is not egalitarian when it comes to adultery. In biblical times, adulterous women were stoned to death, whereas men could have a number of relationships going on at the same time. I have a feeling that deep down this double standard still persists. In any event, since you are about to become a mother, it is obvious that we should not meet again. I hope that I will hear about you, at least indirectly, from time to time from our Brandeis or Hadassah partners.

Stay well. And congratulate the father of your child for his impeccable taste. He seems doubly blessed.

Menachem

PS. The attached <u>haikai</u> was written in the sixteenth century by Arakida Moritake. I wish I had written it.

To the blind minstrel

from the blind accompanist--

comes a letter.

Welling up from the eyes,

the tears come tumbling down.

"Tell me," Frankenthaler asked, "when, precisely, do you expect
to give birth?"

"At the very end of the year." Melanie's eyes sparkled with
amusement.

"But that's impossible," he exclaimed. "Weren't you in Belgium
just after New Year?"

"Felix," she laughed. "The year 5738 ends on the twenty-ninth
of *Elul.* Or to translate, on the tenth of September."

"Okay," he said. "*Anno Domini* 1979 for this ignorant Jew. And
where did you learn the Hebrew calendar?"

Melanie held up her hand. "In a moment. First a question: what's
the time interval between 100 B.C. and A.D. 100?"

"Two hundred years, of course. Why ask such a question?"

"Because it shows you one of the advantages of the Hebrew over
the Gregorian calendar. 'Two hundred years' is wrong. There's no
year zero; and since the numbers increase in opposite directions,
whereas time flows in the same direction, the elapsed time across
the B.C./A.D. boundary cannot be calculated algebraically. In other
words, the answer is *198* years!" Melanie looked triumphant.

"I'll be damned," said Frankenthaler. "Have you converted?" He
sank back in the sofa.

"Not yet, but I'm well on the way. Your advice about calling JTS
turned out to be just the ticket. They referred me to a Reform
rabbi — a woman — who admitted me to her conversion class."

"You just told the rabbi you wanted to turn Jewish so that your
son could be born a Jew?"

Melanie hesitated. "No," she finally said. "The rabbi would not
have agreed. I'd already found that out from a Conservative rabbi
at JTS."

"So?"

"So from the same Conservative rabbi I also learned what questions a potential convert to Reform Judaism would be asked. When I heard what those five were, I concluded I could agree to them in good faith — more or less."

"Five? No more, no less?"

"Five. First — and this one the rabbi will ask at the actual synagogue ceremony — is whether I do all this out of my own free will. In my case, the answer is obviously yes, since no one is forcing me."

"What else?"

"Whether I have given up my former religious affiliation. Since I never had a formal one, there's nothing to give up. Also whether I pledge my loyalty to the Jewish people and to Judaism; and then, of course, whether I promise to bring up any children of mine in the Jewish faith. I don't see any problems with any of them — particularly not the last."

"That leaves one more."

Melanie stared in surprise. "Were you counting? I must have skipped one. Anyway," she shrugged, "I told the rabbi I wanted to do this as quickly as possible. She assigned me a tutor, to whom I go three times a week, so we can cover the required material as quickly as possible. I want to be finished next month — just in case Adam decides to appear prematurely."

"I hope I'm not being intrusive," said Frankenthaler, "but I — a born Jew — have no idea what the conversion process is all about. Could you tell me what you have to learn?" He leaned forward in anticipation.

"Sure," Melanie said good-naturedly. "I'd love to show off what I've acquired. First, I have to learn about the holidays: Yom Kippur, Rosh Hashanah, Chanukah, Pesach . . . even you must know those. And of course the Sabbath. Then the life-cycle ceremonies — birth, Bar Mitzvah, marriage, death. And Jewish literature, like the Bible, Halakah — the Jewish Law, the Midrash, the Talmud and others." She waved her hand. "I'm just starting on the *Responsa* literature, which I find the most intriguing. These are rabbinical answers to Jewish questions that they keep right on issuing, even today. Let me show you. I've got the book on my night table."

Melanie appeared with a paperback, entitled *American Reform*

Responsa: Jewish Questions, Rabbinic Answers. "It would be difficult to think of a question that hasn't been posed . . . or hasn't been rabbinically answered." She flipped open the table of contents. "'Surgical Transplants'; 'Eulogy for a Suicide'; 'Jewish Attitude Toward Sexual Relations Between Consenting Adults'; or here, 'Artificial Insemination.' Clearly, this subject is not to be found in Talmudic or rabbinical sources. So the interesting aspect of the *Responsa* is how modern rabbis deal with modern topics. Or even old ones." Melanie's finger ran down the page. "'Masturbation.' Here is the text of the question."

Melanie moved next to Frankenthaler on the sofa, so that they could both read the text. "'What does the tradition say about masturbation?'" she read. "'Are any distinctions made between males and females, young or old, married or unmarried?' That's not a bad question, is it?" She closed the book.

"So what was the answer?"

She gave a dismissive shrug. "I'll lend you the book when I'm through."

Frankenthaler raised his palms. "No thanks. I already have too much to read. Just abstract the answer for me."

"Masturbation is neither harmful nor sinful. In men or women. At least that's the Reform view."

"Is that all they're teaching you?"

Melanie glanced at him. Was he mocking or was he interested? "I have to learn all the basic prayers — "

"In Hebrew?"

"Not with this rabbi. Maybe with others. All I need to learn are the Hebrew names and key Hebrew words involved in those prayers: *Kaddish, Shema, Amidah.* . . . And finally, in addition to the liturgy, I am also getting some exposure to Jewish history, from the time of Abraham and David all the way through the establishment of the modern state of Israel."

"Are you taking an exam?"

"I will in the end. But my rabbi insists on meeting with me privately on occasion. Since I'm in such a hurry with my conversion, she wants to be sure that I don't take any shortcuts. Actually, she doesn't use the word 'conversion.' In her congregation, it's 'confirmation' or 'affirmation.' At our last meeting, she gave me a small quiz, which I passed brilliantly." Melanie snorted with mock deprecation. "She asked me which Jewish holiday was the most important. I was about to say 'Yom Kippur,' but then I thought that's too simple."

"So what did you say?"

"The Sabbath! And it turned out to be the right answer, because it's the only holiday mentioned in the Ten Commandments."

"So you're really turning into a Jew." He shook his head in wonder.

"That depends on your definition. But I like my conversations with the rabbi. We aren't just talking about rules and prohibitions; we discuss values — the importance of family, education, and community service in Judaism — as well as small tidbits. Like the difference between the Gregorian and Hebrew calendars — the quiz you flunked. By the way, you do know, don't you, that all Jewish names *mean* something."

"I suppose so."

"I asked the rabbi about the meaning of 'Menachem.' It means 'consoler' or 'comforter.' Rather apt, I thought."

"Tell me Melanie," Frankenthaler asked quietly. "Menachem Dvir is the father, isn't he?"

22

Felix and Shelly Frankenthaler were a social couple. Through judicious pruning and grafting, they had cultivated over the years a grove of acquaintances, most of them academics in the Boston area, with whom they indulged in a languorous, social Ping-Pong consisting of invitations and counter-invitations. They also had good manners. Once they had accepted an invitation, they stuck by it even if a more intriguing one was extended subsequently by someone else.

"What are we going to do about this one?" Felix asked, sliding the invitation along the polished dining room table toward his wife. One of their habits was to eat breakfast — even a modest one — with good china and silverware in their dining room.

"We've got to turn it down," Shelly declared flatly. "We accepted weeks ago at the Wilsons. Between you and your Harvard colleague, we practically needed a computer to finally settle on September 20. Besides, I want to hear the latest news on sociobiology straight from the — would 'horse's mouth' be right?"

"I don't know," he said frowning. "Probably 'ant's mandible' would be more elegant." He waved the question irritably aside. "But this is different. I don't recall ever having been invited for a dinner to celebrate the conclusion of Yom Kippur — "

"It doesn't say 'dinner.' " She slid the invitation back. "It says 'break fast.' Two words. Not breakfast. And no one has ever invited you before because you're such a lousy Jew. Melanie converted so recently, she doesn't know that yet." She smiled affectionately across the table. "I know she didn't invite us to the fast, but have you ever fasted? I bet you can't even recite the Ten Commandments."

"Thou shalt not commit adultery," he began.

"That's not the first, but I'm glad you remember it. Seriously, though, why can't you turn her down? Felix, be honest and tell Melanie we already have an earlier engagement."

"I can't tell her that. You yourself pointed out how recently she became a Jew. I still can't quite believe it. But she's taking it seriously and I was the one she first called for advice. You call her, Shelly."

"I won't." She rose and picked up her plate and cup. "The envelope is addressed to you."

———

In the end, the Frankenthalers arrived at a Solomonic solution. Shelly upheld at least a portion of the Frankenthaler reputation by dining with the E. O. Wilsons, while Felix took a four o'clock shuttle to New York. The traffic from La Guardia Airport through the Midtown Tunnel was surprisingly light. He arrived at Melanie's apartment before sunset.

"You're early," the au pair said, shaking her head to brush a strand of blond hair out of her eye while holding Adam against her hip. "Dr. Laidlaw is still at the synagogue. Adam, say 'hello' to our guest." She put him down on the floor and raised his hand for an assisted handshake.

"Ma Ma," the boy gurgled.

"No," the au pair laughed. "This is not Mama. This is a Papa. Adam, say 'Papa.'"

"Pa Pa." His big brown eyes shone with excitement. "Pa Pa," he repeated, clutching Frankenthaler's right leg with both his hands to steady himself.

A cute boy, thought Frankenthaler, but what am I supposed to do with him now? I'm not his papa.

The au pair seemed to have read his mind. "Please excuse us. I need to finish feeding him." She looked at her wristwatch. "Dr. Laidlaw should be back by six thirty."

"Don't worry about me," he assured her. "You and Adam do your thing, and I'll just make myself comfortable in the living room."

"Pa Pa . . . Pa Pa," the sound receded as the boy scooted with remarkable speed toward the kitchen.

The Laidlaw apartment was spacious, but it lacked a formal dining room, the short end of the L-shaped living room serving as the dining area. To his surprise, Frankenthaler noticed only two settings at the table. He had expected a much larger gathering.

———

"And now, let me really welcome you." Melanie hugged Frankenthaler. "I always try to put Adam to bed, especially when he hasn't seen me all day. It's something I never delegate. I'm sorry Shelly couldn't come. Oops, I shouldn't have said that." She smiled sheepishly. "The Day of Atonement is all about being forgiven for lies. I certainly shouldn't say a half-truth with the sounds of the shofar still resounding in my ears. I invited the two of you because I have an important subject to discuss. The end of Yom Kippur seemed just right for it. But when I learned Shelly couldn't make it, deep down I was relieved. The topic I want to raise is more easily discussed first with you alone." Seeing his puzzled expression, she hurried on. "But later. I'm a terrible hostess to start that way. Besides, I'm starving. Have you ever fasted from one sundown to the next?"

"No," he said — a bit curtly, before recovering himself. "But I could use some fasting." He patted his stomach. "I'm getting a spare tire."

"Fasting on Yom Kippur may do you some good, but I'm afraid it wouldn't help your waistline. For that, you should exercise. But now, let's eat." She led him to the oval dining table. "You light the candles while I bring in the food. I told Kirsten to go out for the evening. We won't be disturbed, unless Adam wakes up. If he does, I'll let you watch me change his diapers."

Melanie brought all of the food at one time. "Sort of a breakfast," she apologized. "But of high quality. The pitcher contains orange juice that Kirsten pressed this afternoon. Fresh bagels, real cream cheese, smoked salmon cut very thin, sliced nectarines mixed with passion fruit." She grinned proudly. "And the pièce de résistance." With a flourish, Melanie lifted the porcelain dome covering the serving platter. "Blinis with caviar; and sour cream on the side. Start helping yourself while I put on some music. And then I won't get up from the table."

Melanie lifted the dust cover of the turntable and stacked three records, evidently preselected, on the changer.

"Is this all kosher?" Felix asked jokingly.

"Who knows? You're breaking the fast of a Reform Jew who doesn't follow kashruth. As for you Felix, I suspect you're one of those Jews who didn't even know that this year, the Day of Atonement was the twentieth of September."

"*Nolo contendere.* But this caviar is delicious. By the way," he stopped eating, "what are you playing?"

Melanie smiled with satisfaction. She had hoped he would notice. "Max Bruch's *Kol Nidrei.*"

"But — "

"I know what you'll say. 'But it's composed for cello and orchestra.' I'll play that next. But I wanted to start with this arrangement: just viola and piano. It's much more intimate . . . should I say, more religious? I heard the Kol Nidre prayer three times at today's service. You do know it's a declaration of annulment of vows taken by a person?"

"Don't embarrass me, Melanie. Just tell me. But wait." He raised his hand to stop her. "The subject you want to discuss with me: is it, by any chance, an attempt to convince me to become an observant Jew?"

Melanie guffawed. "Heaven forbid. That's your business. I'll spare you the rabbinical history, but the anti-Semitic interpretation of Kol Nidre has been that Jews can't be trusted, because this offers them a way of backing out of any vows or oaths. Of course, they're forgetting that it's supposed to apply only to unintentionally broken commitments, and only to those made by man to God."

"Rabbi Laidlaw, you amaze me," he said good-naturedly. "Still, all this annulment of vows on the Day of Atonement is just a crutch. Like the Catholic bookkeeping around the confession. All these rituals simply allow people to do terrible things and then forget about them, by assuming that some Almighty Power has forgiven them. Thanks, but I don't approve of such crutches."

"You're a rational man, but don't knock crutches. Take the *Marranos*, the Jews converted forcibly in the fifteenth century to Catholicism. Their 'crutch,' Kol Nidre, enabled them to reject in their minds their baptismal oaths; to renounce what the church had compelled them to do under threat of torture and death. You'd think few people — at least Jews — would argue about *that* use of Kol Nidre. And yet," Melanie waved a cheese-smeared knife for emphasis, "there was a synod of German Reform Jews in the middle of the last century who recommended total expunction of this prayer from the liturgy. Thank God, they lost or we wouldn't be hearing what's about to come through the loudspeakers: Richard Tucker, singing the Kol Nidre Service. For me, it brings back the most moving part of this morning's service. Listen."

Should I tell Felix why I'm starting tonight with Kol Nidre? Would such a non-practicing Jew even understand? Last year, when I first learned about Kol Nidre during my conversion tutorial, I realized that not all of the five commitments I was expected to make as a convert to Reform Judaism were as straightforward as I told Felix. "Do you promise to establish a Jewish home and to participate actively in the life of the synagogue and of the Jewish community?" Silently, I

*hedged in my answer by not inquiring further about the operational
definition of the terms* Jewish home *and* participating actively. *My
real objective was to become legally a Reform Jewess before deliver-
ing my son. Adam was born just a few days before the 1979 Day of
Atonement. On my first Yom Kippur Service, I didn't even fast. While
my son suckled my breast, I read in English the following words about
my vows, bonds, promises, obligations, and oaths: "They shall be
absolved, released, annulled, made void, and of none effect; they shall
not be binding nor shall they have any power. Our vows to God shall
not be vows; our bonds shall not be bonds; and our oaths shall not
be oaths." I concluded that if there really is a God of the Israelites,
any hedged vow of mine during the conversion, and hence my son's
Jewishness, was now kosher.*

*During the past year, my relationship with Alice Goldklang crossed
the border from rabbi-and-convert into incipient friendship. She is a
few years younger than I and still single. Following tradition, I
scheduled Adam's circumcision on the eighth day following his birth.
"Where is the father?" Asked Rabbi Goldklang. Until then, she had
not pursued the question of Adam's father, when I had made it plain
during our very first interview that he was not around. But for the
circumcision, the father ought to play the key role. "We'll use a Jewish physician," I stalled. But the subject of Menachem's paternity
never left me for a day.*

*But what is a rabbi for if not for such problems? First problem:
Did I steal Menachem's seed as Felix had put it with elegant bluntness? Second problem: What if he never wanted a child? Why con-
front him with the fact of his paternity even if I assumed all parental responsibility? But that question had now become moot, ever since
I received Menachem's letter.* I know that I would have wished to have
been your child's father. *He had written about a hypothetical event.
No ambiguity there. But what about problem number three: his
present marriage, about which I know next to nothing? How can I
justify burdening his marriage with such knowledge?*

*Alice Goldklang's transition from pure rabbi to friend occurred on
the day she answered my second question. To the first — had I stolen Menachem's seed? — she answered unequivocally, "Yes." Her position was identical to Felix's, but it still didn't convince me.*

Menachem had thrown his seed away as useless some hundreds of times. My taking one of his spermatozoa was not going to land me in any jail — in my judgment not even a spiritual jail. Sorry, Rabbi Goldklang, I said silently, that's my analysis. Let's get to the real question. "Alice," I said out loud, "how can I burden the man with this problem, which is not of his making. It may destroy, or at least damage, his marriage."

"'May damage his marriage'?" she repeated with rabbinical scorn. "You have already damaged it irrevocably by participating in his adultery. You cannot undo this. Just consider yourself lucky that his adultery doesn't affect Adam from being considered a Jew."

When Alice Goldklang saw my relief, she really let me have it. "That business about 'why burden them?' I hear all the time," she said dismissively. "I totally disapprove of it; even when they talk about cancer — whether the patient or the family should be 'burdened' with that information. In my opinion, dishonesty is always a bigger burden than honesty. People should be allowed to make reasonable choices based on knowledge. When you say, 'I don't want to burden them,' you're taking away their options."

"Options for whom?" I asked. "For what?"

She looked at me for a long time. I could see disapproval turn into compassion. "For the biological father and you. It may turn out that he'll say, 'This is fabulous. I'd like to come and visit my biological child even though I will remain married to my wife.' He might think it fantastic that his infertility was shown not to be absolute. Or he might tell you that he wanted to have nothing to do with your son or you; that you and Adam were totally on your own. If he says that, then you're no worse off than you are now."

"But that's not really true," I remonstrated. "You presented two alternatives. There are all kinds of options. What if he demands shared custody?"

"And is he not entitled to it?" she asked quietly. "Don't be so Talmudic." *It was a strange note on which to end a conversation with my rabbi.*

"Felix," Melanie said, "let's move to more comfortable seats and talk."

"You mean we haven't talked yet?"
"Not about what is really on my mind."

My dearest Menachem,

You may wonder why I asked Felix to take this
envelope with him to Israel and to deliver it in
person. First, I don't want to take the risk,
however remote, that this letter might fall into
someone else's hands. Second, the date of
delivery is not crucial, since you will
undoubtedly ask why I had not written this letter
one or even two years ago. And finally, Felix has
gradually guessed much of what I am now writing.
Therefore, he is the only messenger I can trust.

I did not respond to your last letter because I
was not ready then for a confession. Important
confessions should be made in person. But even
though this confession is the most important one
of my life, I felt that you should not have to
face me when you learn this: You are the father
of my son.

I know there is much to explain here. I imagine
you want to know more about the how right now
than the why. But please (if I can ask you for
any more forbearance) bear with me and let me
tell you about the why. The how is far, far
simpler to spell out.

As you know, I have never had a child before.
While there were times during my marriage when I
considered motherhood, circumstances, as well as
Justin's own ambivalence, led me to postpone it
until too late. It was only when I was a widow,

and the choice seemed utterly irrevocable, that I
came to appreciate what I had lost. And it was
only then, by ways I never could have foreseen,
that the lost choice came back to me again--only
after I thought I had put the possibility aside
forever and buried myself in my work.

It was my new work that gave me back what I had
lost. The REPCON directorship provided me with
security--professional as well as financial--and
perhaps most importantly, self-confidence and
total independence. At the same time, my
biological clock ticked louder and louder, and
with it I became aware of an increasing desire to
become a mother. I felt that in my present
position, I could achieve it functionally, and
that I could afford it emotionally, for myself
and for my child. But as you know, I had no
sexual partner after Justin's death until I met
you. Yes, I had speculated about artificial
insemination with an anonymous sperm donor, but
the idea of my not knowing anything about the
father of my child repelled me. I could not
divorce myself from the importance of the
biological identity of the father.

Suddenly, you, my Menachem, appeared out of
nowhere, like a sexual angel from the sky. More
than that: the only proper choice for the father
of my child. But I knew almost as immediately
that living together with you would not be
realistic. You are in Israel and I in New York;
and while I am free, you are not.

By now, I can imagine you are wondering whether
you are not dealing with a romantic lunatic. How
could you, "infertile" Menachem, impregnate me?
Remember that first night in Kirchberg, when you
told me that Solomon visited the queen of Sheba
only three times each month, but that it was

quality rather than quantity that counted? One of
the great advantages of my position with REPCON
is that I am one of the first in the world to
know about advances in reproductive biology,
including those in the field of male infertility.
Do you remember when you asked me in London what
the Belgians were working on, and I said "ICSI"?
I didn't tell you then, but ICSI stands for
"intracytoplasmic sperm injection," a procedure
permitting fertilization of a woman's egg with
one single normal sperm.

I gambled that my Solomon, Menachem Dvir, still
had enough viable sperm to penetrate a woman's
egg in a petri dish--an assumption that made me
lie to you. This is my first confession and you
must believe me when I tell you that it is the
only deliberate falsehood I ever told you. There
are times when I did not disclose the entire
truth--just as you did not--but that was done
invariably by omission of a fact rather than by
deliberate commission of an untruth. Remember
when I surprised you with a condom because of
some supposed yeast infection? I know you could
not have forgotten, because I can still see that
hilarious expression on your face, and the effect
on your wonderful cock as you saw me apply the
rubber band so that none of your precious seed
might be spilled. What you may not remember is
that immediately after you had come in me, I ran
to the bathroom, ostensibly to discard my condom
with your priceless semen. But I did not discard
it. Rather, I dropped it into a small Dewar,
containing liquid nitrogen, and the rest you can
imagine.

You did, indeed, have some normal spermatozoa;
not sufficient to impregnate anyone on your own,
but adequate for ICSI of a healthy egg, which I

provided. When Felix Frankenthaler told you, some
months later, that I had gotten pregnant, I did
not lie about the father. I just did not
volunteer his identity to Felix. I thought that
it was sufficient for me to know who the father
was.

(There is, of course, the question of when and
what Adam needs to know, but that will depend, in
part, on your response to this letter.)

Now that I am opening up to you as if I were in
a confessional (what a terrible simile for a new
Jewess), I will admit that during my pregnancy
and the first few months after Adam's birth, I
felt no guilt about having deprived you of that
single sperm. But subsequently, on more than one
occasion, at dinner parties or one-on-one
conversations, I brought up, as if it were a
hypothetical case, what I had done. It was easy
for me to bring up the subject. I just told
people about ICSI, one of the hot new projects
supported by my foundation, and then asked, "What
if . . . ?"

I was flabbergasted by the depths of feeling my
question generated. "But she stole his sperm!" was
one of them--a comment I didn't just hear from
men, but also women. Initially, I was very
defensive, pretending I was speaking on behalf of
the accused sperm thief. I kept insisting that
the man couldn't do anything with this one sperm.
"But neither could you!" one woman once yelled at
me, as if she had actually known it was my egg
your precious seed had fertilized. "You and your
egg couldn't do it alone. You needed ICSI. And
that does not belong to you!"

I still remember that exchange, because in the
end it touched me so deeply. I almost wanted to
explain that, in a way, ICSI did belong to me;

that indirectly, I, through REPCON, had made
possible its invention; and that the biological
father, believing himself to be infertile, could
not possibly have thought his semen of value. And
if something is valueless, how can you steal it?
Felix had a reply to that. "There is no
difference between the goods stolen and the value
of the goods."

Another question asked of me was what if the
man did not believe in reproduction, convinced
that too many people were already in this
miserable world? I just shrugged, because in your
last letter you had already presented me with
prima facie evidence of your interest in
procreation. Most Jewish men feel as you do. And
how do I, your shikse lover as you have called me
more than once in bed, know that? Because, as I
hinted earlier in this letter, I am a new Jewess,
having converted, though not to Orthodox Judaism--
but that is almost beside the point. Although we
never really spoke about religion on the all-too-
few occasions we spent together, I felt that it
would matter to you that any child of yours be
borne by a Jewish mother. So you see, deep down I
always thought of Adam also as your son.

I have told you of an overwhelming fact of
life. I must end with a more theoretical fact--of
death. When I had my last physical exam, it was
discovered that I had a fibroid tumor. I am going
to have a hysterectomy. Tens if not hundreds of
thousands of women have hysterectomies annually.
It's certainly not life-threatening (other than
that no future conception of life is possible--
making Adam even more precious to me), but it did
make me think. What if?

I am an only child whose parents are dead. I
have no close relatives, although I do have

friends. At least two of them, Felix and Shelly
Frankenthaler, are close enough that they agreed
(shortly after Yom Kippur, of all days!) to act
as parents for Adam if something happened to me
and no one else was prepared to assume that legal
role. But I felt that for Adam's sake and my own
guilt, you should know that you are his father. I
do not wish to place a burden on you that you did
not seek. Nor does anyone, except the
Frankenthalers, know of your paternal connection.
All you need to tell Felix is <u>yes</u> or <u>no</u> after you
have read this letter. He promised not to
persuade you in any form to assume legal
guardianship of Adam in the event of my death.

Let me end on a mythological note related to
Solomon and the queen of Sheba--after all, that
story brought us together. Did you know that
there exists also an Ethiopian version? I only
learned about it recently from Edward Ullendorff,
a professor of Ethiopian Studies. According to
him, the <u>Kebra Nagast</u> (to Ethiopians, in terms of
importance, the equivalent of the Old Testament
or the Koran) states that Solomon and the queen
of Sheba indeed had carnal relations, but it also
implies that Solomon did not know that the queen
was pregnant when she returned to Ethiopia, where
she gave birth to a son, Menelek--the founder of
the Ethiopian imperial dynasty. What is so
poignantly relevant to us two--hence the reason
why I am citing my references to show that I have
not made up any of it--is that, eventually, the
queen sent the boy Menelek back to Jerusalem with
the request that Solomon educate him. Attached is
a photo of an Ethiopian representation of the
entire legend, divided in the original into
forty-four small pictures in cartoon-strip
format, taken from one of Ullendorff's articles.

Perhaps some day, you and I could look together
at the original in the Ethiopian part of the
Church of the Holy Sepulcher in Jerusalem,
notably at number twenty-six, showing Solomon and
the queen "sleeping" with each other; at number
thirty-one, in which Menelek asks, "Tell me about
my father"; and number thirty-five, depicting
father and son. We would ignore number forty-
three, the queen's deathbed confession.

You and I enjoyed in the deepest sense of the
word a Handel opera in Vienna. A couple of months
ago, I heard Handel's oratorio, <u>Solomon</u>, for the
first time in my life. The last duet by Solomon
and the queen of Sheba ends Handel's piece; in
its last line, the two sing of "Praise unbought
by price or fear." Adam's birth does indeed
deserve praise.

Stay well, my Menachem and my Solomon,
Melanie

24

The Tuesday June 9, 1981, *New York Times* carried a 108-point
headline,

ISRAELI JETS DESTROY IRAQI ATOMIC REACTOR; ATTACK CONDEMNED BY U.S. AND ARAB NATIONS

spread across the entire width of the front page — the type of scare
headline more usually seen in the *Daily News*. The lead article,
under a June 8 Jerusalem dateline, started with two stark sentences:
"Israeli planes yesterday bombed and destroyed an atomic reactor
near Baghdad that would have enabled Iraq to manufacture nuclear
weapons, the Israeli government announced today. Prime Minister

Menachem Begin justified the action as having been essential to prevent the 'evil' President Saddam Hussein of Iraq from attacking Israeli cities with atomic bombs of the type dropped on Hiroshima during World War II."

Continuing for nearly half a page on the inside of the paper, the Jerusalem report included the brief Israeli government statement that "from sources whose reliability is beyond any doubt, we learned that this reactor, despite its camouflage, is designed to produce atomic bombs."

Times editorials rarely deal with news of the same day. June 9 was an exception. The lead editorial, entitled "Israel's Illusion," began, "Israel's sneak attack on a French-built nuclear reactor near Baghdad was an act of inexcusable and short-sighted aggression," and ended, "Israel risks becoming its own worst enemy."

The official reactions from foreign governments were equally scathing. The British Foreign Office categorized the raid as "an unprovoked attack," adding that "we can only condemn such a grave breach of international law which could have the most serious consequences." In Moscow, Tass labeled the attack "barbarous"; Saudi Arabia, through its Information Minister Mohammed Abdo Yamani, termed it "the peak of international terrorism practiced by Israel"; and Iraq's other neighbor, Kuwait, issued a call for "collective Arab action to prevent further Israeli attacks."

The initial response of the French government, though most involved because of its open support of the Iraqi nuclear facility, was curiously ambiguous. On the one hand, the new Socialist prime minister, Pierre Mauroy, condemned the Israeli raid as "unacceptable and a further complication in a situation that is already explosive." Yet he gave no indication whether France would help rebuild the Osirak complex or continue to supply Iraq with highly enriched uranium fuel.

Among the barrage of banner headlines, and editorial condemnation, the one-paragraph Reuters report from Jerusalem, reporting the release of 750 Palestinian prisoners, went virtually unnoticed. Only one British newspaper — hardly known for pro-Israeli leanings — commented on the prisoner release in the form of an editorial sneer to the effect that the Israeli government must have lost whatever residual PR savvy it still possessed: What good, the editorial asked, would such a quixotic gesture buy from the Arab world, or anyone else for that matter? A release of prisoners on the very day of such humiliation of an Arab country and such flagrant violation of national sovereignty?

————

More than two months passed between the Osirak bombing and the scheduled 1981 Kirchberg Conference on Science and World Affairs at Lake Louise in the Canadian Rockies — sufficient time to organize a special working group on the Middle East Conflict. Menachem expected fireworks. He was not disappointed — he was on the carpet for nine grueling hours, while participants denounced Israel's destruction of Osirak. Had the Iraqis not assured their French patrons and the rest of the world of their peaceful objective in developing a nuclear center? And did the international inspection framework not guarantee that Iraq's deviation from these aims would immediately be noted? The highest moral road was traveled by the most senior member of the British Kirchberg contingent, who quoted in funereal tones the famous sentence from the Russell-Einstein manifesto: "We feel that scientists should assemble in conference to appraise the perils that have arisen as a result of the development of weapons of mass destruction, and to discuss a resolution. . . ."

Menachem had predicted that someone at their session would mouth these words. He could not help but throw an I-told-you-so glance at *le gourou*, who had earlier refused Menachem's bet to that effect. When Menachem's turn to reply finally came, he took the Briton's citation of the two saints of Kirchberg as his starting point.

"First, I would like to say a few words about the uses and abuses of the Russell-Einstein Manifesto. Its fate is not unlike that of the words of Christ, from whom competing churches and warring states claim to derive their authenticity; or that of Mohammed, whose name is invoked in similar fashion. I should not like to read the Russell-Einstein Manifesto as a moral imperative. Not when morality is being twisted to suit ever so many nefarious purposes." Menachem raised one finger and waited. The room was still.

"We at Kirchberg should promote reasonable thinking and solutions to problems. *Reasonable*, I say, not *moral*. Reason and good sense are currently not the prime movers in human affairs, but it can be our job to promote them to the place of honor that they deserve." He rose for the rest of his speech, forcing the participants to look up to him.

"And now to the issue at hand: the neutralization of the Osirak nuclear reactor. Let me say at the outset that the Israeli government was and is convinced that the international inspection framework is totally unsuitable for countries such as Iraq and others."

"What others?" one of the Indians interrupted.

"Libya, for instance. Iran. I could go on."

"Oh," the Indian exhaled, and sank back in his chair.

"In fact, highly reliable sources supplied us with two dates for the completion of this reactor and its operation: either the beginning of July or of September of this year." He looked around for challengers. "And that enough uranium for an atomic bomb of the Hiroshima class had become available through French collusion. Incidentally, our source of information was impeccable." Menachem's sweeping gaze skipped over Ahmed Saleh, who seemed to be doodling, his eyes focused on the paper in front of him. "My government released the following statement, which I quote. 'Within a short time, the Iraqi reactor would have become operational and hot. In such conditions, no Israeli government could have decided to blow it up. Such an attack would have brought about a massive radioactive lethal fallout on the city of Baghdad and tens of thousands of its innocent citizens would have been harmed.'" Menachem looked up. "Let me digress for a moment and give you a further illustration of our concern for preserving lives. Our operation was set for Sunday on the assumption that the 150 foreign experts — primarily French and Italian — who, according to our impeccable source, were working in Osirak, would not be there on the Christian day of rest. And indeed, as you know, no foreigners were hurt. Now let me finish with my government's statement. 'We were, therefore, forced, to defend ourselves against the construction of an atomic bomb in Iraq, which itself would not have hesitated to use it against Israel and its population centers.'

"Before you pass the expected resolution condemning my country, I want to remind you that when the French-Iraq collaboration started around 1974, Iraq requested from France a gas-graphite-type power reactor, which is also capable of producing weapons-grade plutonium." Menachem stopped for a few seconds to check some file cards held in his hand. "When the French refused, offering instead a conventional pressure-water or boiling-water power reactor, the Iraqis instead opted for a very advanced Osiris-type research reactor, which has a much higher power rating compared to other light-water research reactors. France agreed to supply it, together with highly enriched uranium, in return for long-term oil deliveries on favorable terms." Menachem had started to focus on *le gourou*, who hid behind clouds of cigarette smoke. "Osirak was *not* a simple power reactor. It was one of the biggest nuclear *materials testing and research* reactors, a type that makes sense only for countries engaged in developing and producing reactors. Clearly, Iraq is not one of those countries. However, of all available research reactors, the French Osiris-type is one of the most suitable for the production of weapons-grade plutonium in significant quantities. I will not burden you with additional technical information, since I have already taken too much time and the outcome here seems already preordained." Menachem sat down again to finish, as though acquiescing in the inevitable.

"The Iraqi Osirak reactor highlights the essential division between countries that constitute a threat and those that do not. A Non-Proliferation Treaty is ultimately a reasonable proposition, but insisting on it in complete disregard of the circumstances is just not right. The world is not uniform. Pressure in nuclear matters should be applied to countries from whom threats and evil designs emanate.

"In June, Israel performed a legitimate act of self-defense against a country about to acquire a nuclear capability — a country still maintaining a state of war with us; a country persisting in its denial of Israel's right to exist. One must divest oneself of the mindset that one rule applies to all. We know this proposition to be completely fictitious; scientists at Kirchberg, at least, ought to have the fortitude to acknowledge it as well. Whether such fortitude exists in September 1981 at Lake Louise is another question."

"Where are you taking me?" Saleh asked as he entered the car.

"To Banff. It's not very far. We'll be back in time for dinner."

"Why to Banff? I didn't come to Canada to be a tourist. No true Palestinian can allow himself to be one."

"Stop being righteous." Menachem barely hid his rising irritation. "We are going to meet someone there."

"Oh?"

"It's part of my confidence-building. I want you to meet a man from our government who until June 7 swore never to deal with the PLO. I persuaded him to make an exception."

"You mean Begin will meet us in Banff?" Saleh laughed sarcastically.

"Don't be silly. But someone very close to him."

"And what will we discuss?"

"That's up to you . . . and him. I will leave the two of you alone. You have two hours with the highest contact the PLO will ever have until there is real peace. Don't waste it."

Some minutes passed. Neither man spoke another word until the impatient blowing of a car horn startled Menachem. He looked into the rear mirror. "Good God, look at that line of cars behind me. I must be driving too slowly for the Canadians. I haven't driven a car for years — I just started again a few months ago." He started peering at the roadside ahead, looking for a place to pull off. "I'll stop for a moment and let them pass. I hope you aren't worried. You can see how cautious I still am."

Saleh dismissed the concern with a wave of one hand. "I'm taking a bigger chance being seen in the same car with you than anything you could do behind the wheel. Let's talk about more serious matters."

"Let's."

"Now that you have taken Osirak out of commission, what next? You've read the newspapers. You heard what everybody said yesterday. Do you think it was worth it?"

"You tell me."

"I don't count."

"You're wrong. And since you know why we had to do it, I'll tell you something that few outside our government know. It won't hurt you to be aware of it. It will also show you that I trust you: Just because people condemn us in public does not mean that they are all against us in private. Have you met Krimapov?"

"Of course. Aren't the Soviets our friends?"

"Only when it suits them."

"As if I didn't know that. So what about Krimapov?"

"He's the ultimate quango example at Kirchberg. That's what makes it worthwhile going to these conferences — even if they weren't held in such beautiful places as this." Menachem waved at the Canadian Rockies closing in on either side of the highway. "Not that you and I aren't also prime quango specimens."

Saleh frowned. "Quango? What language is that?"

Menachem laughed. "English, although I'll admit it doesn't sound so. I learned it first in South Africa: 'quasi non-governmental organization.' You'll find it in any good dictionary."

Saleh's grunt was the closest he permitted himself to laughter. "So I've finally learned something useful here that I may bring back to Tunis. I didn't know the PLO's status has actually been defined in dictionaries."

"Would you be surprised if I told you that Krimapov is not for total condemnation of Israel at tomorrow's plenary session? That the Soviets will not demand that we be thrown out of the IAEA if we don't sign immediately the NPT?"

Saleh cut him off. "Enough about Israel. What about our prisoners?"

"We released 750 the day after the bombing."

"Seven-hundred and fifty! A drop in the bucket," he said bitterly.

"Ahmed, be reasonable. You know it's not a drop, not when the faucet was totally closed before."

"I think it should have been at least two thousand."

"Ahmed," Menachem said calmly. "If it were up to me, I would probably oblige you. You know how I feel about confidence-building. But just harping on numbers is not productive. You asked for the release of some specific persons. Don't think for a moment that our Mossad did not know what those men really meant to you. There were some *real* terrorists among them, not just putative ones.

Yet every one of *them* was released. Listen," he reached over to touch the Arab by the sleeve, "for once, let's not act like Middle Easterners haggling in a bazaar. Or this 'eye for an eye' posturing. You know where that will get us."

"Total blindness," muttered the Arab.

"Precisely. I have cashed in almost all my chips with my government to meet my side of the bargain — or at least what I considered the most important part of it. You and I know that what you found out at Osirak was not only important for Israel's survival, but also for that of the Palestinians living around us. Otherwise, you wouldn't have done it. Yesterday afternoon, you were one of the few persons — maybe the only one other than me — who knew how dangerous the situation in Baghdad had become. Let's worry about the future. Let's talk about what we can do for the next generation."

"Next generation? Will my son, who is now fighting your people, ever forgive me if he knew of our bargain?" he asked bitterly. "But you wouldn't understand. You have no children."

"You're wrong on both counts."

"Both?"

"I do understand." Menachem clutched the steering wheel as he accelerated to pass the Mercedes in front of them. It was the first car he had overtaken all afternoon. "I also have a son."

Afterword

In preparation for *Menachem's Seed*, I interviewed a large number of individuals — scientists, clinicians, rabbis, experts in other fields, and many students and colleagues — in Israel, Austria, Belgium, Germany, the United Kingdom, and the United States. Although all of them were extraordinarily open and helpful, I am certain that, given the sensitive and even personally intrusive nature of my inquiries, and the manner in which the information was woven into my plot, some would prefer to remain anonymous. Therefore, I decided to thank all of my informants privately, while still acknowledging in public the enormous debt I owe them.

But there is one exception: Shalheveth Freier, to whom this book is dedicated. He read early versions of several chapters, but he died unexpectedly on 27 November 1994, before my novel was completed. Among numerous positions in Israel, he served at different times as director general of the Israeli Atomic Energy Commission, as director of the Scientific Department of the Ministry of Defense, and at the time of his death as vice president of the Weizmann Institute of Science and advisor to the government of Israel on atomic policy. During World War II, he fought in the Jewish Brigade of the British Army and was responsible for smuggling thousands of Jewish refugees into Palestine. In most of these respects, he bears a strong resemblance to my fictional hero, Menachem Dvir. But unlike Dvir, who was born in the former Belgian Congo, Shalheveth Freier was born in Eschwege, Germany, and left his native country during the rise of Hitler.

I have known Shalheveth Freier for approximately twenty years. Many of our meetings took place at Pugwash Conferences on Science and World Affairs, which are the inspiration for my fictional Kirchberg Conferences on Science and World Affairs. The January

1995 Pugwash Newsletter carried an obituary, from which I would like to quote a few sentences because of their relevance to my novel and its title character:

> Freier's defense of Israel's nuclear stance put him frequently in the position of one versus everybody else, but there was never any rancor in the debate with him. Indeed, some of his Pugwash activities, not generally known, arose from the feelings of friendship and trust which he induced even in his political opponents. Thus, at a time when there were no diplomatic relations between the Soviet Union and Israel, he arranged a confidential visit of a senior Soviet academic to Israel for a meeting with its Prime Minister. Without a higher academic degree (he always insisted that he was plain mister, not doctor or professor), he amazed people with his profound knowledge in many disciplines, and his involvement in a multitude of activities outside his professional life.

In his eulogy at a special memorial service, Israel's then foreign minister, Shimon Peres, paid tribute to Freier's contribution, in his capacity as scientific counselor in Israel's embassy in Paris, to building trust and fruitful cooperation between Israeli and French scientists. At the time of his appointment in 1956, his was a one-man office. When he left Paris in 1959, his Israel-France Science Liaison Office employed a staff of 150!

For more than one year, I had numerous interviews with Freier on the subject of this novel, both in Israel and London. I was also fortunate in being the beneficiary of his legendary abilities as a correspondent. I would like to end this tribute to an extraordinary man by quoting excerpts from two letters.

> [12 May 1994] If your novel extends into 1981, let me know. I was the only intermediary between the Israeli and Soviet governments from 1970 to 1985, and the aftermath of the bombing of the reactor was really quite dramatic with certain understandings reached on the extent to which Israel should, and would allow itself, to be punished. My Soviet partner was then Mr. Primakov, at the time Director of the Insti-

tute for Asian Research of the Soviet Academy and now Director of Russian Foreign Intelligence. [Note: On January 9, 1996, Yevgeni Primakov was appointed Foreign Minister of Russia in the Yeltsin cabinet.]

[23 May 1994] After the raid on the Osirak reactor in 1981, the Board of Governors of the International Atomic Energy Agency (IAEA) decided to recommend to the General Conference that Israel be expelled from the IAEA. The General Conference generally convenes in late autumn. Even though the atmosphere was charged, the U.S. did not want to go to such lengths. I had no doubt the USSR, its allies, and the non-aligned countries would whole-heartedly support Israel's expulsion and I wrote the attached letter to Primakov. I received no reply, but at the Pugwash meeting in Banff in early September of that year, at which I was on the carpet for about 9 hours on account of the raid, the Soviets told me they knew of my letter, but did not wish to share with me any confidence.

At the Pugwash Council discussion on its statement which wanted to condemn Israel unequivocally and demand its immediate accession to the NPT [Nuclear Non-Proliferation Treaty], I insisted that reference be made to Israel's apprehensions; that no reference be made to the NPT, in which I had no confidence; but that reference be made to a NWFZ [Nuclear-Weapon-Free-Zone] in the Middle East. Everyone being enamored of the NPT, the council was deadlocked until the Russian on the Council suggested to acquiesce in my objection to NPT and settle for a NWFZ. The Russians being — along with the U.S. — stalwart initiators and supporters of the NPT, everyone was taken aback. The chairman recessed the meeting and asked the Russians whether they were sure Moscow would agree to the omission of the NPT. The Russians said they had no problem and the following text was finally published: "The Pugwash Council deplores the use of military force by Israel against the experimental Iraqi nuclear reactor, whatever Israel's perception of a threat to its security. We oppose in general the use of military force to settle questions for which peaceful solutions must be sought. The Council urges on all the governments concerned to act on the proposal for a Nuclear Weapon Free Zone in the Middle East and to put their nuclear facilities under international surveillance and control."

[12 May 1994] Of course, I cannot help a feeling of affinity for Menachem. Indeed, it occurred to me that one day people will discover that I had copied passages from "Menachem's Seed" for official dispatches. Even with what little imagination I have, I can think up an imbroglio which might be the plot of an entertaining short story.

In the final analysis, *Menachem's Seed* is a novel (or perhaps "veri-fiction"), but not a historical account. It would have been a very different novel had I not known Shalheveth Freier. Whatever is good and fair and decent in my Menachem Dvir should be considered my homage to Shalheveth Freier. The rest is simply fiction.

Carl Djerassi

is a professor of chemistry at Stanford University.

His books include the novels *Marx, Deceased* (Georgia, 1996),

The Bourbaki Gambit (Georgia, 1994), and *Cantor's Dilemma*;

the autobiography *The Pill, Pygmy Chimps, and Degas' Horse*;

and essay, short story, and poetry collections.

Djerassi has been awarded the National Medal of Science in 1973

(for the synthesis of the first steroid oral contraceptive),

the National Medal of Technology in 1991

(for novel approaches to insect control), and the 1992 Priestley Medal,

the highest of the American Chemical Society awards.

He is also the founder of the Djerassi Resident Artists Program,

an artists' colony near San Francisco that supports

working artists in various disciplines.

Meet Carl Djerassi on the World Wide Web

http://www.djerassi.com